Don't Call It Night

AMOS OZ

———

Don't Call It Night

Translated from the Hebrew
by Nicholas de Lange

A HARVEST BOOK
HARCOURT BRACE & COMPANY
San Diego   New York   London

Requests for permission to make copies of any part
of the work should be mailed to: Permissions Department,
Harcourt Brace & Company, 6277 Sea Harbor Drive,
Orlando, Florida 32887-6777.

This is a translation of *Al Tagidi Laila*

Library of Congress Cataloging-in-Publication Data
Oz, Amos.
[Al tagidi lailah. English]
Don't call it night/Amos Oz;
translated from the Hebrew by Nicholas de Lange.
p.   cm.
ISBN 0-15-100152-9
ISBN 0-15-600557-3 (pbk.)
I. De Lange, N. R. M. (Nicholas Robert Michael), 1944–
II. Title.
PJ 5054.09A7813   1996
892.4'36—dc20   96-14587

Printed in the United States of America

The text was set in Sabon.

First Harvest edition 1997
A C E D B

Don't Call It Night

A T seven o'clock in the evening, sitting on the balcony of his second-floor apartment, he is watching the departing day, and waiting. What does the last light promise, and what can it deliver?

Below lies an empty garden with a patch of lawn, some olean-der bushes, a bench and a neglected bougainvillaea bower. The garden ends in a stone wall marked with the outline of an opening which is blocked with courses of stones that are newer, lighter in colour – in fact, at this moment they even seem slightly lighter in weight than the original stones of the wall. Behind the wall rise two cypress trees. Now, in the evening light, he finds they look black rather than green. Beyond stretch barren hills. That way lies the desert, where, every now and again, a grey eddy whirls up, quivers for a moment, wriggles, sweeps away, subsides. Only to start up somewhere else.

The sky turns grey. There are some still clouds, one of which faintly reflects the glow of the sunset. The setting sun itself is not visible from this balcony. On the stone wall at the end of the garden a bird shrills excitedly, as though it has just discovered something that cannot be bottled up. How about you?

Night is falling. Around the town the streetlights are coming on, and windows shine out between intervals of darkness. The strengthening wind carries a breath of campfires and dust. The moonlight casts a mask of death on the nearest hills, which are no longer hills but like the notes of a muffled tune. This place seems to him like the end of the world. He does not mind being at the end of the world. He has done what he can, and from now on he will wait.

He leaves the balcony, goes indoors, sits down, his bare legs on the coffee table, and his arms hanging down heavily on either side of the armchair as though being pulled towards the cool floor. He does not switch on the television, or the light. From down the street comes a whispering of car tires, followed by the barking of a dog. Someone is playing a recorder, not a whole tune but simple scales repeated without any apparent variation. These sounds agree with him. In the bowels of the building the elevator passes his floor without stopping. In a neighbouring apartment a woman's voice is reading the news on the radio, probably in a foreign language, though he is not certain of that right now. A man's voice on the stairs says, It's out of the question. Another replies, Okay then, so don't go, it'll come.

When the throbbing of the refrigerator stops, crickets can be heard in the wadi, as though punctuating the silence. A faint breeze rustles the curtains, ruffles the pages of a newspaper on a shelf, crosses the room, stirs the leaves of a houseplant, exits through the other window and returns to the desert. He momentarily hugs his shoulders. The pleasure reminds him of a summer evening in a real city, maybe Copenhagen, where he once stayed for a couple of days. Over there the night does not suddenly pounce, it feels its way gently. There the veil of twilight stretches for three or four hours, as though the evening aspires to reach out and touch the dawn. Various bells were ringing, one sounding hoarse, like a cough. A soft drizzle joined the evening sky to the water of the strait and the canals. An empty, brightly lighted streetcar passed in the rain, and he thought he saw the young conductress leaning over in conversation with the driver, resting her hand on his, then the drizzle again, as if the evening light were not passing through it but coming from it, and the droplets met with the spray of a fountain in a small square, where the quiet water was illuminated from within all night long. A shabby middle-aged drunk was sitting on the parapet dozing, his grey-bristled head sunk deep on his breast, and his feet, sockless in his shoes, immersed in the water, motionless.

What time is it now?

He peers in the dark at his watch, but as he looks at the luminous hands he forgets what the question was. Is this perhaps the beginning of the gradual decline from pain into sadness? Dogs start barking again, furiously this time, in backyards and empty lots, and from the direction of the wadi, and beyond, from the distant darkness, from the hills, Bedouin shepherd dogs and strays, perhaps scenting a fox, one bark subsiding into a whine and being answered by another, piercing, desperate, as though mourning an irreparable loss. This then is the desert on a summer night, ancient, impassive, glassy. Neither dead nor alive. Simply there.

Looking at the hills through the glass balcony door and across the stone wall at the end of the garden, he feels a sense of gratitude, but for what he is not sure. Could he really be grateful to the hills? A man in his sixties, stockily built, with a broad, peasant face and a suspicious or doubtful expression with a hint of concealed cunning. He has close-cropped grey hair and a distinguished-looking brindled moustache. In any room he seems to occupy more space than his body really takes up. His left eye is almost always half-closed, not as though he were winking but as though he were staring fixedly at an insect or a tiny object. He sits wide awake yet limp, as if after deep sleep. He finds the calm connections between the desert and the darkness satisfying. Let others be busy this evening having fun, making arrangements, feeling regret: for his part he willingly endorses this moment, which does not seem empty. The desert seems right to him and the moonlight justified. In the window opposite, two or three stars glow sharply over the hills. Softly he declares: Now you can breathe.

Iᴛ's only in the evening you can breathe a bit, when the heat lets up. Another crazy day is over. I've spent all my time just running after time. From eight o'clock till one forty-five, at school: two hours' general literature, two hours' matriculation revision, and an extra hour for Russian immigrant kids whose minds were definitely not on the Exile of the Godhead. A pretty girl called Ina or Nina said in a lesson about Bialik: His words are Biblical, the sentiment he took from Lermontov, the poesy is anachronistic. She went on to recite some lines of poetry in Russian, perhaps to demonstrate the sort of poetry she liked. I silenced her. Even though I was not entirely captivated with the subject and had difficulty restraining myself from saying that, as far as I was concerned, the Godhead could stay in exile.

During my break, at eleven fifteen, I sat down near the air conditioning in the reading room to prepare for my next lesson, but almost at once I was called to the Deputy Head's office for a meeting with a younger teacher who had taken umbrage at something an older one had said. I agreed to some extent with both of them and suggested they forgive and forget. It's a miracle how this kind of cliché, and especially words like forgive, provided they are used at the right moment and with impartiality, can make tears flow and bring about a truce. Such petty words can soothe the hurt, perhaps because it was petty words that caused it.

I skipped lunch and ate a falafel on the hoof to make a meeting at twelve fifteen at the Workers' Council office. We were going to try to stir up some sympathy for the idea of the refuge. The square was empty and sunscorched. In the middle of the mangy bed of rosemary stood a pudgy bespectacled immigrant with a black beret, leaning motionless on a hoe as though he had passed out. The sun above him was cloaked in a fiery haze. At four o'clock, an hour late, Avraham Orvieto's lawyer, Ron Arbel, arrived from Tel Aviv, a spoiled child whose mother had made him dress up as a businessman. We sat in the California Café with him and listened to a complicated explanation about the finances. By quarter to five, when I took him to meet the Town Treasurer, the perspiration had turned sticky and my armpits smelled sour like a strange woman's; from there to a consultation with Muki, who had promised to write a memorandum but hadn't, instead of which he spoke for half an hour about himself and what the government hadn't got the hang of. Across his T-shirt was a loud print of a new rock group called Devil's Tear. Then to the Education Centre and the pharmacist's in the square and I just made it to the supermarket a quarter of an hour before it closed, and managed to get some cash from the machine and collect the iron which was being repaired. It was dark when I got home, wiped out by the heat and exhaustion, and I found him sitting in an armchair in the living room, with no light on and no sound. Another sit-in to remind me that the cost of my activities is his loneliness. It's a ritual that has more or less fixed rules. I am, on principle, to blame for the difference of fifteen years in our ages. He, on principle, forgives me because he's such a thoughtful person.

He prepared supper by himself: You're tired, Noa, sit down, watch the news. He made an onion omelette, produced a geometrical salad, sliced some black bread and served it on a wooden board with some cheeses, and radishes that he had carved in the shape of rosebuds. Then he waited for my admiration as if he were Count Tolstoy who had once again deigned to light the stove in the hovel of one of his serfs.

After the news he put the kettle on, made us some herbal tea, placed a cushion under my head and another one under my feet and put a record on. Schubert. *Death and the Maiden*. But when I picked up the phone and called Muki Peleg to ask if the memorandum was typed yet, and Ludmir and then Linda to sort out something to do with the planning permission, his generosity ran out and he got up, cleared and washed the dishes, and shut himself in his room, as though I were liable to chase after him. If it hadn't been for this demonstration I might have had a shower and gone to him, to tell him what had happened, ask his advice. On the other hand, I'm not sure I would have done. He's hard to take when he gets going – he knows exactly what's wrong with our project and what I should never have said to whom – and even harder when he says nothing and listens, trying not to let his attention wander, like a patient uncle who has decided to devote some precious moments to listening to a little girl explaining what it was that frightened her doll.

At quarter past ten, after I had taken a cold shower and then a hot one, had collapsed on my bed and was trying to concentrate on a book about the symptoms of addiction, I half-heard from his room the sound of the BBC. The World Service. Recently, like Menachem Begin in his years of seclusion, he has taken to tuning in to London every night. Is he on the lookout for some item of news that they're keeping from us here? Or searching for a different perspective? Or using the broadcast to talk to himself? Maybe he's only trying to get to sleep. His insomnia infiltrates my sleep and robs me of the few dreams I might have had.

Later, groggy with tiredness, when I'd abandoned my glasses and the light and the book, I could still catch the underwater sound of his bare feet in the passage, no doubt on tiptoe so as not to disturb me, and the refrigerator opening and the faucet running and the lights being systematically switched off, and the apartment being locked up, his stealthy nocturnal wanderings that year after year have made me afraid a stranger has broken in. Some time after midnight I thought I sensed his touch on the door and I was so exhausted that I nearly submitted to his sadness and said yes, but he was already tiptoeing away down the passage – perhaps he had gone out onto the balcony without turning a light on. He likes the balcony on the summer nights. Or perhaps there was nothing, the footsteps, the touch on the door, his wall-piercing sadness, it may all have been mere fog, because I was already asleep. I had had a hard day and tomorrow after school there's another meeting at Muki Peleg's and I may have to go to Beersheba to try to finalize the planning permission at long last. I must get some sleep and try to be even more wide-awake tomorrow than I was today. Tomorrow is another hard day. And there's the heat. And the way time flies.

THIS time it did not go straight past on the other side of the wall, up to the next floor, but stopped with a faint scratching sound, and at once slammed and continued on its way. Cold and silent, a gecko, stony-eyed in the darkness, watching a colourful insect fluttering in the light, that is how I receive her: the swish of her skirt, the electrical impulse of her will before she moves, then the motion itself, the rumour of her heels between the door of the elevator and the door of the apartment the lock already turning: as always, with no fumbling, the key slips straight into the slot.

She went from room to room, talking in full spate, voice young and bright, abandoning the ends of her sentences, she crossed the apartment from one end to the other, turning on lights one after another in the hall, the kitchen, the toilet and above my head in the living room, wafting a trail of honeysuckle scent and setting up a row of electric lights in her path as though to illuminate the runway for her landing. The whole apartment screwed up its eyes, dazzled.

When she reached me she dropped her shopping basket and her briefcase and two overflowing plastic bags on the coffee table and asked: Why are you sitting in the dark, Theo? And she answered herself: You fell asleep again, sorry I woke you, actually you should thank me, otherwise how would you get to sleep tonight?

She bent over me and gave me a hasty comradely kiss on my hair, then removed my bare feet from the coffee table and made as if to sit down next to me, but no, she kicked off her shoes, whirled round in her light skirt with the blue pattern of diamonds, and flounced off to the kitchen, came back with two tall glasses of mineral water saying, Dying of thirst, drank, wiped her mouth with the back of her hand in a childlike gesture and said, What's new? She leaped up again to switch on the TV and only then did she sit down for a moment on the arm of my chair, almost leaning on me but not really leaning, she pulled her blonde hair away from her eyes as though drawing back a curtain, and said, Let me tell you what a crazy day I've had.

She stopped. She suddenly slapped her forehead and leaped away from me to the other armchair, saying, Sorry, Theo, just a minute, I must just sort out a couple of quick phone calls, do you feel like making a salad? I've had nothing to eat since this morning apart from a falafel, I'm starving, I'll only be a minute or two, then we'll talk. She pulled the telephone over onto the curve of her lap and held it there for an hour. While she was talking she wolfed down the supper I made and served her without noticing, alternating suggestions, feelings and snap judgments, munching the food only in the pauses when she permitted her interlocutors to defend themselves. I noticed that she said several times, Come off it, You're joking, and also, What the hell, Come on, Don't make me laugh, and Great, Perfect, Grab it with both hands. Her hands are much older than the rest of her, her labourer's fingers wrinkled, the skin shrivelling, the back of her hand with its crisscrossed blue blood vessels and patches of pigment resembling a clod of earth. As if her true years have been temporarily driven back from her body to her hands, where they are patiently building up their reserves of decay in readiness for some weakening.

Then through the bathroom door for twenty minutes I could hear the jets of water and her young voice singing a song from years back, about a white rose and a red rose, followed by the sounds of the hairdryer and a drawer being opened. She eventually emerged scrubbed and scented, in a light blue cotton bath robe, and said, I'm whacked, I'm knocked out, let's talk in the morning. She did not seem tired to me, but lithe and fetching, her thighs alive and breathing under the light bath robe, as she said, Good night, Theo, don't be angry, don't stay up late yourself. And again she said: What a crazy day I've had. And she closed the door behind her. She rustled the pages of a book in there for a few minutes and apparently she came across something amusing that made her laugh softly. A quarter of an hour later she switched the light off.

As usual she had forgotten to turn the shower faucet right off. I could hear water running from where I was in the hall. I went and turned the faucet as hard as I could, put the cap back on the toothpaste, turned the light off in the toilet, and went right round the apartment turning off the lights after her until there were none left on.

She has this gift of falling fast asleep in a moment. Like a popular little girl who has done her homework, tidied her desk, remembered to brush her hair and confidently believes that everything is all right and everybody is happy with her and tomorrow is another day. She is so much at peace with herself, with the darkness, with the desert at the end of the garden beyond the two thick cypresses, with the sheet that she has wound round her and the embroidered cushion that she clasps tightly to her chest in her deep sleep. Her sleep arouses a sense of injustice in me, or perhaps it is just plain jealousy; in the midst of the anger it is clear to me that there is no reason to be angry, but this knowledge does not quell my resentment and simply irritates me all the more.

I sat in my undershirt at the desk in my bedroom and tuned my transistor to London. Between news bulletins there was a programme about the life and loves of Alma Mahler. The presenter said that the male world was incapable of understanding her heart and saw in her a different character, not who she really was; then she began explaining what Alma Mahler was really like. I cut her off in mid-sentence, to show her that the male world has not improved, and went barefoot to the kitchen to raid the refrigerator. I was only after a sip or two of cold water but the soft light inside the refrigerator ambushed me like a caress. So as not to lose it and be left in the dark I poured myself some cold wine and peeled a triangle of cheese and meanwhile I found that I was tidying up the shelves. I sniffed the open carton of milk a couple of times, suspicious both of the milk and of my own sense of smell. I dropped a cluster of sausages in the garbage can because their colour looked off. I drew up the yogurts in a rear line in order of date and closed the ranks of the eggs in the plastic trays. I hesitated before a jar of tuna, but compromised by covering it in plastic film. I pulled down some bottles of juice from a cupboard and slotted them into the door of the refrigerator to plug some gaps in the line. I arranged an orderly display in the vegetable tray and again in the fruit basket. It was only with difficulty that I fought off the temptation to attack the freezer compartment. I advanced on tiptoe to the door of her bedroom: I'm here if I'm called for. If not, at least I can try to catch a whiff of her slumber; perhaps I will absorb some of her surplus sleep.

From there, to the balcony, and the faded, old-fashioned chair. The night is almost transparent. The whole world is bathed in a cold silvery light. It is not breathing. The two cypress trees seem to be carved out of basalt. The moonlike mountains look swathed in lunar wax. Hazy creatures crouch here and there, and they too look moonlike. In the valleys there are shadows within shadows. There was a single cicada that I notice only when it stops. What did the men mistakenly see in Alma Mahler and what was she really? If an answer to this question was possible, I missed it. It is almost certain that the question is meaningless, that it is framed in an empty fashion, and that no answer is theoretically possible. The presence of the barren hills in the darkness cancels words like "almost certain" or "theoretically possible", and empties out the question, What did I see in you, Noa, or what do you see in me? I shall stop. Let's suppose that you see in me what I sometimes see when I look at the desert. And how about me? Let's say: a woman who is fifteen years younger than I am with a pulse like that at the core of life itself, a protoplasmic, rhythmic pulse, from before words or doubt existed in the world. Sometimes, without meaning to, she suddenly touches your heart. Like a cub, or a chick.

Years ago I learned to find my way around the map of the stars. It was something I learned in the army, or even earlier, in the youth movement. On clear nights I can still identify the Great

Bear and the Little Bear and the Pole Star. As for the planets, I can still locate them but I forget which one is Jupiter, Venus or Mars. Right now in the total silence everything seems to have stopped and even the planets seem to have ground to a halt. It seems as though the night will go on forever. All the stars look like tiny pinholes in the floor of the upper storey, droplets of luminosity from the light of the sky shining on the other side. If the curtain is drawn back, the world will be flooded with radiance and everything will become clear. Or be burned up.

There is a good telescope indoors, behind the bed linen on the second shelf on the left. I could go inside and get it so I can see better. Maybe Nehemia left her the telescope that used to belong to Peeping Gorovoy. Or to Yoshku, her cousin. There are still three or four such objects lurking around the house. The rest have gone. Disposed of. Even more spoiled than he was, she once said during a row, even more of a Neanderthal male. She stopped short. She never repeated it. Even when we fight she keeps tight control of herself, and of me, her foot always firmly on the brake pedal. I am careful too, I know the limits: like touching glass with glass and drawing back just in time.

From the east, from the mountains, comes a gust of piercing desert wind. Like a cold sharp scythe. The wilderness is secretly breathing. The dust and stone look like an expanse of calm water in the dark. It is even, suddenly, cool. Nearly two o'clock. I'm not tired but I'll go to my bedroom without switching the light on, I'll get undressed and go to bed. Radio London will tell me what is not known here yet. How is the world tonight? Tribal clashes in Namibia. Floods in Bangladesh. A big rise in the number of suicides in Japan. What's coming next? Let's wait and see. What comes next is punk music, merciless, penetrating, rough and bloodthirsty, from London, at a quarter past two on Wednesday morning.

I WOKE up at six and managed to write the memorandum. Muki Peleg will go over it and Linda has offered to type it out. At lunchtime I'll send it to Avraham Orvieto, with copies for the Mayor and the Treasurer. Who else should I send it to? I must find somebody who has some idea. Perhaps I should get hold of a copy of the official regulations and learn them all. Should I consult Theo anyway? That's all he's waiting for, like a hunter. He knew from the start that I'm not up to the challenge. He knew that after one or two slip-ups and failures I'd come running straight to him. Meanwhile, he's tactful enough to say nothing and not interfere. Like a grown-up who allows a toddler to climb wherever he likes but keeps a close watch and holds his hands out, where the child can't see him, to catch him if he falls.

I began the memorandum with an account of the "development of the idea". I found this expression unsuitable, but I couldn't find a better one. One of our students died in an accident "consequent upon drug-taking". There are various conflicting accounts circulating in the staff room about the circumstances of the incident. I was interested in the young man in question, even though I never actually managed to exchange more than a few words with him. Immanuel Orvieto was a quiet pupil. One of three boys in a literature class containing thirty girls. In recent years shy pupils have disappeared, they are all noisy during break and drowsy during literature lessons. Tired, disconnected, they stare blankly at Flaubert and me with a stubborn expression of amused contempt, as if we were trying to sell them fairytales about storks and babies. But there was something about Immanuel that always reminded me of winter. Once he was late handing

13

in an essay on Agnon. I stopped him in break and asked why. He lowered his eyelashes, as if he had been asked a question about love, and answered softly that the story in question was not particularly relevant to him. I interrupted sharply, Who's talking about relevance, we're talking about an obligation. He found no answer to this, even though I kept him there cruelly for a whole minute before I said coldly, All right, let me have it by next week.

He handed me the essay ten days later. It was a fine, carefully reasoned, understated piece of work. After the concluding sentence he had added a personal line in brackets: In the end I did find some relevance in the story, despite the obligation.

Once I asked him on the stairs why he never put his hand up in class, surely he had things to say, I'd have liked to hear him talk occasionally. Again he had to pause before he answered hesitantly that he found words a trap. Not long before Pesach, I voiced the opinion in class that Yehuda Amichai wanted to express his opposition to war, and suddenly there was Immanuel's introverted voice, as though talking in his sleep, and with an interrogative note at the end of the sentence: Whatever the poet did or didn't want to say gets in the way of the poem?

I decided I should find the time to get him to talk.

But I didn't find the time. I forgot. Put it off. I have three classes and two literature sets, including the special set for recent immigrants. Each one has close to forty pupils most of whom have a tortured look. I'm rather fed up myself, after all these years. Now I don't even bother to remember their names. They're almost all girls; they mostly wander around all through the summer in bright-coloured shorts with a tear at the very edge of the crotch; they're almost all called Tali. Actually, there's always one in every class who keeps correcting me, it's not Tali it's Tal, or vice versa.

The truth is that until after it happened I didn't even know as much about Immanuel Orvieto as his class teacher and his counsellor did: that he had been living here in Tel Kedar from the age of ten with an unmarried aunt who worked in a bank. That his mother was killed a few years ago in the Olympic hijack. That his father is in Nigeria as a military adviser. There was a vague story circulating in the staff room that the boy had fallen in love or got involved with some girl in Elat, several years older, who was a junkie and might even be a pusher. Before the incident, I listened to this with only half an ear, because the staff room is always full of all sorts of gossip. So is the whole town, for that matter.

He was found not far from the abandoned copper mine near Elat, after he had disappeared from his aunt's home and been missing for ten days. He had fallen off a cliff. Or jumped. He had broken his back and apparently lay dying at the foot of the cliff for a day and half a night before he finally expired. It was to be hoped that he had not been conscious all that time, but there was simply no way of knowing. He had previously been taken there and been drugged, or drugged himself, or been tempted. I tried not to listen to these things, which here always come accompanied by excitable voices and gestures of stunned self-righteousness and a hint of secret glee: Look, what do you mean a backwater, look, we've made it to the national news, real-life excitement has come to us, too, and there's a well-known journalist and a photographer, they've been prowling around outside since this morning but the executive have decided that none of us must be interviewed, we have to answer No comment.

The funeral was postponed twice because the father was delayed. A couple of days later the aunt died too, and the talk in the staff room was of a stroke, guilt feelings, the hand of fate. All kinds of cackle that I tried not to listen to. The fact is, I loathed the father even before seeing him. An absentee father, an arms-dealer, in Nigeria, probably full of complaints, probably only blaming us. It isn't difficult to pass judgment from a distance, on the basis of a few hints that converge into a conclusion. I imagined the father as a kind of ex-stormtrooper, prosperous, judgmental and self-righteous. I made up my mind not to participate in the delegation from the staff room that went to see him in his room at the Kedar Hotel even before the funeral. From the African jungle, here he was at last condescending to come here only to blame us for the awful fate of his son, how did we

15

fail to see, why did we ignore, surely it was inconceivable that the entire teaching staff? In the end I went anyway, maybe because I recalled the boy's way of standing, quiet yet nevertheless disturbing, shy, as though plunging to his own seabed before surfacing and telling me almost in a whisper that words are a trap. There was a quiet plea for help in these words that I either didn't catch or caught and ignored. And so, refusing to recognize and recognizing and rejecting the recognition that if I had chatted with Immanuel, if only I had tried to get a little closer to him, and shrugging what the hell, drop it, you're crazy, I went along with the other teachers to meet Avraham Orvieto a few hours before they buried the boy and his aunt. There, in the hotel, in the father's room, this thing began that has filled the whole of my being ever since.

There was also the episode of the dog. Immanuel Orvieto had a dog, a depressive creature that always kept its distance. From the morning to the end of lessons he would lie and wait for the boy in the sparse tamarisk grove which grew, or rather decayed, opposite the school gate. If you threw stones at him he would get up wearily and pad a few yards away and lie down again to wait. After the calamity, this dog started coming into the classroom each morning, oblivious of the chaos in the corridors, mangy, floppy-eared, his drooping muzzle almost touching the dusty floor. Nobody dared to shoo him away or bother him during the days of mourning. Or even afterwards. He lay there the whole morning, with his sad, triangular head resting, motionless, on his front paws. He had selected a regular spot in a corner of the classroom next to the wastepaper basket. If anyone threw him half a roll or even a slice of salami in break, he did not bother to sniff it. If he was spoken to, he did not react. He had a pitiful, brown, bewildered look that forced you to look away. At the end of lessons he would slink out abjectly with his tail between his legs, and vanish until the eight o'clock bell the next morning. A Bedouin dog, not young, the colour of the earth hereabouts: a faded grey. Dusty. Now, in hindsight, I think he may have been dumb, because I don't recall him ever uttering a bark or even a whine.

Once he made me want to take him home with me, to bathe and feed him and make him happy: his undying devotion to a boy who would never return suddenly touched me. If I fed him milk from a spoon and got the vet to take care of him and made him a bed in the hall, he might eventually get used to me and let me stroke him. Theo detests dogs but he'd be bound to give in because he's the giving-in sort. If only I knew how to make him understand how oppressive I find his overwhelming consideration. I could see him screwing up his small eye, the left one, with his silvery retired British army major's moustache concealing a slight quiver: Look here, Noa, if it really matters to you, and so forth. So I gave up the dog. He was a pretty repulsive creature and the truth is that he showed no sign of needing a new attachment.

One morning he was run over. Nevertheless, he still arrived in class precisely on the first bell. His hind legs were smashed and looked like broken twigs. He dragged himself to his regular spot and lay there as usual. There was not so much as a whimper. I made up my mind to call the Public Health Department vet to come and take him away, but at the end of the day he vanished and the next day he didn't come back. We thought he must have dragged himself away to die in some secluded place. A couple of months later, the evening of the class party, after the greetings and the sketches and the refreshments and the headmistress's speech, when we left at one o'clock in the morning, the dog appeared again, bony, misshapen, cadaverous, wriggling along on his forelegs and dragging his paralyzed hindquarters, crossing the light of the lamp in front of the grubby tamarisk grove opposite the school gate, creeping from darkness to darkness. Unless it was another dog. Or just a shadow.

Avraham Orvieto stood to greet us, leaning back against the door of the balcony from which the mountaintops to the east could be seen shimmering in the heat haze. A small suitcase was lying shut on the hotel double bed. Two lemons on the table. A lightweight summer jacket draped over the back of the chair behind it. He was a small, frail, narrow-shouldered man, his thinning hair was turning white, his wrinkled face was suntanned, he looked like a retired metal worker. This was not the image I had of a military adviser or an international arms-dealer. I was especially surprised when he started talking to us, without waiting for the formal condolences, about the need to prevent other schoolchildren from falling victim to drugs. Speaking in a colourless voice, with a kind of hesitancy, as though he were afraid of making us angry, he asked whether Immanuel was the only one of our pupils to succumb. And he asked us to tell him how long we had known about it.

There was an embarrassed silence, because the truth is that we knew nothing until afterwards, discounting the staff-room gossip. The Deputy Head, stammering with tact, pronounced the opinion that Immanuel started taking drugs only at the end, in Elat, after he disappeared, that is to say more or less in the last days perhaps. Even the aunt had not noticed any problematic changes, although it was hard to tell. To which the father replied that we would probably remain in ignorance forever. There was another silence. This time it was protracted. Avraham Orvieto put his two wrinkled hands to his face, brown peasant-like hands with scaly fingers, then he laid them back in his lap, and the Deputy Head began saying something, and at the same moment Avraham Orvieto asked which of us knew Immanuel best. The Deputy Head resorted to vague mumbling. There was a silence. A young Bedouin waiter, dark-skinned and slender like a pretty girl, wearing a white bow tie, wheeled in a trolley covered with a white cloth and holding fruit and cheeses and a selection of soft drinks. Avraham Orvieto signed the bill and added a folded banknote. Help yourselves, he said, twice, but nobody touched the refreshments. Suddenly he turned to me and said quietly: You must be Noa. He liked your lessons, he had a talent for literature.

I was so startled I did not deny it. I muttered a few banalities, a sensitive boy, withdrawn, rather, um, reserved. The father smiled in my direction like someone who is not used to smiling: like someone opening a crack in a shutter for an instant to reveal a beautiful room with a chandelier and bookcases and a fire burning in the grate, then closing it as though it had never opened.

Six weeks later Avraham Orvieto turned up one morning in the staff room during the mid-morning break to ask our help in realizing an idea: he was considering giving some money to set up here in Tel Kedar a small rehabilitation centre for young people, schoolchildren, perhaps from other parts of the country, who were addicted to drugs. He wanted this centre to be a memorial to his son. Tel Kedar was a quiet little town, the desert itself might help: seeing the wide open spaces could inspire various reflections, it might be possible to rescue one or two. Of course there would be local opposition which he could well understand, still, why not try to sort out some basic terms that would allay the fears.

I was startled when he chose to ask me, who was not Immanuel's class teacher, to agree to put together a sort of informal team whose task would be to make a preliminary study and jot down on a sheet of paper what the difficulties would be and what aspects were liable to antagonize the local residents. He himself came to Israel only every few months, but he had a lawyer, Ron Arbel, who would be at my disposal whenever I needed him. If I refused, he would understand and would look for someone else.

Why me in particular?

Look, he said, and again he smiled at me as though momentarily opening that shutter a crack to reveal the fireplace and chandelier, you were the only one he was fond of out of the whole school. Once he wrote me a letter and told me you had given him a pencil. He wrote the letter with the pencil you gave him.

I couldn't remember any pencil.

Still, I agreed to do it. Perhaps because of a vague urge to maintain a link with Immanuel and his father. What link? And why maintain it? When Avraham Orvieto talked about the nonexistent pencil, there flickered a fleeting resemblance, not between him and his son, but to a man I met many years ago. His face, his sloping shoulders, and particularly his gentle voice and the way he chose and put together his words, like the phrase "inspire various reflections", reminded me of the poet Ezra Zussman, whom I met once in a Health Fund rest house on Mount Canaan. We used to sit in the late afternoon, my father and Zussman and his wife and Aunt Chuma and I, on the sloping lawn while the evening colours were changing and an invisible breeze played around the hills. Father in his wheelchair, paralyzed from the waist down, looked like a boxer or a wrestler who had grown old and put on weight, his face rough and craggy, the weight of his body pressing down on the taut seat, his black transistor clasped in his huge hand like a grenade ready to throw, a dark woollen blanket covering his useless knees, his hunched shoulders expressing violent fury as though he had been turned to stone in the middle of delivering a blow. We sat round him on deckchairs facing the light of the Galilean mountains on the rim of the sky that was yielding to the evening twilight. Ezra Zussman showed us hand-written poems that seemed far removed from the sort of poetry then prevalent in Israel and touched me like the sound of harp music. One evening he said: Poetry is a kind of spark trapped in a piece of glass, because words are pieces of glass. He hurriedly gave a sad smile and regretted the metaphor. Then the holiday came to an end, the Zussmans said goodbye humbly, as though wordlessly apologizing for abandoning us, and went on their way. Next day Father smashed his portable radio in a fit of blind anger, and Aunt Chuma and I took him home in a taxi. When a few weeks later I came across a short announcement of the death of the poet Ezra Zussman I went to a bookshop in Netanya to buy his poems. I didn't know what the book was called and the bookseller had not heard of it. Aunt Chuma bought Father a new transistor radio, which lasted about a fortnight.

I made it a condition with Avraham Orvieto that I should not receive any payment for my work in the fact-finding group. He listened and said nothing. Three weeks later I received a first check in the post. Since then he has sent me three hundred dollars each month via his lawyer, and leaves me to decide how much of this sum should be allocated to office expenses and to reimbursing travel, and how much should be a recompense for the time I spend on the project. Four times in vain I have asked the lawyer, Ron Arbel, to stop the checks coming.

Theo warned me, You're getting sucked in, girl, a financial arrangement like this is just asking for unpleasantness and trouble. It's difficult to believe that a hard-headed businessman would do such a thing out of absentmindedness. If all he really wants is to give some money for a memorial to his son, why doesn't he simply set up a trust? With a treasurer and proper accounts? If on the other hand what he wants is to set up a business venture, a private clinic for rich kids, an exclusive cuckoos' nest, three hundred dollars is peanuts for what you're worth to him by way of softening up public opinion, and you haven't even begun to realize how you're being used, Noa. Anyway, since when have you been into setting up institutions or refuges for junkies? There isn't a chance of getting the residents to agree to it – who wants an opium den in their backyard?

I said: Theo, I'm a big girl now.

He screwed up his eye and said nothing more.

He went back to the hall to continue ironing his shirts.

Of course he was right. The whole town is against it. Somebody wrote anonymously in the local paper that we won't let ourselves be turned into a rubbish dump for the whole country. There are so many things I'll have to learn from scratch. Things I've sometimes half-heard on the radio or skipped in the paper, operations, costs, capital fund, association, board of directors, budgeting; it's all still very vague but I'm already finding it exciting. Woman of forty-five finds new meaning in life: possible headline for a colour feature in one of the weekend supplements. Actually I've already been approached for an interview in an evening paper. I turned it down. I wasn't sure if such an interview would help or harm the project. There are so many things I've got to learn. And I will.

I sometimes say to myself in the third person: Because Noa can do it. Because it's a good thing to do.

There are three more members of the team, apart from me: Malachi Peleg (known to the whole town as Muki), Ludmir, and

Linda Danino. Linda is an asthmatic divorcee, an art lover; she volunteered for the team so as to be near Muki. Her contribution is typing on a word processor. Muki Peleg came because of me: he would have joined even if I had been setting up a finishing school for carrion crows. As for Ludmir, a retired employee of the electricity company, he is a rambunctious member of a number of protest committees: an enemy of the quarries and the discotheque, denouncer of defective signposting, and writer of an impassioned weekly column under the title "A Voice in the Wilderness" in the local paper. He roams around the town in summer in a pair of baggy khaki shorts, with battered flip-flops on his veiny, sun-browned feet, and every time he sees me he greets me by saying, There's Noa smoke without a fire, and then apologizes with a smile: Don't take offence, my lovely, I was only joking.

In practice I have all the responsibility. I've been caught up in it for several weeks now: running around the southern offices of the Departments of Social Security, Health and Education, tugging at the sleeve of the League Against Drug Abuse, besieging the Agency for Young People in Distress, coaxing the Parents' Committee and the Education Committee, begging the Development Agency, responding to the local paper and chasing after the Mayor, Batsheva, who has so far refused even to put the idea on the agenda. I've been four times to Jerusalem and twice to Tel Aviv. Once a week I make the pilgrimage to the regional government offices in Beersheba. Here in Tel Kedar friends and acquaintances have taken to eyeing me with a sort of worried irony. In the staff room they say, What do you want with all this extra bother, Noa? What's biting you? Anyway, nothing'll come of it. I answer: We'll see.

I have no complaint against these friends and acquaintances. If one of the other teachers suddenly started agitating to set up, let's say, a laboratory for infectious diseases here, I suspect I'd be bewildered or angry myself. Meanwhile, the Mayor shrugs her shoulders, the Workers' Council is noncommittal, the parents are hostile, Muki Peleg keeps trying to distract me with his stories about what women give him or the things only he knows how to give a woman, and Ludmir coaxes me to join the campaign to close the quarries as well. In the public library the librarian has collected all the literature on treating addiction on a special shelf for me. Somebody has stuck a label on the shelf: Reserved for Noa the Addict.

Theo keeps his mouth shut because I've asked him to.

As for me: I'm learning.

IT is a small, new town with eight or nine thousand inhabitants. The first thing to be built were rectangular quarters to house the families of servicemen from the military bases. In the seventies there were some encouraging drillings in the vicinity, and the decision was taken to create a town. These drillings subsequently turned out to be disappointing, and the plans were put on hold. The principal thoroughfare, Herzl Boulevard, is ambitiously laid out: six lanes extending along the barren ridge of a rocky desert plateau, separated by flower beds containing red earth brought from far away, planted with palm trees that are shaken by the strong winds. On either side of the boulevard, inside iron cages wrapped with sackcloth for protection against the sandstorms, poinciana saplings fed by a drip system look as though they are still uncertain whether there is any point in their existence. From this main boulevard some fifteen identical streets, named after presidents and prime ministers, branch off to east and to west. Each street contains a row of green street lamps and matching green municipal benches set out at regular intervals. There are mailboxes and a bus station and signs indicating pedestrian crossings, even though the traffic is sparse.

The ornamental gardens are forlorn on account of the wind that comes gusting in from the desert, lashing them with dust, despite which meagre lawns subsist in front of some buildings, along with a few oleanders and rose bushes. The buildings themselves are eroded by the heat and the wind. Four- and six-storey apartment blocks stand in rows, with front balconies closed in with cement blocks or aluminum-framed sliding windows. They were originally coated with white plaster, but their colour now is a murky grey: year by year the plaster grows closer to the colours of the desert, as though by assimilating to those colours it can assuage the fury of the light and dust. Solar panels gleam on every roof, as if the town were trying to appease the sun's blaze in its own language.

There are wide gaps between the apartment blocks. Perhaps years ago a heat-dazed planner laid out a garden suburb, with spaces left for parks and garden plots, with patches of fruit trees intended to blossom between the buildings. Meanwhile, these empty plots are strips of desert dotted with heaps of junk and a few bushes straddling the line between plants and inanimate objects. There are also a few eucalyptus trees and tamarisks, blighted by droughts and salty wind, hunched towards the east like fugitives turned to stone in mid-flight.

On the north-west of the town stretches the chic residential district, containing a hundred individual houses. Most of them exploit the slope so as to enjoy several levels. There are no flat, tar-coated roofs here, but red tiles turning grey summer by summer. There are some wooden houses built in Swiss-chalet style, interspersed with others in Italian or Spanish idiom, in a reddish stone brought from the mountains of Galilee, with projections, surrounds and arches, rounded windows and even weathercocks on the gables, sighing for forests and meadows in this desert. This is where the better-off residents live, professional people, regular army officers, managers, engineers and senior technicians.

On the opposite side, to the south-east, in a long narrow valley, stretches a potholed road invaded by shifting sands. Along this road there are ceramic and metal works, a small washing-machine factory and, after that, workshops, garages, depots, corrugated-iron huts and cement-block sheds, and structures without foundations constructed of blocks of bare concrete and planks. All kinds of workshops proliferate here: locksmiths, carpenters, electricians, bodywork shops, aerials, television repairs, plumbing and solar water-heaters. The sheds are separated by barbed wire that has collapsed and rusted and been buried by the sand. The dust at the entrances is thick with engine oil and grease. All through the summer there is a smell of stale urine and burning rubber. The sun blazes down harshly on everything. Further down the hill is a dumping ground for old vehicles and then the municipal cemetery. Here the road ends opposite a row of cliffs crowned with a double wire fence. It is said that on the other side there is a forbidden valley containing secret installations. Beyond this valley there is another row of dark cliffs pierced with caves and crannies. That is the hiding-place of the ibexes that occasionally appear on the horizon and descend towards the curtain of the evening twilight; that too is where the foxes have their dens and the scorpions and asps their holes. And, further still, are expanses of chalky boulders and slate slopes scarred by gullies and deposits of dark scree extending to the edge of the barren mountains, which are sometimes shrouded in shimmering haze and sometimes seem blue in the distance like a mirage of clouds rising from an invisible sea to which they will soon return.

Six times a day the bus arrives from Beersheba and stops outside the shopping centre, in the square that is popularly referred to as "by the lights", although its real name is Irving Koshitsa Square. Here the passengers from Beersheba alight, and the driver disappears into the California for twenty minutes for a cappuccino and a smoke while the passengers travelling to town gather at the bus stop. Opposite the square is an unpaved parking lot, from which the fine grey dust that settles like a veil on the shops, restaurants and offices constantly billows. The square is enclosed by four multi-storey buildings in the style of the coastal plain, two banks, the renovated Paris Cinema, a number of cafés that double as restaurants, and a run-down billiard hall that also sells tickets for the national lottery. Within the area defined by these structures is a square expanse paved with alternating red and grey tiles. In the centre of the square is a column of bare concrete in memory of the fallen. Four cypress trees have been planted at the four corners of the monument. One of them has died. On the column are inscribed in metallic letters the words THE BEAUTY OF ISRAEL IS SLAIN UPON THY HIGH PLAC S. The penultimate letter is missing. Beneath is fixed a tablet in the form of the tablets of the Law bearing twenty-one names, from Aflalo Yosef to Shumin Giora Georg. The tablet is cracked right across, and bindweed is growing in the crack. Beside the monument is a drinking fountain made of concrete, inscribed in Hebrew and English with the biblical verse, Ho, EVERYONE THAT THIRSTETH, COME YE TO THE WATERS – ERECTED IN MEMORY OF DONIA AND ADALBERT ZESNIK, 1983. Three faucets curve down towards the basin: two of them are weeping.

On the roof of the bank building among a jumble of tin billboards is a gigantic slogan: IVE DONE THE POOLS TODAY. In the building on the left of the Town Hall, opposite the Health Fund, is Theo's office. The name on the office door is "Planning". On the same floor there is also the dental surgery of Drs. Dresdner and Nir, and, further along, Dubi Weitzman, notary and accountant, also photocopying and full service for documents of all sorts. In his leisure hours Dubi Weitzman paints the desert landscape in gouache; five of his canvases were once shown in a collective exhibition in a private gallery in Herzliyya. On the wall of his office in a frame decorated with mother-of-pearl hangs an enlargement of a review in *Ha'aretz* newspaper in which his name is mentioned. Dr. Nir is a rock-climber, while Dr. Dresdner's wife is a distant relative of a singer who gave a performance here the winter before last and distributed autographed photographs of herself to her fans.

A couple of Bedouins, no longer very young, sit side by side on the steps of the Workers' Council, both wearing jeans. One sports a brand-name T-shirt, the other is in tatty battle fatigues. The shorter of the two is sitting with his forearm resting on his knee, palm upwards, his thumb repeatedly stroking a dead cigarette resting on his four cracked fingers. Slowly. The other has a bundle done up in old newspaper between his knees. His eyes are fixed on the sky or the glint of the radio aerial on the roof of the police station. Waiting. An old Ashkenazi pedlar walks past dragging his feet, with a tray fastened round his neck by a string. On it are frogs that can be made to hop by squeezing a rubber bulb, tops, soaps, combs, shaving foam and tubes of shampoo made in Taiwan. He is bespectacled, hunched, with a black skullcap on his head. He smiles absentmindedly at the two Bedouins who, uncertain of his intention, nod their heads politely.

"Hollywood Photos – films developed and all photography requisites": the shop is shut and barred. Inside the dusty window, under a photograph of Menachem Begin presented to its readers by the newspaper *Ma'ariv*, a notice has been put up: "On account of simultaneous and concurrent reserve army service on the part of the proprietors Yehuda and Jakki these premises will be closed starting as from today with affect until the first of next month. The public is kindly requested to exercise patients". In front of the funeral parlour, on metal stools, sit three religious youths, one of whom is an albino, exchanging opinions. The old pedlar pauses next to them, eager to join in their conversation; he coughs, sighs and makes a sign with his fingers: So Jew and non-Jew are like oil and water? Well, the same holds good of Jew and Jew. Each and every one. Even if they are brothers. One of the youths goes inside and brings him a glass of water. The old man thanks him, drinks, groans, picks up his tray with the frogs and soaps, attaches it round his neck, and plods on his way in the direction of the traffic lights. In a small cubbyhole sits the bookbinder, Kushner. He is not bookbinding, because he is immersed in reading a crumbling book. His gold-rimmed spectacles have slipped halfway down his nose. To judge by his faint smile it is evident the book pleases him, or perhaps it is bringing back memories. Three Indian birch trees have been planted on the far side of the square. Their foliage is sparse and they cast hardly any shadow.

In Schatzberg's pharmacy a notice has been pinned up: "No medicines on credit". A heavy man with a Romanian accent mutters: What is this word "credit"? A tousled youth with dusty sandals and a sub-machinegun hanging from his shoulder by a string instead of a strap volunteers an explanation: Credit is like a discount.

They are extending the Computer Palace by knocking down a wall. Opening soon: a special display of the last word in computer networking. Meanwhile, the stock is shrouded in plastic sheeting, to protect it from the dust. On the wall that is being demolished is a poster showing an icy, bespectacled beauty sitting with crossed legs at a computer screen: she is so engrossed in her programming that she does not realize she is allowing passers-by to peer up her skirt. A blond child is playing intently with a ball against a side wall of the Paris Cinema: catching, passing, throwing, catching, passing. He plays for a long time without varying his game. His face is concentrated, with an expression of deep responsibility, as though the slightest slip could result in disaster. An elderly man in civil defence uniform tells him to stop before he breaks a window. The boy obeys at once, stuffs the ball in his pocket and does not budge. He is waiting. The air is dusty and hot. The light is almost white. Overhead, on high power lines, a kite has been hanging for months now like a corpse on a gallows. Meanwhile, from today they are selling shawarma in pitta bread at the Entebbe falafel bar: Avram has been to Beersheba and purchased the equipment. He is anxious to know whether it will be a success or not. Still, there's no way round it, you have to give it time. We'll just have to wait and see. And keep our fingers crossed.

At quarter past seven in the morning, when we were drinking our coffee in the kitchen, I said: I've got to go to Beersheba again after school today. I've got to see Benizri from the Department. If they won't help I don't know which way to turn. Don't tell me what you think. Not yet anyway. Maybe this evening when I get home I'll want you to. We'll see.

He looked up from his paper, still in his undershirt, those tanned shoulders, he's sixty and his body's still so spare and fit. He shot me a look of affectionate curiosity. The way people sometimes look at a child who refuses to go to nursery school and complains of a tummy ache. Should you believe him, or be strict with him? A flicker of suspicion or irony twitched his immaculate military moustache. Suddenly he laid his broad hand on mine and said, You're a big girl now. You'll find a way.

Theo, I said, I'm not a half-wit. If you want me to drop this project, then just say, Noa, drop it. Try. See what happens.

You asked me not to get involved. Request granted. End of story. Another cup of coffee?

I didn't answer. I was too afraid of a row.

With his grey hair, his experienced face, his silvery, precisely trimmed moustache, his half-closed left eye, he sometimes reminds me of a prosperous peasant, a suspicious landowner, a man whom life has schooled in how to confront an adversary, a woman or a neighbour: with a combination of generosity and toughness.

Meanwhile, as though deriving incidental pleasure from the situation, he rolled a ball of bread between his fingers and said:

Let's go to the movie this evening. There's a sexy comedy on. It's ages since we had an evening out together. Drive carefully to

Beersheba, it's okay, I can manage without the car today, only watch out for potholes and those juggernaut trucks. Don't pass them, Noa. The less you pass the better. And remember to fill up with gasoline. Wait a minute, I know your Benizri. I trained the people who trained him. Shall I give him a call? Have a word with him before you see him?

I asked him not to.

He went on reading *Ha'aretz*. He muttered something about those Japs. I snatched my briefcase because I'd have to run if I wasn't to be late for my first lesson. I stopped at the door and came back to give and receive a cousinly kiss on the head, on the hair. 'Bye. And thanks for the car. Again this morning I didn't manage to ask him what was new at work. Not that anything ever is: Theo long ago lost interest in new things. This evening after Beersheba I'll go out to eat with him and we'll see a film at the Paris. He's always following me around. Though he's not really, just being sympathetically anxious. If he didn't worry about me I'd be bound to get hurt. I'm the one who's unfair to him. Maybe that's the reason almost everything he says irritates me now. And what he makes a point of not saying. And that overwhelming considerateness of his.

At ten o'clock, during the main break, I'll phone him at work. I'll ask him what's new. I'll thank him for doing without the Chevrolet all day. I'll say I'm sorry, I'll promise to remember to fill up the tank and to go to the movie with him this evening as he suggested.

Sorry for what, though?

Anyway, the staff-room telephone always has a long queue during break, and they always prick up their ears, and then they'll be saying they heard Noa apologizing to Theo, who knows what for. Such a small town. And it's all my fault we're here. This is the place I chose, and Theo gave in and agreed. If only he'd stop giving in and stop making a note of it each time in the debit column of his accounts.

What accounts? There aren't any. There, I'm being unfair to him again.

Muki Peleg was standing at the school gate waiting for me.

What's up? Nothing's up, as the virgin said to the carpenter when he asked her why her belly was so big. He just wanted to let me know that as from today he was looking for an architect who would draw up plans for us for nothing. Theo would have done that for us, if I had asked him, or if only I hadn't said no. When did I say no? And who said anything about plans? When did I give Immanuel a pencil and forget about it? It was all a dream. A strange boy, alone, he thought words were a trap, his eyes lowered, shy, plunging down to his own seabed, and that ghost dog of his waiting for him on the sidewalk outside the school. He must have invented the story about the pencil. But why should he have invented it? Have I started forgetting what's happened? Did I give it to him without noticing?

Six weeks after the funeral, when Avraham Orvieto had come to ask me to agree to put together an informal task force to examine the possibility of setting up an experimental boarding school for the rehabilitation of addicts, the two of us sat together in the California Café towards evening. We ordered iced coffee in tall glasses, and in his soft voice he described to me how the town and the desert might be able to facilitate the process of rehabilitation, could even inspire various reflections. As he spoke his rough hands had seemed to be trying to encircle an invisible object that did not want to be moulded into a ball. I watched them, fascinated. Take my sister for example, Immanuel's aunt, she lived here for about ten years, and she also found something soothing in this special combination of great light and silence. Immanuel, too, who was hoping to be a writer, and maybe he really did have a talent for it, you probably know more about it than I do, but how did I end up talking about him again? He's always here. He stands in front of me, pale, hugging his shoulders, it's a habit he has, to hug his shoulders all of a sudden, as if he's not warm enough. As if he hadn't left me but had come to me from far away to be with me and share my grief. Not a memory of him, not thinking about him, but him. In an old green sweater. He stands in front of me, pale, unsmiling, not saying anything, with his hands round his shoulders, leaning against some wall, with all his weight on one of his legs and the other one slack. Perhaps you can understand it: present.

He himself, Avraham Orvieto, had visited several times during those years, hiking among the hills with his son, who spoke little, or they would stroll around the streets together for an hour or two at sunset, silently observing how the town was growing, another park, another lane paved, another bench. Sometimes they even walked at night, between visits new lights appeared up the hill, the avenues were extended, a new housing development was being opened up to the east. He belonged to the generation that still found it exciting to see buildings creeping out over the wilderness, though Immanuel was apparently more on the side of the wilderness. Yet they both seemed to enjoy those nocturnal strolls, along empty streets, hardly speaking to each other. They were both about the same height by then. If it had not been for his commitments he would have stayed longer: the desert suited him. He might have stayed permanently. It was hard to say what was the truth in such matters, because who knew what was true and what was wishful thinking. Anyway, what was the point, now? As he said this he looked up from the tablecloth and offered me his bright smile that rose quickly from the depth of his blue eyes in his wrinkled brown face and then at once withdrew and sank back, like the head that was lowered again. I laid my fingers on his hand without meaning to, like touching rough soil, and at once I reconsidered and withdrew them, almost unable to refrain from apologizing for touching him without permission.

He said, you see, it's like this, then he thought better of it and said: It doesn't matter. I was so embarrassed that I asked: Are you short of deserts in Africa then, in the part where you live? I immediately regretted the question, which seemed at once foolish, rude and indirectly critical of him, when I had no right to criticize. Avraham Orvieto ordered us each a mineral water to wash away the sticky taste of the sweet iced coffee and said: Deserts in Africa. Well, the fact is that in the part of Africa where I work there really aren't any deserts. On the contrary. It's dense forest. If you've got another few minutes I'll tell you a little story. Well, I'll try to anyhow. During our early years in Nigeria we rented a colonial house that belonged to an English doctor. No, not in Lagos, but in a small town on the edge of the forest. The town wasn't much bigger than Tel Kedar, only very poor. A dilapidated British post office, a generator, a police station, a church, a score of wretched shops, and a few hundred huts made of mud or branches. Immanuel was only three. He was a dreamy boy in a tartan tam-o'-shanter, who blinked whenever anyone spoke to him. Erella, his mother, my wife, had a full-time job as a pediatrician in an immunization centre, a sort of clinic, that had been set up by the Mission in a nearby town. She had always dreamed of being a doctor in the tropics. Albert Schweitzer had conquered her imagination. And I was away travelling most of the time. The house was looked after by maids, one of them Italian, and a young local gardener. In the yard there were goats, dogs, some hens, a whole menagerie, there was even a schizoid parrot that I'll tell you about another time. In fact, there's nothing to tell. We also adopted a baby chimpanzee that we had discovered one weekend in the forest, apparently lost, or an orphan. It was Immanuel who noticed him, peering at us with heartrending eyes from a discarded tire by the roadside. He targeted us at once. It's a known phenomenon, I think it's called imprinting, but I'm not an expert. That ape became a little member of our family. We were so taken by him that we would compete to see whose arms he would go to sleep in. Immanuel fed him at first with canned milk from a bottle with a teat. When Erella sang a lullaby to Immanuel the baby ape would wrap himself up in a tiny blanket. In time he learned to set the table, hang out the washing and take it down when it was dry, and even to stroke the cat until he made it purr. He was particularly good at ingratiating himself. Kisses, caresses, embraces, there was no limit to his thirst for receiving and giving signs of affection. Much more than us, perhaps because he felt he had to maintain and intensify the physical contact between us. Although in fact it is rather hard to tell. He was such an emotional creature that he could tell or sniff when one of us was sad or lonely or hurt, and would outdo himself to entertain us:

he would put on little parodies, Erella making herself up in the mirror, Immanuel staring and blinking, me at war with the telephone, the gardener bullying the cook. We laughed till the tears came. And Immanuel was inseparable from him. They ate from the same plate and played with the same toys. Once he saved Immanuel from being bitten by a venomous snake, but that's another story. Another time he presented Erella with a magnificent scarf that he had stolen from somewhere and we never discovered to whom we should return it. Whenever we went to visit acquaintances and had to leave him behind, he would run after the Jeep sobbing heartrendingly, like a small child that has been unfairly treated. Whenever he was reprimanded he would take umbrage and disappear, climb a tree, or go on the roof, as though he had made up his mind to hand us his final resignation, but then he would come back to make peace, with transparent attempts to make friends all over again, to compensate us with all kinds of endearing efforts, polishing Erella's glasses and putting them on the cat, until we had no choice but to forgive him and stroke him. On the other hand, he was also capable of going on strike when he felt that we had been unfair to him. For instance, once when I smacked him because of some fruit that had vanished from the storeroom. On such occasions he would stand with a chastened air in a corner of the room eyeing us reproachfully, as if to say, How could you sink so low, the world will judge you as you deserve, until he forced us to feel that we had wronged him, and the only way to make amends, he indicated with an unmistakable gesture, was to open the sealed can where we kept the sugar lumps. When Immanuel was ill with jaundice, the ape taught himself how to fetch a cold drink from the refrigerator and how to hand over the thermometer, he even took his own temperature non-stop, as if he were afraid he'd caught the disease. Well, after a few years this chimpanzee reached the age of puberty, he grew a hermit-like thatch of white hair on his face and chest. The first thing he did was to fall in love with Erella. He clung to her. He hardly left her for a moment. That is, I must explain, he courted her in a rather touching way, combing her hair, blowing on her coffee to cool it, handing her her socks, but also in sexual ways that became harder and harder to take. He would feel her skirt, pick at it, cling to her back when she bent over. And so forth. I won't go into detail. When we locked ourselves into our bedroom at night he was overcome with jealous rage and stood outside our window groaning as though he'd been wounded. At first it seemed amusing and even charming, soon he'd be serenading her under her window, but it wasn't long before we realized we had a serious problem on our hands. For instance he took to biting me and Immanuel if we so much as touched her in his presence or if she touched one of us. Immanuel was so startled he began blinking and fluttering his eyelids again. You have to understand, Noa, if you want to follow the rest of the story, that a chimpanzee is a strong, fast-moving animal, and when he's angry or aroused he can be quite dangerous. Once or twice he got her into a clinch from which she couldn't break free and I had to prise her loose by force. It was the merest chance I happened to be at home. Suppose I'd been away? The vet occasionally gave him shots of estrogen, but it didn't cool his ardour. We didn't know what to do: we couldn't get rid of him and we didn't want to hurt him, he'd become one of the family. Can you understand: we'd raised him almost from birth. Once when he swallowed some broken glass we flew him to Lagos for treatment. We sat watching over him in a shift system for four days and nights to make sure he didn't rip off his dressing. After the incidents with Erella, the vet advised neutering, and I was in a torment of indecision, almost as if I were the intended victim. I came to the conclusion that the least terrible solution would be to return him to the wild. So the weekend before Christmas I put him in the Jeep, he was always eager to go with me on one of my long trips, and to be on the safe side I drove more than sixty miles into the forest. I didn't tell Erella or Immanuel. It was better they should think he'd just vanished. That he'd heard the primeval call of the forest and been drawn back to his roots. It's a recognized phenomenon, but I'm not an expert and I can't say for sure. We stopped for gasoline on the way, and as usual he put the nozzle in the tank for me and worked the pump by himself. We stopped for a meal, and afterwards he ran to the Jeep and brought me some paper tissues, he must have sensed something of my distress, or got a whiff of treachery, I can't tell you how attentive he was during that last journey. I looked at him over and over again thinking, Like a sheep being led to the slaughter. He picked up my thoughts, and throughout the journey, for nearly three hours, he sat huddled on the seat next to me with his arm round my shoulder, like a couple of childhood buddies going off together on holiday, and at first he chattered childishly, as though guessing what was in store and trying to secure a reprieve. But as we drove deeper and deeper into the forest he fell silent. He shrank down in his seat and started shivering violently and gazing at me with wide eyes just like the day we first found him in the forest, an abandoned baby looking at us trustingly from inside a ripped tire that had been jettisoned by the roadside. I drove the Jeep with one hand and stroked his head with the other. I felt like a murderer about to plunge a knife into the back of an innocent soul, who was also dear to me. But what other way out did I have? Less than a year later Erella was killed in the Olympic hijack, but then, on that journey of abandonment, I could not possibly imagine the succession of disasters. Well, I finally reached a small clearing. I switched off the engine. There was a dreamlike silence. He climbed onto my lap and laid his cheek on my shoulder. I told him to get down and gather me some sticks. He understood the word "sticks", but nevertheless he hesitated. Still shivering, he stayed where he was on the seat next to mine. Perhaps he didn't entirely trust me. He fixed me with a mute stare that to this day I can't find the right word for. I had to rebuke him roughly before he obeyed me and got out. As I shouted at him I was hoping that he wouldn't believe me, that he would be stubborn and refuse to go. When he was twenty yards away I started the engine, turned round quickly, stepped on the pedal and made my escape. So the last thing he heard from me was not a word of kindness or affection but a harsh reprimand. At that moment he realized that I was not playing hide-and-seek. That he had been tricked. That this was it. He chased me as hard as he could for hundreds of yards, in stooping apish bounds, with loud piercing shrieks: I have never heard such heartrending cries in my life, and I have carried wounded men on my back in wartime, and even when I could no longer see him in my side mirror desperately running after me I could still hear that shrieking receding in the distance behind me. For weeks afterwards I couldn't stop hearing it. Immanuel, who had stayed at home, maintained that he could also hear it, although that was absolutely impossible over a distance of sixty miles. But his blinking, which the doctors from Erella's clinic had not been able to do anything about, disappeared after a while and did not return even when his mother died. For a long while we all used to creep out sheepishly, at different times, to the garden gate, hoping or perhaps fearing that he might have found his way home. And if he did suddenly turn up, how could we make it up with him and would he ever forgive us? We did not open the can of sugar lumps for ages. Then when Erella was killed I put it to Immanuel that we should get another ape, but he would not hear of it and just said, Drop it. But the question is, Why did I tell you about the chimpanzee? What was the connection? Can you remember how we got on to it? What were we talking about before?

I said that I couldn't remember. That we had been talking about something else. And again without noticing I laid a finger on his hand and at once removed it, and I said: I'm sorry, Avraham.

Avraham Orvieto said that he wanted to ask a small favour of me. He was sorry he had told me the story. If it's not too hard, Noa, please let it be as if I hadn't told it. Then he asked me if I would like another iced coffee, and if not he asked my permission to accompany me wherever I was going, that is to say, unless I felt like being alone right now? He smiled hastily, as though he already knew what I was going to reply, and as hastily wiped away his smile. We walked awkwardly, almost in silence and somewhat out of our way, along a deserted avenue of tipuana trees that were slowly dropping a fine rain of withered yellow blossom on the sidewalk. It was getting dark outside, and we may even have slowed down unconsciously between one street lamp and the next, not talking, until we parted twenty minutes later on the steps of my school, as I had remembered that I had a staff meeting of some sort that evening. The meeting was already over when I arrived, and I hurried out again after Avraham Orvieto – to my surprise I suddenly sensed that sometimes I, too, couldn't stop blinking – but of course he was no longer on the school steps. He must have gone to his room at the Kedar Hotel, or somewhere else.

THE school year will be ending in another week. In the early years she used to be smitten from the middle of April with the urge to migrate, and start putting her name down for summer activities, a conference in Jerusalem, a festival in Galilee, a nature lovers' ramble in the Carmel range, a refresher course for teachers in Beersheba. This year she is too caught up in this crusade of hers to think of putting herself down for any summer sortie. I asked her on Saturday, apropos of nothing, what plans she had for the long holidays. When she said, We'll see, I dropped the subject.

Most people are always busy with arrangements, preparations, leisure activities. I am happy with my home and the desert. Even my work is gradually becoming superfluous. I'll give it up soon. My pension, our savings, and the rent from the property in Herzliyya will be enough to keep us going to the end. What will I do all day? I'll examine the desert, for example, on long walks at dawn before everything starts to blaze. During the hot hours I'll sleep. In the evening I'll sit on the balcony or have a game of chess with Dubi Weitzman at the California Café. At night I'll listen to London. Those hills over there, the mouth of the wadi, the scudding clouds, two cypresses at the end of the garden, oleanders and that empty bench next to the bougainvillaea bower. At night you can see the stars; some of them change their positions after midnight according to the seasons of the year. Not according to the seasons, parallel to them. There is a field of golden stubble on the nearest part of the plain, just behind the garden wall. An old Bedouin sowed it with barley in the autumn and harvested it in the spring and now the goats come and chew the stubble. Beyond, there are barren wastes extending to the top of the hills and further, to the mountainous mass that sometimes looks like mist. The slopes are a jumble of brown-black lumps of flint and paler rocks of chalk that the Bedouin call *hawar*, between patches of sand erosion. All in black and white. Everything in its place. Forever. All present and silent. To be at peace means to be as much like the mountains as possible: silent and present. Vacant.

This morning on the news they broadcast an excerpt from a speech by the Foreign Minister, who talked about the hoped-for peace.

The phrase "hoped-for" is mistaken here. Either hope or peace: you can't have both.

Today she said she's going to Beersheba again after school. She promised to fill up with gasoline and to try to be back not too late. But I hadn't asked what time she was thinking of getting back, nor had I asked her to be back early. As if she'd flown into this room by mistake and now she's in such a panic she can't find the window. Which is open as it always has been. So she flutters from wall to wall, crashing into the lampshade, hitting the ceiling, bumping into the furniture, hurting herself. Just don't try to point her towards the door: you can't help her. Any movement from you makes her panic worse. If you're not careful, instead of guiding her outside to freedom you'll scare her into an inner room where she'll keep on beating her wings against the glass. The only way to help her is by not trying to help. Just shrink. Freeze. Blend into the wall. Don't move. Has the window really always been open? Am I really hoping she'll fly away? Or am I lurking in wait for her, motionless, fixing her with a blank immobile stare in the darkness, waiting for her to drop from exhaustion?

Because then I can bend over her and look after her the way I did at the beginning. From the beginning.

IT turned out in Beersheba that there had been some sort of misunderstanding about my appointment with Benizri. An obnoxious secretary with little earrings like drops of blood was delighted not to find my name in his diary: the woman who made my appointment is, according to her, a half-witted typist who comes in twice a week and does nothing, and has no authority to deal with the public. Mr. Benizri is in a meeting. All day. Okay so I heard you the first time, you've come specially all the way from Tel Kedar. What a pity. I'm sorry.

When I insisted, she agreed, with a gesture of vague loathing, to check on the intercom and see if he could spare me a quarter of an hour anyway. As she replaced the receiver with her crimson nails, she said, Not today, miss, try again in something like two–three weeks like, when Mr. Benizri gets back from the conference. And remember, give me a tinkle first, I'm Doris, if someone called Tikki answers, you're wasting your time. Poor kid, she had a child by a basketball player who doesn't want to know, and now it turns out her baby's a Mongolian. And she's religious too. If it was me that was religious, I'd be tempted to drive on Saturday. Who are you, then? What do you want Mr. Benizri for, maybe I can do something for you in the meantime?

At this point I gave in. I asked her to bother Benizri again and tell him that Theo's Noa is here.

A minute or two later he shot out of his office, all excited, oozing charm, waggling his hips, his paunch, Come in, wazzat, sure, and how's our dear friend? Healthwise? And workwise? Did he send you with the findings? That's nice. He's a great man.

And so forth.

But about your business, see here, Mrs. Noa, quite frankly,

how should I put it: so you've got yourself a nice generous donor, the best thing you can do is send him to us. We'll put him on the right track. Never heard of any drugs in Tel Kedar. Insignificant. What, have we fallen on our heads? Are we going to attract all the you-know-whats of Greater Tel Aviv here? Better he should invest the money in, let's say, an old people's home. The Golden Age as they say. That's one thing we could really do with and it would work a treat. But as for importing a truckload of junkies . . . You know, drugs these days don't come on their own, they come with crime, with AIDS, with violence, with all sorts of kinkiness, if you'll excuse me. How does a nice girl like you come to get mixed up in a story like this anyway? You could even land Theo in the dirt too, heaven forbid. You know how it is these days, everything leads straight to the media, the local rags, in-depths, filth, God preserve us. Still, we can't waste a donor. Just you bring him to me. Generous givers don't grow on trees nowadays. It's because of the bad image of the State, which is thanks to the mess the Arabs in the territories have got us into, damn them. What does Theo have to say about the situation? He must be really teed off. The State is his life's blood. How long have you been with Theo now? Eight years? That's nothing. Insignificant. Just you listen to someone who knew Theo in the old days, when this country was nothing but sand dunes and fantasies. We still admire him from the times he used to blow up British police stations and radar installations. He's a really effective guy. More than effective: exemplary. If only he'd gone on running Development, we wouldn't have had all the foul-ups that have happened since. What a shame it's all gone up the spout. Just you remember you've got yourself a national treasure there, make sure you look after him like the gleam in your eye. Whatever happens, don't forget to give him a big hug from Benizri. And as for your junkies, just you drop them, before the dirty business starts. And your donor: send him to me and I'll put him on the right track. Goodbye.

I drove back from Beersheba to Tel Kedar in the wide old Chevrolet like a terrorist, hooting madly as I passed, cutting corners, all tense inside, seething with a cold rage that beat with a pulse of triumph. As if I'd already had my revenge. Drive straight to Muki Peleg's instead of going home, sit down with crossed knees on his low bed, a record, dim lights, shoes, a glass of wine, blouse, bra, without desire or any feeling except a destructive throbbing. Lips, shoulders, breast, then gradually southwards, by the book, twenty minutes more or less, without any passion on his part either, just collecting points in a catalogue of achievements that will never be full. Afterwards I'll have to hand him his points – sweetheart, how was I, you were great, sensational – and have for myself the satisfaction of getting the better of old "Gleam in Your Eye". I'll have a shower at his place and while I'm buttoning up my blouse he won't be able to resist asking me again, how was it, and I'll reply with Benizri's favourite phrase, Insignificant, thanks. I'll start the car and drive home with my terrorist rage defused. I'll say to Theo that tonight I'm doing the cooking. No reason. Just because I feel like it. With a white tablecloth and wine. In honour of what? In honour of Noa, who has decided to reconsider and climb down. In honour of her belated return to her natural dimensions. And tonight there'll be no jackal padding in the hall and no BBC from London. Tonight I'll put him to bed in my bed and I'll settle myself in his lookout post on the balcony. My turn now to sit facing the dark. In the morning, before going off to teach the poetry of Bialik, I'll write to Avraham Orvieto and tell him to find another sucker. Ezra Zussman's posthumous poems are entitled *Footprints Lost in the Sand* – they finally found me the book in the University Library in Beersheba – and on page 63 I came across a poem that I liked the first half of. Instead of creating refuges I'll volunteer to collect warm winter clothing for immigrants. Or gift parcels for soldiers. I'll find some minor good cause within the limits of my ability, without biting off more than I can chew. Maybe I'll take it upon myself to edit a memorial volume for Immanuel Orvieto on behalf of the school, try to collect some material, though it'll probably turn out that no one has anything to say because who actually knew him – not even his class teacher or his counsellor.

I find it pathetic the way good people tend to volunteer to do good things for sentimental reasons. The right way is to serve the Good like that overworked middle-aged policeman, with an undistinguished round face and a small pot belly, whom I saw at the Ashkelon junction crawling on all fours to help the injured people trapped in an overturned truck while they waited for the ambulance to arrive. It was several years ago but I remember every detail: he was lying on the ground, giving the kiss of life to an unconscious woman through the crushed door. But the moment the rescue team arrived on the scene and a doctor or paramedic crawled up and took over, the policeman stood up, turned his back – there was nothing he could do now to help the injured so he set to work getting the traffic moving again: That's right, straight ahead, miss, keep moving please, the show's over.

Drily. Gruffly even. In a smoke-roughened voice. Oblivious of his mud-caked hair, his flattened cap and the rivulet of grimy blood trickling from his nose. He had sweat patches at his armpits and dusty sweat running down his face. Several years have passed, but I have not forgotten that peculiar combination of gruffness and grace. It is still my ambition to serve the Good in the way I learned from that policeman: not with gushing emotion but with supreme precision. With that air of just doing a job that verges on callousness. Confidently. Surgically. "And where are we meant to be shining, and by whom is our shining required," as Ezra Zussman wrote in the opening poem of his collection.

By the time I reached the traffic lights in the centre of Tel Kedar the poem and the policeman had helped me to get over my humiliation and dispense with revenge. Muki Peleg must find himself someone else. He would have to make do with Linda Danino. What would it achieve if yet another humiliated woman offered herself, between seven o'clock and twenty past, on a hot, damp evening in a small town in the desert, to the music of Ravel's *Bolero*, on a bed still covered with its dusty counterpane, to a boastful, rather shabby lecher, drenched in loud aftershave, so as to punish a man who meant her no harm and who would never discover what she had done? What good would it do? What benefit would it bring her?

None at all. Insignificant.

Muki Peleg once said to me, after his usual perfunctory spate of compliments and endearments, that actually he rather likes the pair of us. Theo and me. Not likes: admires. That's not it either. He never quite manages to say what he really means.

That's his problem. Over the years, he said, Theo and I had come to resemble each other in some indefinable way. Not in our characters, or outward appearance, or gestures, but something else, if I could only understand what he was getting at. You often notice that a sort of resemblance gradually appears in a couple who can't have children. Never mind. Forget it. He'd put his foot in it again. And I was blushing, all because of him, prattling on without sense or sensitivity. Sorry. He always ended up saying the opposite of what he meant. Similar vibes, maybe. No. What the hell. That wasn't it either.

I drove slowly past Muki's office, estate agents and investment consultants, did a U-turn at the lights and returned towards President Ben Zvi Avenue. I stopped there for a moment, trying to remember what I had forgotten, and made up my mind that Noa was not going to climb down after all but would continue working to set up the Immanuel Orvieto Remedial Centre. At least until someone better qualified turned up who was willing to take over from her. That's right, straight ahead, miss, keep moving please, the show's over.

I did, however, park the battered great Chevrolet outside the supermarket. I bought various cold meats and salads, wine, an avocado, an aubergine, some spicy olives, and four kinds of cheese: the sin may have been called off but the ceremony of atonement was on. I found Theo sitting in the living room, his feet bare on the white rug, dressed in undershirt and tracksuit bottoms. He was neither reading nor watching television. Perhaps, like yesterday and the day before, he was dozing with his eyes open. After taking a shower I put on a flowery skirt, a blue summer blouse and a scarf. I unplugged the phone, even though I still had to sort out one thing I hadn't managed to remember to do. I forbade Theo to help me get supper ready, and when he asked what the occasion was I laughed and answered: Gleam in Your Eye.

He sat down at the kitchen table and while I sliced and warmed and poured he carefully folded green paper napkins and fed them into the special holder. In any physical activity, even something as simple as opening an envelope or putting the needle on a record, I observe a sort of precise manual dexterity that he may have inherited from generations of clockmakers, butchers, fiddlers and scribes. Though he once told me that his maternal grandfather was actually the last of a long line of gravediggers in some Ukrainian shtetl. He worked for thirty-two years as a planner, most of the time as a senior planner, in the Development Agency. They say he invented some new concepts, that he led some campaigns, some claim he left his mark. When I met him in Venezuela he was already detached, almost cold. He never wanted to talk about the conflict, the defeat, the collision with the Minister, things I learned about from vague snatches of rumours, dismissal, maybe an intrigue, followed by transfer to a dead-end department. Whenever I tried to ask, he took cover behind remarks like, My time there had come to an end, or, I'd already given them everything I had to give. That was all. About his present work he did not speak. Nor did he want me to meet his acquaintances from back then. When I first suggested that we go to live in Tel Kedar he agreed after a couple of days. When I found a teaching job in the secondary school, he opened a small office called Planning Ltd. Within a few months he had severed his links with his old acquaintances like someone opting for a deep retreat. In any case, he said, in a few years he would be due for his pension. Some evenings he goes to the California Café for an hour or two, and sits in a corner near the window overlooking the square, reading *Ma'ariv* or playing chess with Dubi Weitzman. But most days he gets home from the office at ten past five and stays in till the following morning. As though he is turning his back on something. He has gradually sunk into a perpetual hibernation, winter and summer alike, if one can use the word "hibernation" about a man who suffers from insomnia.

While I wrapped potatoes in foil preparatory to baking them, I told him about Benizri and I almost told him about what I almost did on my way home. I didn't want to talk about the image of the good policeman, even though I knew Theo wouldn't mock me. Slowly, intent as though on an intellectual effort, he folded the last napkin and tucked it into the holder. As if this one were more special or more complicated than the others. He said calmly: He's quite a little genius, that Benizri. He also said: It's not easy for you, Noa. These words made me hold back my tears.

After ice cream and coffee I asked him what he wanted us to do this evening. We could catch the second showing of the sexy comedy at the Paris Cinema. Unless he had a better idea. Whatever. He turned his head and squinted at me, and his broad, peasant head at that moment conveyed an amused blend of affection, suspicion and shrewdness, as though he had discovered some detail in me that had eluded him up to now, and decided that it actually worked in my favour. Glancing at his watch he said: Right now I could take you out and buy you a new dress, for instance. Only the shops are closed.

Instead we left the dishes on the table and hurried to catch the second show at the cinema. The street lamps in the square by the traffic lights were feeble; only the Monument to the Fallen was lighted up, by a pale yellow beam from the bushes. A solitary, skinny soldier sat on the iron railings, drinking beer out of a can. His eyes were riveted to the legs of a girl in a red miniskirt who had her back to him. As we walked past, he turned to look at me. It was a desperate look of desire held in check by cowardice. I put my arm round Theo's waist. I said: I'm here, how about you? He laid his hand on my hair. That supper you made for us, he said, wasn't a meal, it was a work of art. I said: What do you think, Theo? Muki Peleg said to me once that you and I are like each other in some way. I found that quite funny: In what way are we like each other?

Theo said: Muki Peleg. Who's that? You mean that agent. The

clown with six fingers on his left hand. A bit over the top, isn't he? A downmarket Casanova? Wanders around in a T-shirt that says Devil's Tear? Or am I mixing him up with someone else? Stop summing up, I said; you're always doing it.

It was a British film, ironic and too clever, about an intellectual woman publisher who gets worked up about a Ghanaian immigrant. After giving herself to him once out of curiosity she falls for him so passionately that she becomes his slave, physically and financially, and then she becomes enslaved to his two violent brothers as well. The comical side was mainly in the relations between her family, who are radical Third-World-lovers and supporters of downtrodden races, and the boyfriend and his brothers: under a thin layer of broadminded tolerance the most ordinary, base prejudices kept bubbling up. There were some telling visual cuts from elegant modern bohemian drawing rooms to run-down kitchens in the slums, and back to book-lined rooms with displays of African art. Halfway through I whispered to Theo, Love will win, you'll see. A quarter of an hour must have elapsed before he whispered back: There isn't any love here. It's just Frantz Fanon and the downtrodden rebelling and getting their sexual revenge.

When we got home he went to the kitchen and came back ten minutes later with a jug of mulled wine and glasses. We drank almost without talking. Something in his eye made me cross my knees. Theo, I said, there's something you ought to learn. You don't put honey in mulled wine, you put it in tea. In mulled wine you put a little lemon. And why did you bring these glasses? They're for cold drinks. We've got different glasses for mulled wine, the smaller ones. You don't care any more. It's all so insignificant.

In bed we didn't speak. I put on my demure white nightie, like a girl from a religious boarding school, he said once, and he came to my room naked apart from an elastic bandage round one knee because of an old injury. I imagined I could feel with my fingertips the progressive lightening of the hair on his arms and chest, from dark black to grey to ash to silver; his body was tough and compact but his desire tonight seemed almost separate from him, as if what he really wanted was to enfold or encircle all of me, as if he longed to comprehend or include me, to have me in his debt, and he was so intent on reaching all of my skin that he hardly cared what his own body would receive, if anything, as long as I was curled up in the fetal position and wrapped in his body like a chick under a wing. I wanted and yet didn't want to surrender to him, to obey him, to give him the power to give and give and give, and yet I slid out of his embrace, from his delicious pampering, and I made him lie on his back and not interfere in what was being done to him, until the point when we were quits, and from then on to the end we were both for each other, like a duet for four hands, we may even for a moment have resembled two devoted parents bending over a cot, intently, heads touching, playing with a baby who returns love for love. Afterwards I covered him with a sheet and ran a finger across his strong peasant brow and his greying military haircut until he fell asleep and I stood up and walked with bare feet to the kitchen and cleared away the supper things and washed and dried the dishes and the mulled-wine glasses that were really cold-drink glasses and where did he get the idea of putting honey in, strange, old Gleam in Your Eye, what did he mean when he said it's not love, it's the downtrodden rebelling? I put everything away and changed the tablecloth. Theo did not wake up. As if tonight I had passed him all my own powers of sleep. Then I went out and took over his place on the balcony facing the desert. I remembered Benizri saying that at first it was all sand and fantasies here and I remembered the religious typist, Tikki or Rikki, the one who had a baby by a basketball player who didn't want to know now, and the baby turned out to be a mongol, or as the crimson woman said a Mongolian. And I thought about the lovesick chimpanzee, and the can of sugar lumps, and the boy who was once a child with blinking eyelids and who seemed to live inside a bubble of winter even in summer, perhaps because I dimly remembered him in a green sweater and brown corduroy trousers in a class where everyone else wore shorts. Although I was not entirely sure now about the corduroy trousers. Whatever the poet did or didn't want to say gets in the way of the poem? I should have tried to initiate a conversation. I should have invited him here, home. I should have got him talking. All I did was flit across his loneliness without stopping. Another time he said he thought words were a trap. I don't understand now why I didn't realize what he was saying was virtually a cry for help: "And over all there hangs a smile, fading and faint and painful", as Ezra Zussman wrote in a poem about autumn evenings.

Above the hills rose a saracen crescent moon that bathed in pallor the waste plots and apartment blocks. There was not a single lighted window. The street lamps still shone unnecessarily and one of them kept flickering: insignificant. A cat passed beneath my balcony and vanished among the bushes. Beyond the hills there was a faint salvo of shots, followed by an echoing rumble, and again a cold silence, which touched my skin. I also remembered the aunt who worked in the bank and died just two days after they found the boy. A plain, desiccated woman with short coppery hair secured with a kind of plastic bow. And she had a funny habit, when you sat down facing her in the bank and talked to her, of covering her mouth and nostrils with her freckled hand, as though she was always anxious that she might have bad breath, or more likely that you did. She used to end every conversation by saying, "That's one hundred percent okay", which she always uttered in a monotone. A rustling passed through the darkened garden as though my thoughts about the dead had left me and gone down there to crouch among the oleanders. As though the twisted remains of a dog were crawling down there. For a moment I thought the old bench under the bougainvillaea bower was broken: the moonlight had altered the angles, the shadows of the struts of the bench had got jumbled up with the struts themselves, and the bench now looked like the broken reflection of a bench in rippling water. What did Avraham Orvieto mean when he said in the staff room, as though referring to a fact known to everyone except me, that I was the only one the boy liked? Maybe I should have asked him to show me his son's letters, especially the one where he mentioned the pencil that never existed.

I was awakened at a quarter to seven by Theo, brisk, freshly shaved, stocky, wearing a smartly pressed blue shirt with epaulettes, looking like a retired colonial soldier with his broad shoulders and his short grey hair, with the morning paper under his arm, bringing me some very hot strong black coffee that he had ground himself as usual by hand and percolated, as though he were trying to conjure up a scene in that cruel British film. Apparently in the middle of the night, instead of going to bed, I had fallen asleep on the white couch in the living room. I took the coffee from him and said, Listen, don't be angry, I promised you yesterday I'd fill the Chevrolet up on the way back from Beersheba but in the end I clean forgot. Never mind, Theo said, I'll do it myself, later, on my way to the office after I've taken you to school. It's not time I'm short of, Noa.

THEO's office, Planning Ltd., is situated on the top floor of the building by the traffic lights. It has an outer and an inner office, a drawing board, a desk, various wall-maps, a colour photograph of David Ben Gurion staring resolutely into Nahal Zin in the desert, two metal cabinets, some shelves containing different-coloured folders, and in a corner of the outer office a couple of simple chairs and a coffee table.

Friday. Quarter past ten. On Fridays the office is always closed, but this morning Theo has come in to wait for the cleaning woman, Natalia, even though she has her own key. Until she arrives he has decided to go over one or two letters. He switches on the air conditioning and the powerful light over the drawing board. Then, changing his mind, he switches off the light and waits at the window instead. At the counter of Gilboa's, Books and Stationery, he notices a small crowd: they are waiting for the newspapers that normally arrive at nine o'clock in the morning. This morning they are late. They say the police have set up roadblocks on all the roads out of Beersheba because there has been a bank raid. Near the monument, two gardeners wearing broad-brimmed straw hats are stooping to plant new rosemary bushes in place of the old ones that have died. Theo asks himself why he should not do a bit of work this morning. At least until Natalia arrives. He might try to jot down a few preliminary thoughts about the Mizpe Ramon project: at present all that is needed is a schematic outline, perhaps a few simple drawings without any detail and not even to scale. They haven't even got a budget yet, there's been no final decision, and they still haven't asked him to send in detailed plans. He thinks for a while but cannot find within himself that spark of acuity that is essential if an idea is to emerge. What's happened to Natalia today? Perhaps he ought to try to call her, find out if anything's wrong, though he has the impression they're living in the prefabs and it's doubtful if they have a phone, and anyway she once explained to him in broken English mixed with a few Hebrew words that her husband is madly jealous and is suspicious of the faintest hint of a man, even his own old father. He thinks about her, hardly more than a child, barely seventeen and already married and downtrodden, a submissive, timid girl, between smiles her mouth seems pursed as if to weep, if you put a simple question to her she trembles all over and goes white, her waist and breasts are those of a woman but she still has the face of a schoolgirl. Desire suddenly surges up inside him, violently, like a fist clenching.

Friday. Noa is at school till twelve thirty. Then they've agreed to meet here and go to the shops together to try to choose her a skirt. He skipped his shower this morning, to hang on to the odour of her love that he can smell now, not with his nostrils but with his pores. Her laughter, her spontaneity, her body, the speck of light that capers rapidly in the pupils of her eyes – even her wrinkled hands, dappled with patches of brown pigment, so many years older than the rest of her, as though the forces of withering are patiently assembling there, waiting for a sign of vulnerability so as to spread all over her body – all seem to him to be joined to the very core of life itself. Like an electrical current she conducts life to him, too. Even if it was thinking of Natalia that aroused his desire, the flicker came from Noa and returns to her. There is no way of explaining this to her. Instead he will buy her a skirt and maybe a dress as well. And since Natalia has not come to clean the office and may not come today, there is time to stand at the window and watch the square by the traffic lights. What was the mistake that the male world made about Alma Mahler? What was Alma Mahler really like? Both questions are empty. Once, in Mexico City, during a festival of modern music, he happened to hear on successive evenings two performances of the *Kindertotenlieder*, one sung by a baritone with piano accompaniment, the other by a woman with a deep voice, perhaps a contralto, full of longing and yet pure and calm as though in resignation. Theo remembers that the latter was so poignantly sad that he had to get up and leave the auditorium. The second song in the cycle is called "Ah, now I know why oft I caught you gazing", and the fourth, "I think oft they've only gone a journey". These names cause him a dull ache like a single low note on the cello. The names of the other songs he cannot remember, even though he tries very hard. He must ask Noa tonight.

Under his window a woman in a headscarf passes carrying in each hand a chicken freshly killed for the Sabbath. As the woman is short and the square is dusty, the dead combs leave a trail behind them on the sidewalk. Theo smiles for a moment under his moustache and almost winks shrewdly, like an avaricious peasant who, vaguely suspecting that the man he is bargaining with has adopted a cunning ruse, starts to plot a way of eluding the trap. The woman has already vanished.

In front of the Sephardi synagogue an improvised table has been erected, a wooden door resting on two barrels. It is covered in open books, presumably sacred books that have been brought out of the closets on account of the damp and the worm to take the air in the sunshine. Half past ten and Natalia still isn't here: she won't come today. Has her husband locked her up again? Does he beat her with his belt? He must find their address right away, this morning. Go round, see if he can help, break down the door if necessary, to prevent a disaster. There's still time: Noa won't be here for another two hours. But here is the taxi from Beersheba with the weekend papers. Limor Gilboa, Gilboa's pretty daughter, arranges them adeptly, inserting into the outer pages that have just arrived the supplements that were sent on yesterday's taxi. Gilboa himself, a tubby teddy bear of a man, full of energy, reminiscent of a trade-union hack, with his wavy grey hair, his protruding paunch, always looking as if he is about to embark on a speech, has already started selling *Yediot* and *Ma'ariv* to the crowds of people elbowing their way towards him and extending their hands. Theo jots down a little list of things that are needed for the office and decides to go down to

Gilboa's to buy them when the crowd has thinned out, and perhaps also the weekend *Ma'ariv* before they have all been snatched up. As for the sketch he has been asked to do for Mizpe Ramon, it's not urgent, in the course of next week he may have a brainstorm. Let them wait. They certainly won't build their leisure complex over the weekend, in fact they never will. If only everything that had been done there so far could be wiped out and a fresh start made, without the hideous housing schemes, but in a low-key architectural rhythm, in a relation of proper humility to the silence of the crater and the lines of the mountain ranges. He locks the office and goes downstairs.

Pini Bozo has adorned the walls of his shoe shop with a display of portraits: Maimonides, the Lubavitcher Rebbe, the Holy Rabbi Baba Baruch. It may not help, but it can't do any harm. Even though he is not a practising Jew, he has some fear of God in his heart, and also some respect for the religion that has protected us from all manner of evil for two thousand years. Besides these rabbis Bozo has hung up a photograph of the previous President of Israel, Navon, who is popular because he was a man of the people. On either side of him he has stuck up Shamir and Peres, who in his opinion ought to make their peace for the public good and work together again, against internecine strife: we have enough to do combating the external enemies who want to destroy us, the whole nation ought to unite against them and march forward together. Bozo's wife and baby son were killed in a tragic event here four years ago, when a young love-crossed soldier barricaded himself in the shoe shop, started shooting with a submachine gun and hit nine people. Bozo himself was saved only because he happened to go to the Social Security that morning to appeal against his assessment. To commemorate his wife and child he has donated an ark made of Scandinavian wood to the synagogue, and he is about to give an air conditioner in their memory to the changing room at the soccer field, so that the players can get some air at half-time.

At the end of the sidewalk next to Bozo Shoes there are some municipal benches, and a plastic slide with a sandbox at the bottom. In stylish concrete containers among the Indian beech trees a few petunias struggle to survive. Blind Lupo is resting on one of the benches, his face to the strong sun. He is surrounded by pigeons, some of which are perching on his shoulders. His pointed stick is secured like an anchor in a crack between two paving stones. Back in Bulgaria, they say, he had a high-ranking post in the secret service. Here in Tel Kedar he works nights in the telephone exchange, seeing the keys and switches with his fingertips. Every morning he sits in this little park, harnessed to his grey dog, staring straight at the sun and scattering maize for the pigeons that flock around him even before he reaches the bench. Sometimes one of them trusts him enough to settle on his knees and let him stroke its feathers. When he stands up he occasionally bumps into his dog and mumbles politely, Sorry.

An engaged couple, Anat and Ohad, are standing in Mr. Bialkin's furniture shop. They are looking for an upholstery fabric that will suit the three-piece suite and co-exist with the curtains, but their tastes differ: whatever he likes she finds repulsive, and whatever she likes reminds him of a whorehouse for Polish officers. She asks venomously where he has acquired his experience, and he beats a hasty retreat, Look what a state we're in, quarrelling over nothing. Anat replies that it is not a quarrel but a difference of opinion, and that's perfectly normal. Ohad suggests a compromise: Let's go to Beersheba after the weekend, there's a much better choice there. But that's exactly what I said in the first place, she crows triumphantly, and you wouldn't hear of it. Mr. Bialkin intervenes gently: Maybe the lady would like to take a look through the catalogue, and if there is anything that meets with her favour I shall fetch it on Tuesday from Tel Aviv, God willing. Ohad, for his part, corrects her: I don't deny that you suggested it, but you were the one who said let's try Bialkin first, and if we don't find it there . . . His fiancée cuts in: I don't deny that I said it, but don't you deny that you agreed. The young man concedes her point, but asks her to remember that he had certain reservations. Reservations, she says, have you become a lawyer all of a sudden? Next thing you'll be filing an appeal.

When they have left the shop Bialkin says: That's how it is

these days. They eat their hearts out and they die. And what can I do for you, Mr. Theo? A rocking chair? A wooden one? No, I haven't got anything like that. I've got a TV chair that can rock. Nobody makes the old rocking chairs any more. Theo thanks him and leaves. He had an idea the opening song of the *Kindertotenlieder* was called "Once More the Sun", but he is not certain. Might as well ask Noa to check it in the school library, she spends such hours there.

At the Entebbe falafel stand a Bedouin in his fifties is buying shawarma in pitta. The shawarma is a new venture, and Avram is happily explaining to the Bedouin that it's still trying out. If it goes well, in a couple of weeks' time we'll try grilled shish kebab. Meanwhile a haughty white cat with tail erect prances past Kushner's bitch, who had a litter of pups a couple of days ago. The bitch chooses to feign sleep, but opens one eye a slit to observe the extent of the insolence. Cat and bitch alike behave as though the whole situation were beneath their dignity. Old Kushner says to Theo: What's up, we never see you these days. Theo's left eye shrinks as though peering through a microscope and he replies that nothing's changed. If you'd like to have one of the puppies, Kushner says, but Theo interrupts him sharply from under his authoritative moustache: No thanks. Quite unnecessary.

At a quarter past eleven a small funeral cortège passes by the lights, only a handful of mourners, mainly elderly Ashkenazim. From his invariable stool in the doorway of Bozo Shoes, Pini Bozo asks who has died and how, and Kushner the bookbinder replies that it is old Elijah, Schatzberg the pharmacist's senile uncle, the doting old fool who kept escaping and sitting in the post office all day long; every five minutes he used to join the queue and when he got to the counter he'd ask, When's Elijah coming, and however often they chased him away he always came back.

The cortège is in a hurry. The pallbearers are almost running because the Sabbath is approaching and they still have a lot of preparations to take care of before sunset. The elderly mourners are panting with the effort, and even so a gap has opened up between the bier and the mourners and another one between the leading mourners and the ones at the back. With all the commotion the corpse, covered in a yellowing tallit, looks as though it is writhing in agony. A fair-haired, sparsely bearded religious youth hurries at the head, rattling a tin can and promising that almsgiving saves you from death. Theo reflects for a moment and concludes that it is a moot point.

In the Champs–Elysées Hairdressing Salon a noisy argument has broken out between Violette and Madeleine, the two stylists, who are sisters-in-law. Their shouts can be heard on the other side of the square. One wails, You don't even know yourself any more when you're telling the truth and when it's a filthy lie. And the other shrieks back at her, You tampon, you, don't you dare call me filthy. They have both visited Muki Peleg's bed, and perhaps still do. Muki Peleg himself is sitting over a beer in the California Café with a group of taxi drivers, and at the sound of the shouting he embarks on a detailed comparison that has his audience in gales of raucous laughter. Muki clasps the beer glass that is perspiring with cold in the six fingers of his left hand. Then they light up and talk about index-linked shares. Meanwhile, the funeral cortège has disappeared behind the Tel Kedar Local Council building, while at Gilboa's the crowd has dispersed and there are still plenty of papers for sale. Pretty Limor Gilboa is standing at the counter staring after Anat and Ohad, who have left the furniture shop and entered the Electronics Boutique. Kushner points to her with his chin and says to Bozo, Look how that one takes care of herself: she's a regular Princess Diana. Bozo remarks sadly, Until the Russian immigrants arrived, she was considered to be a national-class cello player. Now that thousands like her have come from Russia, she's become no bigger than that. That's celebrity for you: it's like water. Yesterday there wasn't any, today it's running, tomorrow there'll be none again. Do you remember a minister called Yoram Meridor? He was a household name? Always on TV? They say now he's opened a shopping mall at Netanya Junction. That's celebrity.

Theo buys *Ma'ariv* and a local paper, sits down in the California, and orders a grapefruit juice. Muki Peleg invites him over to his table, which he calls the Council of Torah Sages. Theo hesitates and answers, Thanks, later maybe, and Muki adds, As the condemned man said to the hangman who offered him a cigarette while he was knotting the rope.

Theo skims the headlines. Risk of renewed hostilities. Deaf-mute divorcee from Acre burns ex-husband's mistress alive. Transport Minister walks out of ceremony in protest. Gasoline prices to rise from midnight on Saturday. Security forces prevent . . . In his mind's eye he follows the hasty Ashkenazi Sabbath-eve funeral cortège, which must have passed the car dump by now and reached the cemetery. First they lay the stretcher on the gravel path: like it or not, they'll have to wait for the stragglers to catch up. All the hurry was in vain: they can't begin until the last mourner gets here. The lugubrious Hungarian cantor fills his lungs with air, his face turns a furious red, and he starts to trill the prayer "O Lord Full of Compassion". He draws out the phrase, "May he repose in Paradise", he bows at, "he will face his destiny at the end of days", and the mourners say Amen. Now they push Schatzberg the pharmacist forward and tell him to repeat word for word the phrases the cantor mumbles, Magnified and sanctified, in Aramaic with an Ashkenazi accent, speedily and in our own times. Every day he disappeared but they never worried about him because he always turned up on the dot of eight o'clock at the post office, with a shy smile shining in his childlike blue eyes, the smile of a shy man who has forgotten what it was that has made him happy. The cantor begs pardon and forgiveness from the dead man if any offence has inadvertently been committed against him in the course of the preparations for the burial or the burial itself, and formally releases him from membership of any association to which he may have belonged in his lifetime. He used to come up to you in the street sometimes and bow politely, his blue eyes glowing with warmth and feeling, and address you in that soft voice of his: Forgive me, sir, would you be so kind as to inform me when Elijah is coming? That is why he was known in the town as Elijah, or sometimes as Schatzberg-the-pharmacist's Elijah.

Now the gravediggers tip the canvas, a task requiring the cooperative precision and dexterity of an operating theatre, and the sparsely bearded religious youth clasps the dead man's feet lightly and like a skilful midwife lets the wrapped body slide smoothly from the stretcher into the grave. They quickly draw away the tallit, like cutting an umbilical cord. Then they lay down five slabs of precast concrete, and set to work with spades raising a heap of earth that they mark with a rectangle made up of blocks of grey cement. On top of the mound, approximately over the deceased's noble brow, they set a metal plate inscribed not ELIJAH but GUSTAV MARMOREK RIP. The mourners wait for a couple of minutes in embarrassed silence, as if uncertain what to do next or expecting some necessary sign, then one of them stoops and lays a little stone, others follow suit, somebody makes for the gate, impatient for a smoke, and all the rest follow him, hurriedly again, it being midday on Friday, getting late. The gravedigger in charge locks the squat iron gates topped with a coil of rusty barbed wire. A few cars start up and wind their way out of sight behind the hill. Bozo the shoe-man's wife and child are buried here, in the upper section, four rows away from the soldier Albert Yeshua who, in a fit of unrequited love, killed them both with a submachine gun together with all the customers in the shop, and was killed himself ten minutes later by a single shot from a police marksman, in the middle of his forehead, between the eyes. Today's corpse has been laid to rest next to young Immanuel Orvieto from class 12C, and his aunt, who died two days after him of a cerebral hemorrhage. The boy's mother has lain for nine years now in Amsterdam. Everything is peaceful, Friday midday silence in the desert at the foot of the hill. Wasps drone ceaselessly around a rusty, dripping faucet. And two or three birds may continue to sing there, concealed in the pine trees tested by an easterly breeze that carefully rustles them needle by needle. Immediately beyond the last graves is a steep fenced rock face that the army does not let you cross, they say behind it is a wide valley full of secret installations. Theo pays for his drink and heads back to his office. He will have another look for his Russian cleaner, if her husband does not come at him with an axe. Noa will be here in a few minutes. Desert Chic Fashions, he ascertained by phone, is open till one o'clock on Fridays. In the little public gardens the blind man is still sitting with his dog, still surrounded by pigeons. Now he is pouring them some water from an army flask into a little plastic bowl. Theo has forgotten to buy the office supplies that he jotted down on a piece of paper. He'll get them next week. There's no hurry. And it also turns out that he's left his *Maʿariv*, unread apart from the headlines, on the table in the California Café. He's left the local paper behind, too. Meanwhile, the simple answer is, I am sorry, sir, I have no idea when Elijah is coming or indeed if he is coming at all. I do not believe he will come. But that is not what I was asked.

SHE finally chose a light-coloured dress in a rustic, possibly Balkan, style, with a butterfly-shaped bow below the breast. She reacted to the new dress at first with girlish pleasure. In front of the mirror her shoulders and hips circled as in a dance. But after the initial joy came hesitancy. Wasn't it too folksy? Too loud? And anyway, on what sort of occasions would she ever be able to wear a thing like this? And tell me frankly, Paula, isn't it a bit like a costume for a folk-dance company? She spent more than ten minutes agonizing between the mirror and the saleswoman, who declared that the two of them, the dress and Noa, were simply made for each other like music and good wine. Almost in the same breath she promised Noa to take out the shoulder pads, shorten the back a bit, and maybe lower the bow by an inch or so.

I stood in the corner by the cash register and said nothing. I had the feeling the saleswoman was secretly mocking, behind her façade of extravagant friendliness. But I didn't get involved. I went on standing to one side, hand in pocket, trying to identify by touch under my handkerchief the keys of the car the apartment the office and the mailbox, and then I counted the coins in my purse: eight shekels and eighty-five agorot, unless the five agorot was really another shekel coin, in which case it would make nine shekels eighty in all.

About a quarter of an hour passed before she did what she had been hoping she wouldn't do, and asked me what I thought.

Turn round, I said, stand up straight. Now walk away. That's right.

Do you like it, Theo?

It's got something, I said after thinking about it, provided you feel it's right for you. If you're not sure, don't buy it.

Noa said: But it's supposed to be a present from you.

Paula Orlev hastily intervened: It can come with this belt, or with this one. Try it tied like this, on the side, or tied in the middle, either way it's absolutely charming.

Noa looked at me suddenly with a look of Don't leave me alone, as though she were sending me a hot blast from the core of life. I shivered.

Theo?

I suggested that if she was still unsure, and it was Friday afternoon now, the dress would still be here on Sunday morning. What was the hurry?

On the way out she said: What a pity. I'd have quite liked to wear it for the weekend. I let myself be steamrollered by your logical reasoning.

I said that if on Sunday the dress still didn't please her, she could look for something more suitable on one of her next trips to Beersheba or Tel Aviv. Noa told me to stop dropping hints all the time about her trips. She would travel as and when there was a need for it, and without asking me for an exit permit. And anyway, who said she needed a new dress? What was this about dresses all of a sudden? It was you who offered to buy me a dress today, Theo, but as usual you managed to spoil it with your balanced calculations, your what's the problem, what's the hurry, on the one hand this, on the other hand that, and your regular strategy of maneuvering me into the position of a capricious little girl and your hints about my trips. It's not easy with you, Theo.

I said I didn't drop hints.

Noa said: But it's what you think. Don't deny it. You have made up your mind that I have taken on a task, no, not a task, more of a hobby, that is unnecessary, foolish and also too much for me.

I said: That's not correct.

And Noa, almost in tears: But I really do want it now. I want to wear it for the weekend. Do you mind if we go back?

We did a U-turn in front of the Kedar Hotel and drove back to Desert Chic and caught Paula Orlev just as she was shutting up shop. She opened up again for us and Noa put the Balkan dress on again. Paula said she knew we'd be back, she'd spotted at once that the dress liked Noa even more than Noa liked the dress, it looked so fresh on her, so cheeky, so cool, as her daughter always said, You must know her, Noa, Tal Orlev, you taught her in eighth grade.

When I took my credit card out Noa suddenly said, shyly, that she still wasn't a hundred percent sure. She asked me this time to tell her honestly what I thought. I said: Try to concentrate. The question is whether you feel good in this folksy dress or not.

Paula Orlev asked if I wasn't in too much of a hurry. And Noa told me to stop putting pressure on her instead of helping her make up her mind. It's so complicated with you, Theo, it's getting more and more unpleasant. The word "folksy" didn't exactly come out of the kindness of your heart. And turning to Paula she asked if she had anything similar but with less embroidery, or at least where the embroidery was less prominent.

At a quarter past two we left the shop again. Without the dress and also without that subtle affection that had joined us when we went in, left over from the night, from yesterday evening, and now we'd lost it. It didn't help when I pointed out that she, not I, had been the first to use the word "folksy". On the way home we stopped at the Palermo for a quick pizza so we shouldn't have to start making lunch at home, and by three o'clock we had somehow managed to do the weekend shopping in the supermarket and pick up the dry cleaning. Together we put the contents of the plastic bags away in the refrigerator and the kitchen cabinets and our clothes in the wardrobes. Noa said she thought that Paula was one of those nice people who you can see at once get real pleasure out of making you feel good. Such people are a rare commodity. It's as if she was choosing a dress for herself, not trying to sell one to me. I liked it when we went back, and she said the dress liked me. You probably weren't listening, Theo. You didn't enjoy being there. You weren't very nice, never mind about me, but Paula really didn't deserve that Arctic blast.

An Arctic blast on a day as hot as this, I said, actually wouldn't be so terrible. And I went on, Mrs. Orlev didn't strike me the same way as she did you. She seemed calculating. But of course I may be mistaken, I may even be doing her an injustice. This made Noa express some sharp remarks about "my character" – I always feel I'm being cheated, always adopt a negative stance, in advance, and whatever the situation, I'm suspicious, defensive, as though everybody is an enemy. The whole world's against us. Anyway, that's the world according to Theo. My father was a hot-tempered, even an aggressive man, who could fly off the handle and go really wild, raging at me and throwing his transistor at me or smashing it against the wall, but he wasn't a sour man. He wasn't bitter. There are times when you're even more of a spoiled child than he was. Even more of a Neanderthal male.

Isn't your lightning judgment a bit black-and-white, Noa?

With you everything's always black-and-black.

She left the room, flushed, sparking, pushing the door to angrily, but stopping it from slamming at the last moment and closing it gently without making a sound.

She took a long shower, apparently a cold one, and then shut herself up in her bedroom to rest because in the night, she said, she had not managed to get to sleep until she dropped onto the sofa in the living room at around three o'clock in the morning: Your tension, Theo, fills the apartment like a smell.

I knew precisely what to reply. But I restrained myself. Instead I concentrated for a moment and found not tension inside myself but an unrelieved tiredness. After she shut her door I went to my own room, without the weekend *Ma'ariv* or the local paper that I'd left at the California Café. The BBC World Service, from London, via the relay stations in Gibraltar, Malta and Cyprus, brought me a detailed, ruthless description of the destruction of the rain forests in South America, in a series of broadcasts under the title "The Death of Nature". The rain forests brought back a few memories, whereas the expression "The Death of

Nature" left me cold even though it was presumably intended to shock listeners. On the contrary: "The Death of Nature" had such a soothing effect on me that I fell asleep for twenty minutes and woke up only as the programme was ending and another, on changes in shipping routes, was beginning. The only way to help her is not to try to help. I should contain myself and say nothing. How many times have I reduced her to tears simply by trying to be helpful? Once, in her absence, I went through the whole apartment gathering her bits of paper that were scattered all over the place: on the kitchen table, on the coffee table in the living room, by the telephone, on the bookshelves in her bedroom, on shelves in the hall and the living room, and under little magnets clinging to the door of the refrigerator, on her bedside night table and on the floor at the foot of her bed. I carried all the loot off to my room and put it down on my desk, and I spent nearly three hours sorting it out for her: I put letters in one pile, drafts of memos in another, public opinion surveys, excerpts she had copied in her perfect handwriting from the books in Hebrew and English that the librarian had put together for her on drugs, their cultivation and distribution, influences, addiction and rehabilitation, another pile for prospectuses, non-committal or negative replies, some of them polite and some less so, from all sorts of institutes, organizations and bureaus, and hundreds of scraps of paper with telephone numbers or dates of meetings.

After an initial sorting I made a pile on the left-hand side of my desk of everything that had a date. I arranged them by date and subject and addressee. I copied the telephone numbers for her into a little notebook. I cleared out one of my own files for her and organized all the papers in eight compartments separated by coloured cardboard dividers on which I wrote precisely what was in each section.

Great, she said when she got in, wonderful. So logical. Thanks.

And the next moment, almost in tears: Who gave you permission, Theo? They're not yours, they're mine.

I promised. I didn't touch them again, I didn't say a word,

even when the contents of the file quickly dispersed and settled again like feathers over every available surface in the apartment.

Another time I left the office one morning and popped across to the printers opposite the traffic lights to order some headed notepaper and a receipt book in the name of her committee, and I even volunteered our own address and telephone number for their temporary use. This time she neither thanked me nor turned tearful but merely said in a quiet, hard voice, as though she were admonishing a disruptive pupil: Theo, this is going to end badly.

I said: Try to understand, Noa. Concentrate for a minute. I've noticed that apart from your African benefactor, the father of the junkie, you've had at least two further gifts. Small ones admittedly. Insignificant in fact. Still, you must realize that the law of the land stipulates that for any donation, however minimal, you must issue a proper receipt. It's a criminal offence not to. Surely you don't want us to get into trouble.

She stood up, whirling her light skirt, thrusting her fair hair back from her left cheek, as though opening up to me: We're not going to get into trouble, Theo. At least, I might, but you won't. You'll go on being the gleam in the eye. You're not a part of this.

If I were a stubborn man I could easily have explained to her that, even though I had promised not to touch and I was not breaking my promise, strictly speaking any involvement of hers involved us both for the simple reason that we had a joint bank account. Not to mention the three hundred dollars a month that the father sent her to fund the committee, and nobody knew, least of all she herself, what precisely she did with the money. Nevertheless I did not bother. I merely said: Look. These receipts. They're printed anyway. Here they are, on the table, I'm leaving them and you can do whatever you like.

Benizri, she hissed suddenly, that obsequious, brilliantined Levantine, calls you an angel of a man. You know what you are, Theo? A tombstone. It doesn't matter. I've got a headache.

I went back to the hall and continued my ironing. Inwardly I agreed with her: It's hopeless. There won't ever be a clinic for drug addicts in Tel Kedar. Or if there is, it'll close within a month. Nevertheless, it's something she's got to find out for herself, without my help. I've got to be invisible. Although maybe, on the other hand, maybe what I ought to do is locate the Orvieto man and say a few words that'll take this nonsense away from Noa once and for all, making certain she never discovers how I managed to find the crook, what I told him or what I saved her from. But no. I'll wait.

SATURDAY. Three p.m. Theo was lying in his undershirt on the floor of his room with the fan blowing next to him. I was sitting at the kitchen table, with grapes and coffee in front of me, reading an American monograph entitled *The Chemistry of Addiction*. There has been a debate for several years between two opposing schools of thought about whether drug addiction is an illness or whether it is a congenital tendency to be dependent on so-called psychoactive substances, including those found in tobacco, alcohol, coffee, aphrodisiac plants; in fact in a certain sense one might say that substances that cause dependency can be found in almost everything. A parallel was then drawn, albeit with certain reservations, between drug addiction and known diseases, such as diabetes, that display hereditary factors and environmental conditions that accompany the development of the disease or impede it. An addict who has been weaned off the drug still carries with him a chronic latent problem, that is, he is more exposed than other people to the danger of a relapse, qualified in brackets by the Hebrew expression "liable to return to his evil ways", an expression that I find unfair, as I noted on a slip of paper on which I was collecting questions and objections that occurred to me in the course of my reading. Suddenly Muki Peleg appeared: excited, out of breath, dishevelled, with the flowing locks of the young philosopher from the brandy advertisement, in trendy baggy trousers, with an artistic silk scarf at the opening of his crisp red shirt, a fifty-year-old teenager, with dazzling sky-blue shoes, bearing a pattern of little ventilation holes in the form of the letter B. He begged my pardon a million times over, but he had something really urgent to say. He always has something really urgent to say about everything. If it's not one thing it's something else, but always unpostponable. I sometimes enjoy his utterly unquenchable enthusiasm.

I reached up to button the light dress I was wearing and found that it was already buttoned up. Seating Muki across the kitchen table from me I closed my book, using the page of notes as a bookmark. Despite his protestations I poured him a cold Coke and passed him the grapes. Where's Theo? Resting? Sincere apologies for bursting in at such an unsocial hour, I normally hold Saturday afternoon sacrosanct. But something's cropped up that we've simply got to make a decision on today. By the way, in that green dress you look just like a flower on its stalk. Except that any flower would look like a weed next to you. To cut a long story short, if it weren't for the urgent problem he would go down on his knees here and now, if I would only stroke him, as the legless man said to the armless woman. Jokingly he raised his six-fingered hand and put a finger pistol-like to his temple to illustrate the hopelessness of unrequited love. He was probably trying to be funny, but when he realized he had failed he laughed and said, Never mind, and he also said, I've got this thing going with Linda now. But that's not why I've come. The point is, we've got to tell Theo at once that a fantastic opportunity has come up and it would be a crime to miss it. In a word, I've found a building for us. A palace, as a matter of fact. And it's only eighty-five thousand dollars, and there's no agency fees because I'm the agent, the only condition is that we initial an agreement tomorrow and finalize the contract, hand over the cash and do the transfer of ownership, all signed and sealed with no loose ends, by Tuesday morning at the latest.

I told him to begin at the beginning.

Yes, miss. Sorry, teacher. Well, it's like this. You must know that building all by itself, with the tiled roof, near the industrial zone. Everybody knows it. The Alharizi house. Opposite Ben Elul's garage. The one that's been empty for nearly a year. To cut a long story short, it's like this. There was this television importer called Alharizi from Netanya, when the town was just beginning, who had the bright idea of starting up a sort of exclusive business. A house to let to artists who wanted to commune with the desert and so on. Or to have a good time with a little rosebud on the side, if you've heard of such an option. It very soon turned out that it wasn't such an attractive proposition, there's Elat, Arad, Mizre Ramon, there's no shortage of desert paradises. This Alharizi guy let the house to Desert Resources, who used it to house technicians working on the oil drillings. To cut a long story short, you know how it was, they drilled and they drilled and nothing came of it and so the building stood empty, there was nobody to let it to, and now the gent is in a tearing hurry to sell it. The important thing is to pull out in time, as Snow White said to the seven dwarfs. To cut a long story short, he was asking a hundred thousand but I got him down to eighty-five by promising he'd have the money in his hands this week: the guy's under pressure, there's some story, he's got the law on his tail, don't ask me how I found out, Noa. I've got my methods. The trouble is that the old fart, sorry, got in touch simultaneously with Peleg's Agency, i.e. me, and with Bargeloni Bros, those new agents, the bastards, no disrespect intended to any real-life bastards. And they've got a client of their own, a dentist with his own lab, an Argentinian, a new guy, competition for Nir and Dresdner. Don't ask me how I found out. I've got my methods. Will you get me another Coke? Just seeing you getting up and sitting down makes me thirsty, and that dress like cellophane on a stalk. To cut a long story short, it's like this: we've got a couple of days' lead on them because fortunately for us the dentist is on reserve duty filling teeth in the army. We've got to make our minds up today and get in touch with Ron Arbel so he can ring Nigeria tonight. If the money's available, we must rush round there tomorrow and sign a provisional agreement, and pay up and complete on Monday or Tuesday at the latest. So what do you think: aren't I the greatest? Say something nice. A kiss perhaps? And the property's all checked out. It's clean: no mortgage, no lien, no third party. Never mind what it means. Forget it, Noa. You take care of the pretty side of life and leave the ugly side to me. Just you wake Theo up and we'll pop round together to look at this Buckingham Palace, though actually I ought to tell you to do

72

the opposite, let him sleep so you and I can go on having fun here in the kitchen, at least in theory, as the bread said when the butter spread all over it. Okay. I'm sorry. It just slipped out. To cut a long story short, miss, I'm handing you the clinic on a silver tray. It's quite a lot of money, actually, but weren't you afraid it might take us six months to locate suitable premises or that we might even have to build, which would have cost twice as much and taken four or five years, with all the permits? If we ever got there at all. Aren't you going to tell me I'm wonderful? Well don't, then. You're just mean. You know who really did tell me this week that I'm simply divine? You won't believe it: an Ethiopian woman. A divorcee. A peach. Didn't you know they get divorced, too? My second time with a black woman. Believe me, that was class. Classic class, if you really want to know. Eventually at three o'clock in the morning she let out such a loud scream the neighbours thought it was an air-raid alarm. Only make sure Linda doesn't find out. She's sure to take it amiss. To cut a long story short, we've got to the moment of truth. We've got to get Theo to say something about the state of the building and so on, and then we have to decide if we're going for the place or letting the dentist have it. If you want my opinion we should go for it. And I'm speaking as a member of the committee now, not as an estate agent, I've already told you that as an estate agent I won't accept a penny. Personally I'm all for a quick grab, as the Cossack said to the gypsy girl. Even if we haven't got the paperwork tied up just yet. What have we got to lose? Let's imagine the worst scenario, suppose we end up not getting planning permission. Suppose the clinic never gets off the ground. We can still say perfectly calmly to lawyer Arbel and mystery man Orvieto that the eighty-five thousand are as good as in a safe deposit: if our venture gets bogged down, I'll undertake to sell the property in six months' time for ninety or ninety-five. I'm even willing to let them have it in writing. Well, what do you think of me? Will you say something sweet?

I said: You're wonderful, because I was suddenly filled with affectionate pity for this middle-aged lamb with his sky-blue shoes, trying hard to be a wolf. A pitiful, vulnerable wolf, or, rather, a tortoise without a shell: with a single hint of scorn any woman could wipe out all the conquests of his thirty years' seduction marathon. In that instant I could see the twelve-year-old he had once been: pudgy, unloved, noisy, joining in the cruel jokes about his six fingers, a tedious, ingratiating child, attaching himself to everybody, striving in vain to amuse the world, and when the world refused to smile lapsing into buffoonery. Always hurrying to fill every gap in every conversation, to prevent a silence that might deny his existence. Constantly responsible for feeding the communal bonfire with twigs of foolish prattle, and when the twigs ran out he would get up and throw his own heart on the bonfire of mockery. A juvenile also-ran.

For almost twenty years he has been a divorced skirt-chaser (though he himself denies chasing skirts, quipping that he only chases what's inside them). He views the entire female sex as a stern tribunal unanimously condemning him to rush around making ritual gestures so as to please it, but it is never pleased. Subconsciously he knows that he can never obtain the desired pardon, despite the bed-points that he is indefatigably clocking up on a score-sheet of achievement that can never be completed. Despite which, he persists, undeterred, Sisyphean, panting from bed to bed as though the next one will bring him at last the coveted distinction, the formal release, the certificate of exemption from further exertion. Every time he tries to beam me a half-serious gesture of everlasting smouldering desire, what I pick up is not desire but a plea for some kind of feminine receipt that he has no idea what to do with. So he staggers on until his strength gives out, from seduction to seduction, from quip to quip, from bedroom scene to bedroom scene, puffing and panting, boasting, constantly threatened by the fear that the women are making fun of him behind his back, the threadbare hero of an Odyssey peopled by lonely divorcees, cheated wives taking vengeance, middle-aged housewives turning sour.

Muki, I said, you're wonderful, and I'm terribly jealous of all your Ethiopian women. Why don't I ever meet an Ethiopian man? But why don't you tell me what there is in that house? Didn't you say it was empty?

So it emerges that some money will have to be invested in improvements. For example, to put down new floors. For example, the toilet bowls are broken, so are the washbasins, even the roof is a bit so-so. And there will have to be some changes inside, but that really isn't his field. The best thing would be for Theo to pop round with us for half an hour or so, and give it a professional once-over. To give his opinion on the structure and on the possibility of shifting some walls or adding a storey and so forth. Apart from which, addicts, you know, bars on the windows, locks on the doors, the fence as I've said before is none too high. To cut a long story short, it's bound to come to a good few thousand on top, as the photographer said to the naked model. Actually, it depends how much more we want to spend. To cut a long story short, let's be decisive for a change, let's grab Theo and let's pick up Linda and Ludmir on the way, the whole committee, and take a really close look, as that horny Italian once said to Cleopatra. We've got to make our minds up today, because of the dentist. Yes, I've got the key. The unfortunate thing is that Bargeloni Bros have also got a key. Though actually you don't even need a key because it's all so decrepit. Why are you looking at me like that? Is decrepit a rude word? Or have you suddenly seen the light? Have you realized the man you've been looking for all your life is standing in front of you? Okay. Don't be angry. It just slipped out. I never manage to say what I'm really feeling, what I truly mean. That's my whole problem. Here's Theo. Hi, Theo. You jealous at finding us whispering together in the kitchen? If only it were true. Did you get some sleep? Are you awake? Let's put you in the picture.

There's no need, I said. Theo's not involved in all this.

Theo said: I'm just going to make myself some coffee and I'm off.

And Muki: What do you mean you're off? So who's died? On the contrary. Listen to the story, Theo, and then come along with us, take a good look, and decide about the place.

I said in a flat voice: Theo doesn't decide. The committee decides.

Meanwhile the water boiled. Theo made instant coffee for the visitor, for me and for himself. He offered sugar and milk. He took some more grapes out of the refrigerator, washed them, put them in front of us on two plates, and said: Well? To stay or to go? What's the majority verdict?

Without waiting for an answer he turned his back, in his undershirt, suntanned, his shoulders thick and hard, he gave us up, took his cup and went. All he left behind was his sorrow, wrapping it, as it were, round my shoulders. Beyond his bedroom door which he drew noisely to behind him I could guess him bent over his desk, leaning on it with both fists, resembling from behind an old, tired ox, standing silently as though waiting for some inner sound to come and release him from his waiting. I recalled him during one of our first trips in Venezuela, in a Jeep, on a dirt track running along a winding mist-filled valley, as he suddenly exclaimed that even if what was happening to us turned out to be love, he hoped we could go on being friends.

I went to his room to call out to him to come back, to join me and Muki. And while I was calling I knew I was making a mistake.

He sat down on his regular chair in the kitchen, his back resting on the side of the refrigerator, listening silently to the story about the Alharizi building, asking a couple of short questions, and while listening to the answers patiently and meticulously cleaning out the holes in the salt shaker with a toothpick and then going on to clean the pepper mill. Muki concluded with the words: Either way there's nothing to lose. And then Theo declared: It doesn't look right.

But why?

From every point of view.

What can we lose if we go there now? Just for a few minutes? To look the place over?

There's no point in going. It looks wrong from the outset.

Because you're opposed to everything to do with the clinic, or because you think this particular step is wrong?

Both.

Isn't it a shame to miss the opportunity?

There's no opportunity.

Meaning?

I've already said: it doesn't look right.

Up to that moment, my opinion was that it was too soon for us to start looking for a building. I felt that Muki Peleg was too eager, there was no sense in acquiring a building just because there might or might not be a chance of a bargain, and it definitely was not good to make decisions the same day, under pressure of time. But Theo's mockery, his scorn, his faint rudeness, his peasant-like way of sitting, in his undershirt, legs apart, deliberately picking grapes from the middle of the bunch in front of him, all exasperated me. My father's temper suddenly welled up inside me like boiling oil. At that instant I resolved not to let go of the building, if it seemed suitable. Just as when in class some dozy show-off says in a wheedling voice, Oh, that Agnon does go on so, and I tremble with rage and give her and the whole class a stinker of an essay for homework on the functions of the lyrical aside.

Theo, I said, Muki and I certainly don't consider ourselves as intercontinental experts on realizing projects. Or as entrepreneurs who have left their mark et cetera. So you'll just have to explain to us in simple Hebrew why we shouldn't take a step that on the face of it looks pretty rational.

On the face of it, said Theo: a good expression. And one that contains an answer to your question.

Not my question: our question. And now Muki and I are asking you for the third time, what are your objections to the purchase of the Alharizi house, and to going round now to see whether or not the building is suitable? We would be pleased to receive a verbal answer instead of that grimace.

There are eleven reasons, Theo said, with a fleeting shrewd smile under his grey moustache, why Napoleon's guns did not bombard Smolensk. The first was that there was no more ammunition, and the other ten reasons he rightly refused to listen to. The sum that has been mentioned, even without the improvements, is more than your gent has undertaken to donate. Any more?

We'd had two further small benefactions, and I knew Theo

knew about them. But I chose to say nothing. Theo added: Besides which, I thought I read in the local paper that you had volunteered to form a team to investigate possibilities, not to purchase properties. Besides which, there hasn't been even the beginning of a beginning of a proper public procedure. Besides which, has anybody yet calculated the volume of junkies that you are planning to raise here, in proportion to the capacity of the building in question? Eh?

Hang on a minute, Theo, I said.

Besides which, the money, if there is any, isn't yours, Noa. A big girl doesn't go shopping for toys with money which isn't hers. Besides which, you need to get through four or five committees for the change of use of the building, and I'm telling you seriously that you'll get a negative reply from all five. You also need to get local planning approval, and then –

All right. We understand. But why not go along and take a look anyway?

Besides which, there's the Town Hall. The administration. The Local Council. The District Council. Deposit and processing of plans. Hearing of objections. Appeals. Public opposition. Political opposition. Three years at least. Besides which, the Health Department, the Welfare Department, the Education Department. Another two years. Besides which, who owns the land? Besides which, the unanimous opposition of the neighbours, including court proceedings. Minimum five more years of legal hearings. Besides which, who exactly is the purchaser? Whose name is the property registered in? And how do you define the purpose? Besides which – shall I go on? Oh? Why not?

Muki Peleg mumbled softly: But there aren't that many neighbours.

Ah, welcome, Mr. Peleg Agency. So you're here, too. Bride's side or bridegroom's? Very well, give me a definition of neighbour. A legal definition, please, if that's not too hard for you. Go ahead: what is a neighbour precisely? And I'm not talking about a neighbour's wife.

Thank you, Theo. I think that'll do.

As you wish, he sniggered, with one eye contracted, as though peering at an insect through a fine lens, or as though looking at us through the viewfinder of a camera. Besides which – haven't I said that before? – didn't I promise not to interfere with your party? I forgot. Expunge it from the record. Sorry. See you. Carry on.

Having said this, he went on sitting, relaxed, his back resting against the side of the refrigerator, staring fixedly at his coffee cup, systematically plucking grapes from the bunch, his smaller left eye suddenly making him look like a miserly peasant who has managed to put a creditor off the scent.

Come on, angel, I said, Theo's absolved. Let's pop over there just the two of us and have a look, and then we'll call a meeting of the committee and make a decision.

Muki asked: Aren't you coming, Theo? Just for ten minutes?

Theo said: What for?

It was around nine p.m. when we finally managed to contact the lawyer, Arbel, on Muki's office phone. He arrived at midday the following day from Tel Aviv, bringing with him a surveyor and an assessor. We went back to the building four times that Sunday, with builders, roofers, fencers, plumbers, to compare estimates. I felt I was in a trance.

After the nine o'clock news Theo said: Right. I've been. I've seen it. Not bad. Your African can buy it if he likes. His decision. On condition you take care not to sign any document, Noa. No signature. Remember.

During Sunday night there was a telephone conversation between Arbel in the Kedar Hotel and Orvieto in the Ramada Hotel in Lagos. He was prepared to authorize the purchase, he had confidence in the people on the spot, but was unable to transfer the promised sum because there was not enough time. On Monday the school year ended and before the distribution of certificates there was a little ceremony in the School Hall. The Matriculation literature class had bought me a black wooden bowl with a bonsai orange tree in it. And on Tuesday the broken-tiled Alharizi house standing near the entrance to the industrial zone across from Ben Elul's garage was sold for the shekel equivalent of eighty-one thousand dollars, and registered in the name of the Immanuel Orvieto Memorial Fund, whose official address was henceforth c/o Cherniak, Refidim and Arbel, Lawyers, 90 Rothschild Boulevard, Tel Aviv. Theo advanced us most of the money on the surety of Ron Arbel in the name of Avraham Orvieto, and on condition that neither his name nor mine would appear in any connection in the deeds of sale or ownership. And since we went to Tel Aviv that Tuesday to be present at the signing of the contract, we were able to go together and compare various possible options at our leisure. It was in Ben Yehuda Street of all places that we finally found a pretty, light summer dress that delighted us both: the colour was somewhere between blue and green, it had a simplified pattern reminiscent of wide tropical leaves, and it left the shoulders almost bare. We were home before dark, and together from the balcony we saw that the moon was still waning.

Bᴇᴄᴀᴜꜱᴇ once she told me about her mother, who went off with a soldier from New Zealand when Noa was four. They were both torn to pieces by an enraged tigress whose cubs had been killed by an English hunter, so her aunt used to tell her when she was little on winter nights after lights out and before she fell asleep. This aunt, Chuma Bat-Am, was a Tolstoyan vegan, a resolute enemy of any act of violence, a determined woman in thick orthopedic shoes who used to fast every Wednesday, so as to remind her body that it was only a servant, and a pretty lazy, loathsome one at that, an unworthy servant who must not be left alone for a moment. Noa's father, Nehemia Dubnow, a retired employee of the water company, a stocky, hirsute individual, melancholy, always negligently shaved, shut himself up at home from the day her mother ran off with the soldier. Every day when he came home from work at dusk he would shut the gate, lock the front door on the inside, and withdraw to the inner room where he lived in the evening surrounded by his albums of picture postcards. All in a determined silence punctuated by occasional fits of blind rage. Each evening, summer and winter alike, after an omelette and salad, he would sit down and write postcards with views of the Tower of David in Jerusalem or of Bethlehem, which he sent to collectors in other countries. In exchange they sent him postcards from Haiti, Surinam, New Caledonia and other places where the sky is not blue but almost turquoise and the sea at dawn looks like beaten gold. He would sit up till close on midnight sorting and cataloguing the collection according to an organizing logic that changed every month or two. With the passage of the years he became heavier, like an ageing sumo wrestler; he grew fleshy protuberances, his eyes sank under layers of fat, and his occasional attacks of rage were followed by prolonged bouts of sullen apathy. Noa received the duplicate postcards: her task was to arrange a kind of shadow collection between the pages of the telephone directory, parallel to the main collection and subject to the same ever-changing logic. Apart from the aunt and her weird son, Yoshku, not a soul came to the house. Its shutters were closed in winter because of the wind and in summer because of the dust. It was a small house that stood at the eastern extremity of a remote village in the Hefer Valley, facing a ruined synagogue dating from the time of the first settlers. Beyond the house there was nothing but a forsaken henhouse, some remains of cultivation, rusty railway lines and a fence marking the armistice line, on the Jordanian side of which stretched rocks and olive trees. Two years ago we went to look at the spot and found the house had been demolished and a gaudy water park had been built on the site of the house and the synagogue, with a souvenir shop and a kiosk. The border fence had been erased. In 1959 when Noa was fifteen Nehemia Dubnow fell down a disused well and broke his spine. He was permanently consigned to a wheelchair. From that time on she looked after him. She did not want to marry because she did not see how he could live without her and because he did not remarry after his wife left him. During her army service the cripple was cared for by his elder sister, Aunt Chuma, who was opposed on principle to all heating in the winter and banished frying as well as most other forms of cooking. Under her rule the house was run to a strict timetable and in absolute obedience to a rota of household chores, three copies of which were posted at various points around the place. There was a clinging smell of mint, summer savoury and garlic in the rooms. Even when the aunt went off for a day or two in her thick orthopedic shoes to hunt for mysterious roots in the Carmel range, the smell of spices still lingered. Digestive, medicinal and rejuvenating herbs grew in pots and basins on the roof and on every windowsill. When Noa returned from the army she had to fight for three years for her right to care for the invalid whose body was swelling like a soaked sponge. Eventually at the end of a murky day during a heatwave, the aunt bit the secretary of the Local Council during a clash about digging up a lemon tree; the next day she lay in wait for him and poured boiling oil over him, and she was about to do the same to Noa when a neighbour, Peeping Gorovoy, who claimed the title of weight-lifting champion of Lodz in the 1920s, ran across from his garden and, after a struggle, managed to overpower her. After undergoing various treatments, Aunt Chuma was put in a private institution devoted exclusively to vegans afflicted with emotional disturbances, that had been set up by a pacifist family from Holland. Noa got her father back, and in addition to doing the cooking and cleaning she took over responsibility for the post-card collection and the correspondence with collectors around the world. She pulled up the medicinal and rejuvenating herbs and planted flowers in the pots instead. Every Wednesday she went to see her aunt in the Mahatma Gandhi Sanatorium and took her untreated fruit and vegetables that had never encount-ered a grain of chemical fertilizer. At the end of her life Chuma Bat-Am was overcome by a particular hatred of potato crisps, mustard and stuffed intestines, and denounced all kinds of roast meat in detailed and highly coloured language. She died in the garden of the clinic at ten o'clock in the morning, of a knitting needle thrust through the right eye into the brain by a fellow patient, just as the inmates were being served with their morning tea and its accompaniment of three rusks and a tangerine. As for Nehemia Dubnow, the more he aged and grew fatter, till he looked like a beaten wrestler, the more Noa had the impression that he became jollier, as though his anger had run out or he had completed his share of self-mortification. He sang in his hoarse voice, told jokes, imitated politicians, entertained Noa with gossipy stories about the leaders of the third wave of immi-gration and the founders of the water company. He lost interest in his picture postcards. More and more he saw life, ideas, words, human doings in general, as ridiculous, self-contradictory things that revealed only foolishness and hypocrisy. Every morn-ing Noa took him up on the roof in his wheelchair. He had a powerful telescope and the old man enjoyed spending hours on end watching the road below. Sometimes a tractor went past, or a girl on a donkey, or a group of Arab workers on their way home from the orchards. Like Peeping Gorovoy, Nehemia Dubnow too began to use his telescope to explore the neighbours' lives through their windows that were left open all summer long: a lone, amused spectator of a farce involving everyone bar himself. Seventeen years after the first accident he had another. Noa popped out to the grocer's one evening to buy some oil and onions, and when she came back in the last glimmer of daylight she found that her father had fallen from the roof terrace in his wheelchair. Turning the wheels of the chair with his strong hands, he had been propelling his mountainous body as usual like a charging tank from one end of the roof to the other when he had burst through the railings and fallen over the edge. When she discovered that her father had put the house in the name of her cousin Yoshku, she took it as a sign that the last chance had arrived for her to break free and start living, which for her meant primarily going to a university. This Yoshku, Noa's only relative, was the son of Chuma Bat-Am by a violin-maker from Leipzig who had ended up as an officer in the fire brigade in Hadera. Their affair lasted, according to her father, three and a half weeks. By the time Yoshku was born, the violin-maker-turned-fireman was in Brussels, married to a musician in the Flemish Ensemble. For several years the aunt and the child lived in a rented room in Haifa, with two iron bedsteads, a packing case for the clothes, and a washbasin in the corner hidden by a plastic curtain. Islands of mould were spreading over the pale blue of the curtain. The aunt worked two days a week as a secretary for the League of Pacifists and she also had a part-time job with the Vegan Association. Every evening she went out, in battle order, like a frigate dispatched to relieve a besieged port, to a meeting of the Council for the Advancement of Understanding Among Races and Creeds. Yoshku was brought up for several years on the Tolstoy Youth Farm, until he ran away to his mother, and subsequently he sneaked away on occasion to his crippled, irascible uncle and his cousin in whose presence he either talked and talked without stopping or

84

else said nothing all day long. Then he disappeared from Haifa, lived for three months in an Arab village in Galilee from where he sent Noa a passionate twenty-eight-page love letter, took part in strikes and demos, had two poems published in a magazine, and at seventeen made it into the newspapers, which published detailed accounts of the boy from a pacifist home who undertook conversion to Islam to avoid military service; one leading article even called on the leftist camp to stop and do some soul-searching. Eventually the young man made contact with a small Hasidic sect, or maybe the sect's emissaries made contact with him. Once the army had released him on account of his nerves, the Hasidim took him to Brussels. This was in 1962, when Noa was called up and started serving in the headquarters of Army Education. Aunt Chuma, who was alone now, left her rented room in Haifa and went to look after her crippled brother in his house at the eastern extremity of the village on the east side of the Hefer Valley. Until she was killed by a knitting needle in a private clinic. When Noa's father died it turned out that the reason he had left the house not to her but to Yoshku was "in the hope that he will return from the malignant Diaspora and strike new roots in the soil of the Sharon". Yoshku neither returned from the Diaspora nor struck new roots in the Sharon but instead hired from Brussels a lugubrious ultra-Orthodox lawyer resembling a well-mannered coffin salesman, who explained to Noa regretfully in a pleasant tenor voice that the only way she could appeal against the will was to go to court and declare *coram publico* that her late father was not of sound mind when he made it, or that it was intended as a joke, or, alternatively, that at the time he was under pressure from an extortionist, namely his sister Chuma Zamosc Bat-Am, and therefore the bequest was not valid. However, the lawyer declared, you have hardly any chance of establishing either of these claims with evidence that will satisfy a court of law, and you are liable to end up covered in shame and confusion as well as empty-handed, having moreover represented yourself publicly as a daughter who groundlessly reviles the memory of her late father may he rest in peace and also that of her late aunt peace be upon her, and adds one sin to another in an unprovoked offence against your only relative, who only wants to rescue you or at least to assist you. In sum, the family will come out of it covered in mire from head to foot, and you will end up gaining nothing, not a single penny, whereas if you are wise enough to refrain from a lawsuit, I shall sign here and now, here is my power of attorney, in the name of my client Yoshiahu Sarshalom Zamosc, a statement to the effect that he grants you, of his own free will and through no legal requirement, as a gift and not as an obligation, a quarter of the value of the property, as a goodwill gesture and in obedience to the commandment not to abandon one's own flesh and blood.

So it came about that at the age of thirty-two she left the house that had been her home, packing all her belongings in three suitcases, and sending the collection of picture postcards as a gift to the Mahatma Gandhi Sanatorium, and went to study literature at Tel Aviv University surrounded by students who were ten years younger. After that she became a secondary school teacher in Bat Yam, lived once or twice with older men, had an abortion with complications and finally, for six months, lived with a famous professor, originally from Prague, who in his retirement was devoting himself to preparing a revised edition of an *Essence of Judaism* in six large volumes. This professor was a sour, sarcastic man, and his hobby, from his youth on, had been piano-tuning. Whatever the time, whatever the weather, he was always ready to set off for anywhere, with his little bag of instruments under his arm. He was not a young man, nor a well man, and he would tune a piano for nothing. So long as it was a real, pre-war piano. One day the professor accepted an invitation to spend the remaining years of his retirement in the guesthouse of the Catholic University of Strasbourg, where he hoped to discover afresh, peacefully, the essence of Judaism. Noa felt she, too, ought to leave the country for a year or two, to find out whether some other kind of life were possible. Friends arranged a part-time job for her in Venezuela. It was there, in Caracas, thanks to some concert tickets, that we met. Since then we have been tied to each other.

After the nine o'clock news and the weather forecast, Theo said, Let's switch off and go out for a bit. I changed out of the dress I wore around the house and put on jeans, a red top and white walkers. Theo was wearing walkers too, and jeans with a broad belt. Going down in the elevator we hugged and I buried my face in his shoulder. His body was warmer than mine and the belt gave off a smell of old leather and sweat. I said: You're always so warm.

Theo said: You're on holiday as from yesterday. What are you going to do, Noa?

I said: The clinic. Immanuel House. Only I wish we hadn't had to take your money. That wasn't good. I mean, I don't feel good about it. Avraham's going to repay it all next week.

Theo said: Avraham: who's that?

And a moment later: Oh yes. Your African. It's not urgent.

There was no one in the street. A row of parked cars and a row of streetlights, some of them not working. Some pathetic trees, Indian beech, eucalyptus, tipuana, grew as though they had difficulty breathing. The trees, in fact the whole street, suddenly looked to me like an amateur stage set. The windows of the apartments were open and from almost every one came the voice of Housing Minister Sharon shouting at his interviewers. A dry breeze blew from the hills to the east. A startled cat suddenly slunk out from the trash cans and almost tripped us. I put my arm round his waist and laid it on the broad belt, which was rough to the touch. The metal buckle gave my fingers a cold thrill. Shabby staircases showed in the entrances to the buildings in a murky light that seemed to infect the mailboxes, too.

Theo said: The Mayor. Batsheva. The dinosaur. You ought to

try and speak to her, not in her office, privately, about your fantasy. I don't suppose you'd let me speak to her? Would you?

This business will go better without you.

And without you, Noa.

Don't take everything away from me.

Everything. What's everything? There's nothing there.

On the corner of the street, at a point the streetlight could not reach, a couple stood in a motionless embrace, like a sculpture, with lips joined, frozen in a kiss that in the darkness resembled mouth-to-mouth resuscitation. As we walked past it seemed as though the border between them had been erased. I fancied the girl was one of my Talis from class 12, and hoped I was mistaken, though I didn't know why. So I couldn't prevent myself from staring like someone at an identity line-up. For some reason I was blushing in the dark.

From a first-floor window came a sound of regular, even crying, the crying of a satisfied baby who would grow into a calm child. Theo hugged my shoulders and for a moment I had a feeling his squinting left eye was scheming something in the dark. Two streets further on the town suddenly stopped like a ship whose bows were stuck in the sand on the shore. And the desert began. Theo leading, we went down the path that led into the wadi. His shadow covered me and my shadow, because I was walking so close. Black flints cast dark conical forms behind them that seemed to be cut with a knife because of the silvery sharpness of the moonlight. Scattered bones whitened here and there among the stones. From down below in the wadi came a gust smelling of dried thorns. It was as though the pale rocks, the slope, the hills to the east, even the sharp starlight, were all waiting for a change. Which would come at once, in another moment, and then everything would be clear. But what the imminent change was or what needed to be clarified I had no idea.

Theo said: It's night here, too.

I fancied I heard a slight hesitancy in his deep, calm voice, as though he were unsure of his ability to convince me that it was night here, too, as if he doubted whether I could understand.

Once this summer's over, I said, we'll see what comes next.

Theo said: What comes next?

I don't know. Let's wait and see.

At a bend in the wadi a shadow stained the road: a fallen rock. No, not a rock. A wreck. An abandoned car.

It wasn't abandoned. It was a Jeep. Silent. Lights out. From close up we could see the shadow of someone, a head drooping onto the steering wheel. A man by himself, bent, huddled, his coat collar turned up, uttering smothered laughs at irregular intervals. Theo put his hand in front of me to halt me. In three strides he had reached the Jeep and bent over the huddled man. He may have asked if he could help. The man raised his head and stared, not at Theo but at me, motionless, then slowly sank back onto the steering wheel. Theo stayed for a moment, his dark back hiding from me whatever it was he was asking or doing, then he took my hand and pulled us further on towards the lonely poinciana. What was the matter, I asked, but Theo didn't answer. Only when we'd passed the poinciana, as though he'd invested a lot of thought in his reply, he said:

It was nothing. He was crying.

Shouldn't we have stayed a bit? Or else –

It's not a crime to cry.

We had reached the top of the hill known as Hyena Hill. Yellow, sparse, scattered in the darkness, the lights of the town flickered as if they were vainly trying to answer the stars in their own language. On the southern horizon a blinding light flared up then died in a dull explosion. Look, I said, fireworks. Soon there'll be music too. Theo said:

A flare. It wasn't a firework, Noa, it was a flare. From a plane. Their night training. They're firing at dummy targets.

And suddenly, perhaps because of the words "dummy targets", I remembered with a pang the poet Ezra Zussman, and the bereaved father, Avraham, their shy smile shining and dying away in an instant, fine, melancholy smile, like autumn clouds parting. The boy's downcast eyes behind the long lashes, and the father's face furrowed with lines of subdued affection, like a weary retired metalworker. What did he have left now? In Lagos? Waiting for the return of the chimpanzee he abandoned in a clearing in the forest? What was keeping him there, and what did he want from me, really, deep down inside? By means of what spell was that humble man managing to transmit his dim wish to me through the silvery summer night stretching between Tel Kedar and Lagos across deserts and plains, over thousands of moonswept mountains and peaks and valleys and expanses of shifting sands from here to there?

For a quarter of an hour or more we stood at the top of Hyena Hill and I hardly felt him take my hand in his and stroke it with his other palm. We saw patches of milky mist slowly creeping and massing in the bottom of the wadi and rolling towards the unlit Jeep. The sorrow of the darkness and the desolation, the man sitting there huddled over the steering wheel of the Jeep in the mist, the policeman at the Ashkelon junction with blood dripping from his nose and dusty sweat rolling down his face and neck, all of it is on me. But why on me? What have I to do with the suffering of strangers I have met only by chance or strangers I haven't met and never shall? And if it has to be me, how can I distil from myself that essential combination of compassion and detachment? How to bring disaster under control like that policeman, not with a panting heart but with a surgeon's hand? "And where are we meant to be shining, and by whom is our shining required?"

Noa.

What?

Come.

Where? I'm here.

Come closer.

Yes. What?

Listen. Last Friday when I was waiting for you at the California Café a funeral procession crossed the square with a stretcher covered in a tallit and yeshiva students and a Charity Saves from Death box. Schatzberg the pharmacist's gaga old man has died. Elijah. Only his name wasn't Elijah. I've forgotten what it was. It doesn't matter. They buried him opposite Bozo's wife and baby, among the pine trees, just past your pupil and his aunt. Shall I go on? You're not too cold?

I don't understand what you're trying to say.

Nothing. Let's go on a trip. Let's get married. Let's decorate the apartment. Or buy a CD player. Just tell me for once what you really want.

Get married for what?

For what. For you. You're not happy.

And then quickly: Actually, I don't know.

I said: Let's go home. I'm a bit chilly. The kid who died, the clinic, the Alharizi house, and the grieving father, I don't know how it got into me. Something's going to happen, Theo. Don't you have a feeling too, as if the overture has ended?

We started back. And we chose not to return by way of the Jeep and the wadi but to make a detour past the cemetery at the bottom of the cliff that conceals the forbidden valley. Crickets and darkness and the scent of a distant campfire on the breeze. For a moment I felt a vague desire to turn my back on the sparse lights at the top of the hill, to leave the road, to head much further south towards the real wilderness, to cross a threshold and leave. What was the poet trying to say? That words are a trap? If so, why did he not resort to silence? Suddenly, it was as if a mountain had moved, and I recalled in a flash of illumination the pencil that Immanuel really did receive from me one winter's day during a power cut, when I went to the nurse's room to get some aspirin and the nurse wasn't there, but like a shadow he was sitting there by the bed, looking at me with downcast eyes from behind his feminine eyelashes. And yet he seemed to be sorry for me. For some reason I spoke sharply to him, as though it was my job to discipline him on the spot. I asked him gruffly what precisely he was looking for and who had given him permission to go into the room when the nurse wasn't there. I was aloof and entrenched at that moment and irritable like my father in his wheelchair on the roof for days on end while life passed by in a procession through the lens of his telescope. The boy nodded, almost sadly, as though he could read my mind and was trying to minimize the embarrassment he was causing me, and asked if by any chance I had on me anything to write with. Did he blink? Or was it just my imagination? With rough movements, keeping my back to him, I opened one drawer after another in the white medicine closet until I found the broken tail-end of a pencil. Before I left, or rather fled, I growled at him sarcastically: I'm afraid you'll have to look for a sharpener yourself. He had a talent for literature, Avraham Orvieto said, he might even have been planning to become a writer, whether or not he had any ability to write only you can judge, it was only with you that he found any sense in studying, and he even told me in his letter about the pencil you gave him, and he said he was writing the letter with that very pencil. I could not believe what I was hearing. Like a woman receiving by mistake a declaration of love intended for someone else. If we hadn't decided to come back the long way, if we had come up the path through the wadi to the Jeep with its lights out and discovered that the man had vanished, then I could have sat in the driver's seat, with my head on my arm on the wheel, mourning for the child who had been, and I shall never have another. He plummeted to his own seabed. When we got home we locked the balcony door and made some herbal tea and put on the TV to see if there was anything worth watching, and as it happened there was a programme of excerpts from Artur Rubinstein's last concert before he died. Then I went to have a shower and Theo shut himself up in his room to listen to the news on the World Service from London.

THERE is a God after all, chortled Muki Peleg, in baggy burgundy trousers and a sky-coloured shirt, with a violet silk scarf round his neck, as he opened the door of his new Fiat for Noa. Come and see for yourself what's fallen down from heaven for us, as the carpenter said to his virgin wife. Noa put her straw handbag down by her feet, then changed her mind and put it on her knees. And they set off for the Josephtal district to look for the apartment that had belonged to Immanuel Orvieto's aunt. Ron Arbel from the law firm of Cherniak, Refidim and Arbel had received instructions in a wire from Lagos to clear up the deceased's estate. That morning he had announced on the phone that his client authorized Muki Peleg's agency to sell the aunt's apartment and its contents and to use the money to repay Theo part of the loan he had advanced to the Immanuel Orvieto Memorial Fund for fear that the opportunity to buy the building might be missed.

On the way, he told Noa about a red-headed beautician who he was a hundred percent sure was attracted to him, more than attracted, wild about him, and he asked her advice about which of four possible approaches to adopt so as to get her into his bed. Noa suggested he try scenario number three. Why not? And would the same approach work, for instance, with her? Noa said sure. As he described to her what he termed the tactical scenario, and went on to tell her about eleven thousand dollars he had just put into a new partnership for importing ties from Taiwan, sexy fluorescent ties that glowed in the dark like cat's eyes, she detached herself and tried to imagine what it is like when you are dead: a dark non-being where eyes that are no more see nothing, not even the total darkness because they are no more, and the skin that is no more does not feel the cold and the damp because it, too, is no more. But all she could imagine was at most a feeling of cold and silence in darkness, sensations, and sensations are life, after all. So this too has vanished. Plunging to its own seabed.

Elazara Orvieto's apartment had been shut up and locked since her death. They were met by a faint smell of dusty books and unaired wool. The blinds were closed so they had to switch on the light. In the living room there was a sofa and a coffee table and two wicker chairs, all in the style of the austerity years, and a reproduction of a landscape in Galilee by the painter Rubin. In a blue glass vase a bunch of oleander flowers had already withered and started to disintegrate, and beside it, face down and open, was a book on the last ten days of Jewish Bialystok. A pair of brown glasses lay on top of the book and beside it was an empty cup, also brown. On a shelf were a Bible with commentary, some novels and books of poetry and picture books, among which stood a china figurine of a young pioneer holding a tiny stringed instrument that Noa was unable to identify for certain as a lyre. At the bank she had sat on the left, behind the last window, at the savings schemes counter, a woman in her fifties, efficient, desiccated, freckled, with flat-heeled shoes, her short hair fixed close to her head with a plastic bow. Noa could almost hear the flat tone of voice in that set phrase with which she ended every conversation: "That's one hundred percent okay."

In the low-ceilinged bedroom there was an iron bedstead covered with a plain rug and a dark cupboard of a type that Noa seemed to remember from her childhood used to be called a "commode". Dried desert thistles were turning grey in a Bedouin earthenware pitcher that stood on the floor in a corner of the room. On a stool beside the bed stood another empty brown cup and a little jar of pills, and a work about Baha'ism with a photograph of the temple in Haifa and a partial view of the bay.

From the bedroom they reached the balcony, which had been closed in to make a tiny room, little more than a storeroom. Here, there was only an iron bedstead, a shelf, a map of southern

Israel on the wall and a wooden packing case, on its side, in which, meticulously folded, lay Immanuel's clothes: four shirts, two pairs of trousers, one khaki and one corduroy, underwear, handkerchiefs and socks. And also a brand-new leather bomber jacket with a mass of zippers and buckles that Noa could not recall ever seeing the boy wearing. On the top surface of the packing case that apparently also served as a desk were various textbooks and exercise books, a ballpoint and a small electric lamp with a blue shade. A few paperback novels in translation, a dictionary, a dried-up sprig of pine in a glass whose water had evaporated, and some poetry books. The green sweater that she remembered from last winter was lying on the bed. And at the foot of the bed an old, tattered blanket that Noa peered at for a while before she realized that it was where the strange dog used to sleep. This was where they both slept. This was where they sat indoors on winter days. Rolling up the blind and opening the window, she saw in front of her only a grey concrete wall, depressingly close, almost within touching distance, the wall of the next block. She nearly wept. Muki Peleg hesitantly laid his hand on the back of her neck, not quite stroking her, his nostrils quivering at the faint scent of honeysuckle, and said to her gently: Noa?

She reached up to push away his hand but changed her mind halfway and clutched it; she even leaned against him for a moment with her eyes closed.

As though releasing a repressed tenderness that he normally struggled to keep under control, Muki Peleg whispered to her: Okay then. There's no hurry. I'll wait for you in the other room.

He touched her hair and left.

Bending over she picked up the sweater and pressed it to her breast to fold it properly. She did not manage to fold it right, so she laid it out on the bedspread and folded it on itself like a diaper, then carried it slowly over to the packing case and placed it among the other clothes. Then she closed the blind and the window and was about to leave, but instead she sat down on the bed for a few moments, drained. She closed her eyes and waited for the tears. They refused to come. All she felt was how late it was. Rising to her feet she wiped the top of the packing case with the back of her hand and smoothed the bedspread, straightened the pillow, drew the curtain and left. In the next room she found Muki, in a wicker chair, with his glasses on, waiting for her, quietly reading the book about the end of the Jews of Bialystok. He got up and fetched her half a glass of water from the kitchen. Then, in his Fiat, he told her how much he hoped to sell the apartment for: naturally he wouldn't dream of taking a commission for this sale either, but the fact was that the money from the apartment would not be enough to repay Theo, and on top of that we still had to make what we wanted of the Alharizi house, though actually that depended on what we did want, and in fact we had never really discussed what we were going to do, as the Empress Catherine said to her pet Cossack.

Noa said: All right. Listen. It's like this. Bear in mind that if this inheritance turns out not to be enough, I had an aunt of my own and there might be another inheritance, hers, mine, that went to some ultra-Orthodox cousin in Brussels and I gave it up even though I didn't have to and I was wrong to do it. Maybe I could still put up a fight for it. Now take me to the California and treat me to an iced coffee. Iced coffee, Muki, that's what I want right now.

IN late 1971 or early 1972 Finkel was appointed head of the Agency. As a consolation prize or to soften the blow, Head Office offered to send Theo to Mexico on behalf of the Planning Authority to serve as a special adviser for regional planning. After all, you're single, you're more mobile than a family man. A change of air will do you good, you'll see the world, shall we say a couple of years, maybe three, you've heard all about Latin women, well, there are blacks, too, and Creoles, mulattos, Indians. And professionally speaking, too, you're sure to find ample scope. You'll be able to revolutionize things. You can devise new structures. When you've had enough you can come home, by then there may have been some kind of reorganization. In principle everything is wide open and anything may still be reversed.

Within two and a half weeks he had dismantled his bachelor apartment in Hyrcanus Street, near the River Yarkon. He found the phrase "ample scope" vaguely exciting. And the word "mobile", too. This may have been the reason why he decided to travel with nothing more than a single suitcase and a grip. From year to year his contract was extended, his work expanded from the state of Veracruz to Sonora and Tabasco and eventually to other countries as well. Within a few months his superficial ties with his circle of acquaintances in Tel Aviv were dissolved. One or two women wrote to him via the office but he did not bother to reply, not even with a picture postcard. He saw no reason to exercise his right to home leave every six months. He did without Israeli newspapers. After a while he realized that he had no idea who the Minister of the Interior was back home or the dates of the Jewish festivals. From so far away all the wars, and the rhetoric that separated them, seemed to make up a vicious circle of self-righteousness and hysteria: kicking out at everything that stood in the way and at the same time pleading for mercy and demanding to be loved. A tacky cocktail of destiny, arrogance and self-pity, that was how Israel appeared to him from his vantage point in a hammock strung in a remote fishing village on the Pacific coast. Although he did not neglect to ask himself if all this was simply because that scum Nimrod Finkel had landed the top job in the Bureau. And the answer he gave himself, occasionally, was that that had merely been the last straw.

He felt an urge not to go back home. He tackled his work with a kind of quiet zeal. He managed to design a few models of rural areas that suited the tropical climate and were not at odds with the existing way of life. After the Nicaragua earthquake two districts were rebuilt along lines that he had put forward. New offers started coming in. In 1974 he wrote to the Planning Authority asking for indefinite leave. Nimrod Finkel granted it immediately.

Year after year he migrated from hotels to village inns, from air-conditioned offices to baking townships and Indian villages, carrying everything he needed in a modest shoulder bag, and he learned to speak six dialects of Spanish. Regimes rose and fell, but he steered his way through unscathed because he refrained from forging friendships. When he came across cruelty, corruption, barbarity or grinding poverty he passed no judgment but merely concentrated on his work: he had not come here to combat injustice but, so far as possible, to attain professional perfection and thereby perhaps, however minutely, to reduce disasters. Honour, the labyrinth and death were ever-present here, and life itself sometimes flared up like a festive firework display or a salvo of shots in the air: ruthless, spicy, noisy and cheap.

Women were easy to find, like food, like a hammock to spend the night in, all lavished on him everywhere out of curiosity or hospitality. His hosts expected him to join in conversations late into the night, under the dome of the sky, in village inns, in development-company encampments, in isolated farmyards, in the company of strangers or chance acquaintances. And again, as he had done around campfires in the youth movement and the army, he drew close to the fire and listened. Here, too, they talked halfway through the night about things like the ravages of time, family, honour, vicissitudes of fate, the hypocrisy of society, the atrocities that people inflict on themselves and each other because of excessive appetites or, on the contrary, from excessive indifference. Theo drank little and hardly joined in the conversations. Only very rarely did he contribute a small anecdote from one of the Israeli wars or a biblical text that struck him as appropriate. When close to dawn the men dispersed and he headed for the darkness there was generally a woman who wanted to join him.

Sometimes he mingled with the crowd and from within it watched all night long the lascivious carnival, the Fiesta of Our Lady of Guadalupe, General Saragossa's feast day, the screaming festival, with dancing, carousing, horrific and seductive diguises, and salvos of flares and shooting in the rancid air and the throbbing of the drums accompanying desperate music that writhed till dawn in horrendous, violent desire.

He despatched most of his monthly salary to a bank in Toronto, because his expenses were negligible. Like a travelling artisan he wandered in those years from one godforsaken place to another that was even more so. He stayed in wretched villages at the foot of extinct volcanoes and once he saw one of them erupting in flames. Sometimes he journeyed under thick canopies of ferns and creepers through sensuous jungles. Here and there he would befriend for a while a desolate river or a steep mountain range that the forest seemed to be invading with the savage claws of its roots. Here and there he would stop for a couple of weeks and surrender to total idleness, lying in a hammock all day watching birds of prey in the depths of the empty sky. A girl or a young woman would come in the night to share his hammock, bringing huge earthenware cups of coffee from somewhere for them both. Past and future appeared to him on such nights as two common diseases, slow, destructive plagues that had infected most of mankind and were gradually causing all sorts of strange frenzies in their victims. And he rejoiced that he was not afflicted, and considered himself immune.

Even the present tense, that is to say the given moment that you are at, here and now, travelling, dozing, having sex, or the moment when you are sitting huddled, wide awake and quiet in your battered leather jacket in a window seat on a long night flight in a near-empty plane, even the present moment appears not to demand anything of you beyond being present in it and being as receptive as possible to what you are shown and what is being done to you. Like water running slowly down the inside of eyelids closed with fatigue.

Occasionally he felt fear, or rather a vague apprehension, that in the absence of suffering he might be missing something that would never return. Without having any idea what it was that was being missed, if indeed anything was being missed. Sometimes he had a feeling that he had forgotten something he should remember but when he collected his thoughts he found that he had forgotten what it was he thought he had forgotten. In Trujillo, in Peru, one night he jotted down on a sheet of hotel notepaper four or five questions in Hebrew: Is this a contraction of the life force? Barrenness? Atrophy? Exile? After an hour or two he wrote under these questions a reply: Even if we suppose it really is atrophy etc., why not? What's the harm in that?

And with that he seemed to snuggle down again into his tropical torpor.

But in his work he was as alert as a thief in a treasure chamber. For instance, when he happened to spend three or four days on end in a low-ceilinged broom closet of a room in some village inn, or occasionally in a splendid city office put at his disposal by the company, drawing, writing, altering, calculating, he was electrically sharp, needing neither sleep nor company, not raising his head from the paper even when a petite beauty slipped in with coffee and a tray of food and stood looking at him for a moment, waiting, tense, as though receiving the capering sparks of his energy on the skin of her nipples, until she gave up and left. Or sometimes during a meeting, when he presented his proposals to the decision-making authorities, a cold, sharp inner flame might beam out from him and make others yield to his will. At such times he felt a powerful, delightful upsurge of professional pleasure: the force of invention and perfection glowed white-hot in him like the filament of a powerful light bulb. It was as though deep in the forest, in a hidden cut-off place, there pulsed intermittently a kind of spring that existed independently of you and from moment to moment it bubbled up and vanished, bubbled up and again carved itself a predetermined course, by the force of laws that you were unable to understand but that had you entirely in their power.

And again on long journeys to godforsaken districts in the mountains or on the Caribbean coast, studying the locality, supervising the construction stage, introducing the odd improvised alteration, on the inspiration of the moment, he would sometimes be smitten suddenly with fatigue and lie down for days and nights in a hammock behind a hut. Sometimes he would rise at midnight and walk barefoot to join a conversation round a fire about love, betrayal and the vicissitudes of life. And so, in the courtyard of a miserable tavern, over glasses of native liquor, in the company of workers, technicians, vendors and comfort girls, under a strange night sky that might be suddenly illuminated by the momentary ecstasy of falling stars, he came to learn more and more about episodes full of lust and despair. As though these two were a pair of strolling players who appeared evening after evening before an audience gathered in taverns or in the courtyards of remote inns, never wearying of repeating endlessly the same fixed passion play, watched by Theo time and again without his ever being bored but without his being particularly impressed either.

In bed, or in a hammock, when he was having sex with a woman who had chosen him, usually a woman twenty or thirty years younger than himself, he would make love slowly and precisely, expertly prolonging the pleasure, guiding her confidently along the byways of the forest, and occasionally in the midst of ecstasy he experienced all at once a powerful craving for fatherhood. He would show the girl a loving side that was inappropriate to casual sex and unusual between strangers: a parental side. Glimpsing this parental concern suddenly in the midst of ecstasy, the girl would react at first with bewildered fear and alarm, but then she would be overwhelmed, as though pierced to the secret core of her spine. So their bodies would reach territories that lust alone cannot get to, until it seemed as though the river was not simply passing by on the other side of the hut but flowing out of them. But by the light of day he always reverted to being distant and correct. Polite, considerate, detached. And obliged to go on his way.

In February 1981 I dropped into the Embassy in Caracas to pick up an envelope containing some material I had sent for from the office in Israel. The new receptionist explained to me, with an air of sympathy and particular delicacy, as if she had the task of softening the blow to a patient receiving the results of tests, that the package was locked in the security officer's safe, and he would not be back for another hour or so. Meanwhile, she sat me down on a wicker chair, gave me some coffee that I had not asked for – it was sharp, penetrating coffee, that almost felt alcoholic – and in a few moments managed to make me feel that I had charmed her. She had not a trace of inhibition when she said to me in her young girl's voice, some ten minutes after I entered the office: Stay for a bit. You're interesting.

A woman of medium height, she moved around the room as though every movement of her body pleased her; her blonde fringe tossed lightly on her forehead, and she was wearing a colourful printed dress. When she stood up to pour the coffee her dress whirled round her legs and I noticed something athletic, though unhurried and relaxed, in her bearing. She contrived to hint without really hinting that it was I who was arousing the feminine signal that was emanating from her, you are attractive, I am attracted, why should I hide it, and I discovered, to my own surprise, that almost unawares I had begun to return her signals. All these years I had been avoiding the company of Israelis, and especially those progressive, cooperative Tel Avivi girls with reasoned views for or against everything in the world. In my years of wandering around these parts I had been drawn to a hypnotic tropical femininity that sometimes seemed imprisoned like a dark flame in a cage of Hispanic arrogance. Yet here was this fair-haired, green-eyed, energetic woman with her bell-like voice, her face openly beaming with the pleasure I was affording her, bursting with generous vitality. With a movement of the shoulder and hip that said, Take a look, this is a body, she stirred something inside me that almost resembled the relaxed openness that is experienced sometimes in a meeting between childhood friends. There was also a sudden urge to make a strong impression on her. Yet for years and years I had made no effort, I had not had to make any, to impress a woman.

Within ten minutes I had learned that she was a literature teacher, that she had been born and lived until a few years previously in a village at the eastern end of the Hefer Valley, that she had started really living, as she put it, shockingly late, because she had been saddled with a violent, childlike crippled father, that she had hardly any other relatives, and that her name was Noa. You're Theo, I've heard about you, you're quite a legend hereabouts. I had some kind of breakdown in Tel Aviv, but let's not go into that, some friends arranged for me to come out here partly as a receptionist in the Embassy and partly as a teacher for the little Israeli colony. That's right, how did you guess, the coffee I made us really is radioactive. I slipped an Indian thing into it, a powdered root, no, it's not exactly like the cardamom the Yemenites back home use, it makes your head spin more, and I also added half a glass of French brandy. There, I've given away most of my secrets. Of course I didn't ask you if I could put things in your coffee. Why should I? Here, have another cup. You don't look to me like a man who is likely to get drunk or lose control. Rather the opposite. Always in control.

When the security officer arrived and handed me my envelope I thanked him and her and took my leave. But she wouldn't dream of letting me go: Wait, Theo. They say you've been living among the Indians for ten years. Will you take me? It'll be worth your while. If you say yes I'll teach you how to control pain by regulating your breathing.

I supposed she must have belonged to one of those mystical groups that were so popular in Tel Aviv. I was determined to escape while there was still time from this mercurial schoolteacher with her tricks for regulating your breathing. Despite which I agreed to go out with her that evening to a concert by an orchestra and choir from Berlin: she had a double ticket and without me she wouldn't be able to go, it wasn't that easy here for a woman to go out at night by herself, and she promised that the programme included Schubert's Mass in B Flat Major. For years I hadn't heard Schubert except through the earphones of the little cassette player that went everywhere with me.

That evening it turned out that she didn't know any breathing exercises: she had just fancied me and didn't want me to disappear. If I insisted on my rights, she would take a correspondence course in controlled breathing and discharge her debt when she'd completed it. Fancy wasn't the right word, she said. Actually I had struck her as someone who was imprisoned in my own dungeon and I made her want to try to reach me so I wouldn't freeze down there in the dark. Even now I can't express myself the way I want to, imprisonment, dungeon, it's all your fault, Theo, it's because of you that I'm talking in metaphors and that it won't come out right. Am I ridiculous? Then you must accept the blame. Look what you've done to me. It's your fault I'm ridiculous. It's because of you I'm blushing, too. Look.

After the concert she invited me out to eat roast veal at a restaurant she'd heard was considered one of the best in the Western Hemisphere. The restaurant, empty apart from the two of us, was full of folksy decorations and waiters dressed as gauchos. It was nothing more than a tourist trap. The meat and the wine were crude and tasteless. The candle at our table had a repulsive greasy smell. As for the ensemble from Berlin, it turned out that they had performed the Schubert the previous night. We were treated to Hindemith and Bartók. To cap it all, when we were leaving the concert hall the heel of her left shoe broke, and as we were getting out of the taxi her wristwatch caught my forehead and gave me a nasty gash. I've blown it, she said, with a touching smile by the light of the street lamp outside her apartment: I've lost my Indian village.

The first Sunday after that evening, a rogue cobbler having stuck an odd heel on her shoe, I took her over dirt tracks in the

Development Agency Jeep to see an Indian village not far from Calabozo. We drove for five hours each way. We saw a wedding carnival, half Catholic, half pagan: in a dark, ecstatic ceremony, accompanied by strange songs that at times resembled howls, a pretty widow was paired off with a half-dazed, perhaps slightly drugged, youth, who seemed to us no more than fifteen years old. Next day I flew back to Mexico. We continued to meet each time I passed through Caracas, every few weeks, and I would bring her a bottle of Napoleon brandy so that she would have something to lace her magic coffee with, together with her powerful native brew. Instead of the secret of breathing control that she had made up the first day so I wouldn't get away I discovered another secret in her that came to fascinate me: whenever she met a stranger, even by chance, she would immediately spot any malice. Or hypocrisy. Or generosity. Even people I myself saw as being complicated, enigmatic, well hidden behind a polished image or disguised by perfect manners, she could apparently identify as being good or bad: wicked, naive, generous, stagnant – that was how she classified everybody. And also as warm or cool. In fact she didn't so much classify them as set people, places or opinions on a temperature scale. As though she were grading pupils' work from forty to ninety. What's this supposed to be, I protested, a court-martial? A people's tribunal? And Noa replied: It's easy, anyone who wants to know what's good and what's bad knows. If you don't know, it's a sign you don't want to know. I find you quite attractive. You seem to find me attractive, too. But you absolutely don't have to answer that.

Was she really always correct in her lightning judgments? Or more times than not? Sometimes? I couldn't check any more, because with time I began to see people through her eyes: icy, warm, tepid, generous, villainous, compassionate. How about me? Am I hot or cold, Noa? Or would I be better off not asking? To which she replied instantly, unhesitatingly: You're warm but getting colder. Never mind, I'll warm you up. And she added: Not bad. A bit domineering. You drive the Jeep brilliantly – it's not so much driving, more like a rodeo.

And sometimes she looked to me again just the way she looked the first time we met, at the Embassy, an energetic, well-meaning, judgmental Israeli schoolteacher. Her beauty was written all over her in capital letters. Wafting all around her a faint but unmistakable scent of honeysuckle. But I found nothing repellent in all of this. On the contrary, there were times when her presence filled me with childlike excitement, like a creature that has been brought indoors and from now on is going to be well looked after. I gradually discovered how fine and how effortless was her emotional range, maternal one moment, girlish the next, or seductive, and most of the time sisterly. What's more, she revealed to me a childlike sense of humour, "the horse is the main protagonist in the history of the Latin peoples", a humour that gave me a strange urge to cover her shoulders carefully. Even when it was not cold. Indeed the first present I bought her was a Caribbean woollen scarf. When I first laid it round her shoulders, so white and delicate with a tiny brown birthmark near the nape, there was a moment of mystery and joy: as though it were not me covering her shoulders, but her suddenly covering all of me.

Once when we were visiting the ruins of a gloomy church from the time of the first settlers and as usual I delivered a historical précis, she interrupted me with the words, See for yourself, Theo, how light you are now.

At these words I trembled like a boy to whom an experienced woman, from the heights of her expertise, perhaps as a joke, has revealed that he is apparently blessed with what in due course will make women desire him. I leaned over and kissed her. On her hair for the time being. She did not return my kiss but reddened and burst out laughing, Look, Theo, it's so funny, your bossy moustache has started quivering. And yet when we met in Caracas, Noa and I, I was fifty-two, I had been loving various sorts of women for thirty years, I was, in my own opinion, an expert, I was acquainted with menus of pleasures such as she had not seen in her wildest dreams, if she had ever had wild dreams. I imagined not. Despite which, the words she spoke to me in the ruins of that church, See for yourself how light you are now, moved me so powerfully that I had to remind myself almost by force that I had stopped in the eighteenth century and I had yet to tell her about how the church and the whole town had collapsed in the great earthquake of 1812 and about the cyclical element that really underlay the shifting power-alliances between the Church, the secret service, the Maoists, the army, the Liberals, and the Republican Guards. I recommended my lecture, and continued it passionately, lingering over each detail, digressing, enthusing, embarking on Borgesian myths, until she said, That's enough for today, Theo, I can't take any more in.

In the course of four months we may have seen each other only seven or eight times, we went to art exhibitions and concerts, to restaurants that, after her slip-up the first night, we agreed between us she should not be the one to choose, and sometimes on a Sunday we went off for a few hours in the Jeep to the high mountains of the Cordillera del Litoral. She knew only a few hundred words of Spanish, but nevertheless, directly after listening to a short conversation I had had with a gas pump attendant or a technician from the administration, she would declare without the slightest hesitation that this man was a liar while the other, the fat one, actually liked people but was rather ashamed of it and that was why he was so gruff. What have you swallowed, Noa? A seismograph? A lie detector? She didn't hurry to answer these questions. When she did finally reply, I couldn't see the connection: I grew up, she said, with a paralysed father and an aunt who was demented by her own idealism, I had to keep my eyes open.

At the end of the evening I would accompany her to the apartment that the Embassy had taken for her, on the ground floor of a house belonging to some wealthy Jews. We parted at the gate with a goodnight kiss on the cheek or the hair, she had to stand on tiptoe while I almost bowed to her, breathing my fill of that scent of honeysuckle. Gradually I noticed that my trips were tending to bring me to Caracas more and more often. I bought her a pair of woollen socks and a llama wool scarf. She bought me a pot of honey. Then one night, in the spring, there was a thunderstorm and a long power cut and she decided that this time I could stay the night: she had a sofa-bed. She sat me on her bed, the rain was beating on the windows like stones, she lighted a kerosene heater, poured me a glass of my own brandy, brought some fruit, paper napkins; then all at once she changed her mind, blew out the candle, sat herself down next to me and said, The courting's over, let's make love. And she started unbuttoning my shirt. At that moment I felt a warm flood not just of desire but of protectiveness. Her sensuality turned out to be dead straight, open, and yet – curious, with a strong determination to study me at once and in depth, to skip the niceties, make my acquaintance thoroughly and quickly, establish a foothold in me that very night.

Straight after the love, she fell asleep lying on her stomach like a baby, her face in the hollow of my shoulder.

In the morning she said: You enjoyed that a hell of a lot. Like a stallion. Me too.

After the night of the storm and after the following nights, I was still certain that there was no permanent relationship. I still saw myself ending my days alone. But she and I could not have an agreement of the sort I had had all those years with transient women in hotels, villages, hammocks, Development Agency hostels, the two-clause agreement: fair pleasure and farewell. On the contrary: our friendship became open and playful after the night of the storm. We both felt easier and better. It was a strange experience, because up to then I didn't really believe in friendship, certainly not friendship between a man and a woman. Intimacy, yes, and passion, and fair play, and passing affection, and pleasure for pleasure, give and take, all these I had known over the years, and always in the shadow of the inescapable combination of desire and embarrassment. With the limits marked out in advance. But open-handed friendship, an unembarrassed relationship, no limits, I didn't think that was possible between me and a woman. In fact I didn't think it was possible between any two people. Then along came Noa, in her colourful summer dresses that whirled round her legs, with rows of large buttons fastened with loops down the front, the whole length of her lithe body, teasing me, slapping my shoulder sometimes in a gesture of relaxed comradeship, her deep simple sexuality like warm brown bread, the way she loved to strip us both naked in broad daylight, on the bank of a stream or in a clearing in the forest, free from all embarrassment, of flesh, or cash, or feelings, and the way she seemed to have made up her mind to untie me too and set me free.

Once I stayed with her for three days and three nights. When it was time to leave for the airport I said, Look, no arguments, I'm leaving you four hundred dollars on the shelf here. It's what I'd have spent on a hotel. And you're living such a hand-to-mouth existence. Noa said: Fine. That's okay. Thanks. A moment later she changed her mind, she'd worked out that the three days I'd stayed with her hadn't set her back more than a hundred. So what, I said, you've earned the rest from me honestly, you can use it to buy a television, call it a present from me, if you start watching a bit in the evenings you might learn some Spanish at last. Noa said, I'm all for a television, but they start at six hundred here and I can't make up the difference. I liked that. And I liked the way she could turn her back on me for a couple of hours, immune to all pleas and blandishments, concentrating on marking some tests that she'd promised to hand back the next morning. Even when we only had one evening together. Once she looked up suddenly from her marking and said in a concentrated way, without a smile: You're a man who likes summing up. Don't sum me up just yet.

In April we both fell sick, me first, with relapsing fever. We must have picked up a tick or a louse on one of our Sunday outings. She put me to bed in a sort of flannel prison nightshirt, with a blue wollen turban on my head like an Indian baby's that covered my forehead and my ears, covered me with four blankets, half-drowned me with a boiling-hot infusion of cactuses that her mad aunt had taught her to make, took several days off work in the Israeli class and the Embassy to nurse me and, wrapping herself in a thick brown grandmotherly dressing gown, she sat next to me and told me in a soft, soporific voice all about her father the paralyzed boxer and her Tolstoyan aunt and Yoshku the born-again Jew and some clown of a Peeping

Tom by the name of Golovoy or Gorovoy. The story got more and more complicated and more and more misty until I fell asleep, and I slept for three days and woke cured and cancelled my flight to Veracruz because Noa herself fell sick. She was a demanding invalid. She wrapped her two fists in my hands and wouldn't let me open them for several hours, it was the only way she could keep warm, despite the four blankets and my leather jacket that I wrapped tightly round her legs and zipped up. By the time we had recovered there was such a deep intimacy between us that Noa commissioned me to buy her some German cream for a vaginal inflammation in a pharmacy in Mexico City. At Easter I took her for a weekend to see the place where they were building a new town with a ring of six modern villages round it, all according to my plans, all in the first phases of construction in the south of the state of Tabasco. Noa said: It's spectacular; no it's not, it's human – if only they'd realize back home that it's possible to build like this before it's too late. I said: Maybe in Israel they don't need to build like this, they certainly don't need to build the kind of barracks they build there. In Israel the horizon is different. At least, it used to be. Incidentally, what makes you think that spectacular is the opposite of human?

Noa said, with no obvious connection: Look at us, a pair of teachers with no children, correcting each other all day long. It won't be easy, but at least it won't be boring.

In June, at the end of the school year, she suddenly said: I'm through here. I'm going back to Tel Aviv. Are you coming?

Look, I said, it doesn't work like that. I've got a contract till December, and unfinished projects in Tabasco and Veracruz, and there's nothing waiting for me in Israel at all. Noa said: Me neither. Are you coming or staying?

We got to Tel Aviv in July, during a suffocating week-long heat wave. The steamy city repelled me at first glance. After ten years away it looked more ugly than ever: a mess of grimy suburbs with no centre. Wars, rhetoric, greed, punctuated by raucous fun and the same sweaty mixture of destiny, arrogance and despair. We rented a furnished two-room apartment on

Prague Street, behind the central bus garage, and began to settle in. In the late afternoons we went out for long walks along the seashore. In the evenings we tried out restaurants. Then in August she went on a one-day tour of the Negev for teachers and when she got back that evening she said, Let's go and live in Tel Kedar, it's the end of the world, the desert is like an ocean and everything's wide open. Are you coming?

I hesitated for the best part of a week. I remembered Tel Kedar from before the town existed. I'd worked there for a few weeks in the late sixties, in a barbed-wire encampment of tents that was visited once a day by an army tanker that brought us water and the newspapers from Beersheba. For three weeks I roamed all over that bare plateau roasting in the sun at the foot of the cliff from before dawn to after dusk. At night by the light of a pressure lamp I sat in the administration tent sketching rough preliminary ideas for a master plan that was intended to get away from the usual Israeli approach and create a compact desert town, sheltering itself in its own shade, inspired by photographs of Saharan townships in North Africa. Nimrod Finkel looked at the sketches and shrugged his shoulders, Same old Theo, carried away by his fantasies, it's brilliant, it's original, creative, the trouble is, as usual you've left one factor out of account: when all's said and done, Israelis want to live in the Israeli style. Desert or no desert. Just you tell me, Theo, who do you imagine suddenly wants to be transported back to North Africa? The Poles? The Romanians? Or the Moroccans? The Moroccans least of all. And just remember this, chum: this isn't going to be an artists' colony.

That was more or less the end of my contribution to the construction of the desert town of Tel Kedar. I had never experienced the slightest urge to go back and see how it had turned out. I imagined they had built row upon row of identical prefabs with a first floor held up by bare concrete pillars and with sliding shutters on the balconies. They'd have fixed all sorts of notices to the concrete pillars, and mailboxes, and receptacles for collecting old newspapers for the Soldiers' Support Committee. And rows of trash cans in rectilinear containers in front of each building.

By the end of the week I said to Noa, All right, why not, let's give it a try. Something inside me responded and wanted to follow her to the desert. Or anywhere. I transferred half my savings from the bank in Toronto, put part of it in index-linked government bonds and part of it in shares and pension plans, bought this apartment, and purchased the property in Herzliyya that brings in a thousand dollars a month. Noa immediately got a job teaching literature in the secondary school. I opened a small planning office. Seven years have passed and we're still here, like a couple that's come through the child-rearing wars and is living in a quiet routine, looking after the houseplants to pass the time between visits from the grandchildren. We've furnished the living room with a white three-piece suite and matching rug. Noa usually invites a few people over on Friday nights, some teachers with their professional army-officer husbands, the local choirmaster, a couple my age from Holland who are both doctors, a hydraulic engineer, a neo-cubist vegan artist who objects to leather shoes, a drama instructor. We talk about national security and the Occupied Territories. Joke about government ministers. Deplore the way the town has stopped growing, the better residents are leaving and are being replaced by people who are only so-so. Perhaps the immigration from Russia will give us a bit of a boost. Though in point of fact, what will they *do* here? They'll dry out in the sun like us. Noa serves fruit and biscuits and South American coffee that makes your head spin, concocted with spells and brandy. If one of the speakers pauses, hesitating, searching for the right word, Noa has a habit of jumping straight into the gap, volunteering to finish his interrupted sentence, produce the missing word or free an idea that had got stuck. Not as though she is dominating the conversation but like an usherette whose job is to stand at a particular spot and gently take any latecomers by the elbow to make sure they do not stumble in the dark on some unseen step.

As the evening wears on the conversation breaks up into groups: the men discuss the issue of the deterioration of standards in public life, while the women exchange their impressions of a new play or novel that is causing controversy in the newspapers. Occasionally they come together again around scandals in artistic circles in Tel Aviv or a recent television broadcast, and there may even be a few local affairs, generally thanks to Muki Peleg. The artist may say, for instance: A couple of days ago I went to see an exhibition of young minimalists in Rishon Le-Zion, followed by a display of contemporary multimedia. Art is galloping ahead, culture is booming, and all we do is sit here slowly evaporating in the sun. There's a charming pedestrianized street now in Rishon Le-Zion with galleries, artists' clubs, restaurants, and the other streets are brightly lighted and full of life, people come back at midnight from a night out in Tel Aviv and fill the cafés and talk about new directions in the theatre, here all we can do is have a game of backgammon, watch TV and go to bed with the birds. The aerobics teacher says: If only they'd link us up to the cable television, like everyone else. And her husband, the lieutenant-colonel, adds bitterly: You can be sure of one thing, darling, that those settlers in the territories will get cable TV long before us, we're at the back of the queue as far as they're concerned, if we're in it at all. Noa says: We could bring that display here too. We could rig up some spotlights and turn the corridor of Founders' House into an art gallery. And why shouldn't we invite an art historian from Beersheba occasionally to give a lecture?

As for me, I go round the room serving the drinks in a gesture of democratic politeness, emptying the ashtrays, offering the occasional anecdote from the Caribbean islands or an example of Indian humour. Most of the time I just sit and listen. Trying to guess what sort of judgment Noa will pronounce after the guests have left: good or bad, hot or cold, desperate. And it's she who says to me, You're such a summer-up. Don't sum up, just watch.

At midnight or twelve thirty the guests disperse, promising that we'll meet again next Friday. Noa and I clear away and wash up and then sit down for another half an hour or so over a glass of mulled wine in winter or iced coffee in the summer.

Her blonde hair masks half her face from me, but her printed dress leaves her shoulders bare and they are delicate and fragile like leaves turning brown in the autumn, in places where they have autumn. At moments like these, when we are exchanging views about the acquaintances who have left, I still have an urge to take a shawl and cover her shoulders that are punctuated with a tiny brown birthmark near her soft nape. I start to woo her in my usual way, that enjoys waiting. Drawn by the scent of honeysuckle. Sometimes we go on talking till half past two at the kitchen table about the wonderful sights we used to go and see at weekends in the Cordillera del Litoral. Until Noa interrupts me in mid-sentence and says, That's enough talking, let's make love, and then she undoes my belt and undresses us both and lays her head in the hollow of my shoulder and puts my fingers to her lips. Our life is quiet and steady. The sitting-room rug is white and the armchairs are light-coloured too. Between them is a black metal standard lamp. There are houseplants in the corner. We have separate bedrooms because it turned out that we sleep differently.

On fine Saturdays I sometimes wake her at half past six in the morning, we get dressed and have coffee, then put on walkers and set off to find out what's new in the desert, walking down one wadi for a couple of hours and coming back up by another one. Once home we munch something from the refrigerator without bothering to sit down, then go back to sleep till the afternoon, when she likes to sit at the kitchen table, remote, bent forward, concentrating, planning a lesson or marking, while I sit and watch the red pen trembling between her fingers that have aged prematurely as though betraying her youthful body. One day I'll surprise her and buy her a little desk that can stand in the corner of her bedroom. Meanwhile I put it off so as to be able to watch her sitting at the kitchen table. While she finishes her marking I get some food together for us and switch on the TV, and we sit and watch the Saturday afternoon French film. On Saturday evenings we sometimes go out to a café or to the Paris. We stroll in the evening air for another half an hour in the square. Then we go home and listen to some quiet music sitting at the kitchen table. The next day another week begins here. Seven years have gone by like this, carefully avoiding the troupe of strolling players repeating, as if they were accursed, their old passion play: wandering, suffering, perdition. Until a weird pupil of hers died, in an accident when he was drugged, or it may have been suicide, there's no way of telling, and instead of editing a memorial volume, she agreed to help set up a rehabilitation clinic in his memory. The father of the boy has promised a financial donation, and for some reason I can't fathom decided to pick on her to run a sort of board of trustees. What does Noa know of committees and trusteeship, it's bound to lead to disappointment and embarrassment that I'd have liked to spare her, only I've no idea how. At first I tried to warn her off gently, and she responded with a sarcastic anger that I didn't know she had in her. Then I tried to help with various simple suggestions and was met with her cutting resentment. She did agree in an absentminded way to accept a loan from me, without seeing that as a shackle or a trap.

The only way I can help her is by avoiding any attempt to help. I have to hold back, as if to diminish a pain by regulating my breathing – and that I have no difficulty doing. Her strange project is becoming precious to her, "the gleam in your eye", as Shlomo Benizri says.

As though she had got herself a lover.

What about me? I followed her here, to her world's end, because I wanted only to be with her. Instead of the peace of the desert, all I have now is a sense of approaching danger. Which I can't prevent because I have no idea which direction it's coming from. Once, before all this, in the army, I volunteered to serve for six months in a small reconnaissance task-force in the desert, dashing around the Ramon Mountains in a couple of Jeeps, because I had turned down the command of an engineering platoon. It was before the road was built, before there were even dirt tracks here. Sometimes we would spot the silhouette of a hyena in the moonlight or a group of ibexes seemingly frozen on the line of the hills in the first light of dawn. Mostly we slept all day in hollows in the rocks and came out in the evening to give chase or to lie in ambush at night for caravans of smugglers crossing the Negev Mountain on their way from Sinai to Jordan. It was in 1951, or maybe 1952. We had a Bedouin tracker with us, a gruff, taciturn man, no longer young, dressed in the tattered uniform of the British Border Police, who knew how to read footprints even on rocky ground. He could sniff sun-dried donkey or camel dung and tell us who had passed this way, when, whether heavily laden or not, and even from which tribe. He could say on the basis of the dried-up dung what the beasts had eaten and where, and that is how he could work out where they were coming from and where they might be going and whether they were smuggling. He was a small, wiry man, and his face was not tanned but the colour of the cold ashes of a nomad campfire. It was said that his wife and daughter had been murdered in some tribal vendetta. And that he hopelessly loved a young cripple in Ashkelon. Even on nights when clouds blotted out the stars and the mountaintops he would bend down and pick up a rusty cartridge case, a faded buckle, a dry crust, traces of human excrement on the black scree, a gnawed bone thrown in a crevice, and decipher it with the tips of his fingers. We never let him have a gun, perhaps because he was always awake when we were asleep. It was only when we were all wide-awake and starting up the Jeeps full of the thrill of the chase, making the wadis re-echo in long rolls of dull thunder to our salvos of machine-gun fire, that he would detach himself from us and doze sitting down on the floor at the back of a filthy Jeep, with his foxlike chin between his knees, and his eyes neither open nor closed, waiting for silence to return and cover everything with a veil of greyish dust. Then he would wake without a sound and set off barefoot, stooped and crouching, as though straining to lick the soil, pattering away from us on his own to sniff out a cave or pit whose opening we had not even noticed as we drove past. Aatef was his name, but behind his back we called him "Night" because the night was as bright to him as if he had the characteristics of a nocturnal creature.

But we were careful never to use this name in his presence

because, we reminded ourselves, in Arabic the Hebrew word for night, *laila*, is a woman's name.

I SNATCHED Muki Peleg from a raucous taxi drivers' reunion at the California Café, at the table they call the Council of Torah Sages: he had forgotten that we'd arranged to have a committee meeting this evening at Linda's. Look, men, feast your eyes, just see who's come to pick me up, he said to his friends, with the broad smile of someone having his picture taken with the President.

Walking westwards into the sunset, we crossed the square by the traffic lights. At the Paris Cinema they had a thriller on: so the British comedy had not been a success here. A lefty comedy, Muki said, Linda dragged me off to see it but I talked her into walking out in the intermission. We went back to my place instead to listen to some groovy music, the sort that turns you on, if you know what I mean.

I said I knew what he meant.

Then he told me he had invested thirty-three thousand dollars in a third share of a travel agency that specialized in sending groups of "floating" youngsters on trips to Latin America. Maybe Theo would like to join in, he knows a bit about sombreros, I caught them with their pants down literally seconds before the liquidator arrived, realistically my third is worth at least forty or fifty grand, and if Theo puts another thirty in we'll clear a cool hundred grand inside a year.

It was evening calm in the square. A westerly breeze was blowing, as though it was trying to bring the sea here. An occasional car drove past the line of parked cars. A flock of swallows was swirling to and fro above the streetlights, veering abruptly eastwards then changing its mind and settling in a huddle on the power lines again. I like this square that does not pretend to be what it will never be. The shops, offices and eating places, the simple window displays, everything is made with modesty. The Monument to the Fallen and the drinking fountain in front of it seem to suit each other and both seem to suit the centre of Tel Kedar. And the square seems right for itself, the way weekday clothes are right for a weekday. When Theo suggested seven years ago that they should put up a black basalt fountain surrounded with palm trees and black rocks I thought it was a cold idea. But there was no point in saying so, and anyway the suggestion wasn't accepted and there was never any chance it would be. It's not that he's short of ideas, they say here, the trouble is he's up in the clouds, old Sombrero, he's several sizes too big for our little town. It's some time since they've even said that because Theo has long since stopped making suggestions.

Muki Peleg said: It's a beautiful evening. And you're beautiful too.

Thanks, I said. I liked your expression "floating youngsters". By the way, listening to groovy music at your place and all that, try not to hurt Linda. She's not that strong.

Nothing but love, Muki exclaimed, laying his hand on his chest in a gesture of offended probity. Love and nothing but love, that's what she gets from me. And there's plenty to go round, so if you happen to need some you know where to come. I'll make you float too.

Most of the shops were closed by now. The shop windows were sparingly lighted. People were strolling unhurriedly up and down the square, couples, parents and children, mothers with baby carriages, and four tourists in casual clothes, baked by the desert sun. Pretty Limor Gilboa, in red trousers and high heels, was walking between two suitors, who were both talking to her at once. Anat and Ohad, a young couple, she was in my class not long ago, were standing whispering in front of Bozo's shoe shop. In the window Pini Bozo has hung a photo of his wife and baby son in a black frame decorated with coral. In a fit of unrequited love, a soldier aged seventeen and a half shot them and everyone else in the shop.

A few old people were sitting on the municipal benches near

the beds of petunias conversing in low voices. Among them I could see Blind Lupo, sitting at the end of the bench, surrounded as usual by a flock of pigeons that were bold enough to perch on his knees and shoulders and eat maize from his outstretched hand. His Alsatian dog was dozing at his feet, oblivious to the massed pigeons. The blind man's foot struck the dog's back and the man hastily apologized. Meanwhile, every minute the traffic lights changed colour, even though there were no cars waiting. In front of Ecstasy Boutique, Women's Lingerie, an army officer from Ethiopia in a Givati Brigade beret was staring into the window with his mouth half-open.

As we were crossing Ben Gurion Boulevard the streetlights came on. There was no need for them yet, because the daylight was still fading very slowly. Half the sky was lighted by a red glow broken by wispy clouds. Behind the usual evening sounds, a woman calling a child to come in this minute, sentimental music from the Palermo, the murmur of metal signboards shaken by the westerly breeze, there was a deep, wide silence. At the place where Ben Gurion Boulevard ends and the greying expanse commences, two bulldozers, one of them enormous, were parked, and next to them the night watchman had lighted a smoky brushwood fire and he and his three dogs were motionless on the ground staring into the fire. Overhead a gliding raven made a black stain against the cloud-strewn blaze of the twilight. Here came another. And two more.

Twenty years ago there was still a bare plateau here hemmed in by grey hills. It was crossed only by a vague dirt track leading to the military installations in the valley behind the cliff. Now there are nine thousand inhabitants, a draft of a real town, flat, not entirely clear to itself, and already beginning to expand slowly over the plateau. There are some fifteen thoroughfares, perpendicular or parallel to each other, and all of them lead to the desert. People from thirty different countries live in five symmetrical districts, go to work or to the café, put their money in savings accounts, change the baby's diapers, change their curtains or their solar water-heaters, make an extra room by walling in the rear balcony. As if this has always been here. And there is a health clinic, a library, a hotel, a little industry, and henceforth there is also a string quartet that arrived only a fortnight ago from Kiev. A miracle, Avraham Orvieto said the first time he came after the death, sometimes, for an instant, you could see it as a miracle, a minor one at least. And he added: Immanuel loved Tel Kedar. It was his home.

The soil for the little gardens has been brought from far away by the residents, in trucks, and they have covered the dusty flint gravel with it as if they were dressing a wound. The dust constantly makes its way back from the open expanse, straining to reconquer its original terrain. And yet the gardens hang on and refuse to be dislodged. In a few places the treetops have grown higher than the roofs. Swallows have found their way here from far away, and perch in the treetops. Peaceful, homely, almost gentle, that's how President Shazar Street seems to me at seven o'clock in the evening, at a time when the day is departing and the sky is still on fire. In every flowerbed the hoses start their dripping at the same moment, operated by a tiny electrical impulse from the municipal irrigation computer. As the sun goes down the sprinklers begin to revolve in the little park and the façade of Founders' House is illuminated by beams from a floodlight concealed among the hibiscus bushes.

On a balcony we saw a handwritten cardboard placard: "FOR SALE OR TO LETT". That's the new estate agents, Bargeloni Bros, Muki said: They're such morons it's a wonder they didn't write SAIL. I said that actually I quite enjoyed living in a place that was twenty-five years younger than me, you could watch the life evolving. Muki said with a laugh: Nought out of ten for arithmetic, Noa, what do you mean twenty-five years, you don't look a day over thirty-three and a half, and you're getting younger every day – if it goes on like this you'll be ten soon. Blushing again, are you? Or is it just my imagination? After a minute or two, when he took in what I had said, he added in a different voice: Listen, one of these days I'm going to take things into my own hands and rig up some device with my own eleven fingers that'll hide or change those awful solar panels and TV aerials. Make it look a bit nicer round here.

I said: And the cypresses will grow taller, and we'll have a pretty skyline against the background of the mountains and the cliffs.

Muki said: And then they'll build Notre-Dame here and the Eiffel Tower, they'll fix us up with a river through the middle, with boats and anglers and everything, I'll be the building contractor and take charge of the lot, on condition that you'll kiss me on the bridge at night.

I nearly kissed him on the spot, in President Shazar Street, such a frantic, dishevelled boy; I restrained myself, and only said: It's almost pretty as it is. That is, so long as you remember when it started and what it was like before. A barbed-wire army camp in the middle of nothing. It started from sand and fantasies, where have I heard that?

Hardly started, and now there's no stopping her, as the empress's hussar said when they asked him how he got so thin, Muki said. Sorry. It just slipped out. Don't be angry.

And what sort of groovy music was it that he played to Linda whenever they walked out of the film halfway through and went back to his apartment?

Music for the soul. The Sword Dance. *Bolero*. He had loads of tapes that all kinds of girls had given him over the years. If I went, he'd leave the choice to me, and he'd make me a really explosive cocktail, out of this world. A couple of days ago Linda dragged him to a concert in a private house, at Dr. Dresdner's. That quartet from Russia played something sad and then they put on a record, even more depressing, the song of the dead children. It must have been Mahler, I said, *Kindertotenlieder*. One of them, called "When thy mother dear", gives me the shivers whenever I hear it, or even just think about it. Muki said, Look, I'm not really into all this stuff, Mahler, Germany, philosophies, but the honest truth is, I almost felt like crying there the other night from the music about dead children. It seems to get right inside you through your skin, not your ears. Through your hair even. If there's one really bad thing in the world, worse than bad, terrible, it's children dying. I'm against children dying. That's the only reason I'm on the committee. What did you think? That's why I'm going to this meeting now.

Linda served coffee in little decorated Greek cups. A regular glass menagerie filled three shelves: delicate tigers, transparent giraffes, shiny blue elephants, elegant lions that caught and reflected the light of the lamps, a tiny illuminated aquarium containing a single goldfish and a collection of miniature vases in whose glass little droplets of air are trapped forever like tears. Four years ago her husband the insurance agent left her because he had fallen in love with her sister. For years she has worked part-time as secretary in the little washing-machine factory here. She plays the piano at the rehearsals of the local choir. She signs up for every trip organized by the Workers' Council, takes part in voluntary activities for the Immigration Absorption Committee, art and craft groups, the panel for promoting the art gallery, the support group for the day centre for the elderly. A shy, asthmatic woman in her forties, with an old-fashioned plait coiled round her head, a whispery voice, and the thin, angular body of an adolescent. At our meetings she serves drinks and nuts, and then curls up quietly in a corner of the settee as though her forehead is being drawn towards her knees.

At the beginning of the meeting we asked Ludmir to take the minutes. Ludmir is a tall, suntanned man of seventy, long and thin and slightly stooped; reminiscent of an oddly proportioned ornamental camel made of wire and raffia, he gives the impression that his long, veiny tanned legs in their threadbare khaki shorts and battered flip-flops are attached directly to his chest. He has a prophetic mane of grey hair. Armed only with bitterness and angry pathos, he has been jousting year after year with one dragon or another. And still he never forgets his catch phrase: "Noa smoke without a fire". Ever since they moved to Tel Kedar in the days of the pioneer camp he and his wife Gusta have lived in a small, immaculate shack, overgrown with passiflora, behind Founders' House. Gusta Ludmir, a tall, severe, bespectacled woman with grey plaits wound round her head like rope, gives private math lessons. In her old-fashioned dresses, secured at the neck with a gloomy silver beetle, she sometimes reminds me of an aristocratic English widow from times gone by. Once, four or five years ago, a short while after he retired from the electricity company, Ludmir told me that his only grandchild, a girl of sixteen, whom he and his wife were bringing up, suddenly determined to leave home and go and live on her own in a rented room in Tel Aviv so she could study in a special school of dancing. Ludmir insisted that I speak to her "and prevent her throwing away her young life in the maelstrom of the big city, where all that lies in wait for a youngster like herself is ugliness and degeneracy disguised under the blandishments of a glittering career". So I invited Lailach Ludmir, a nervous, suspicious girl with the eyes of a hunted gazelle, her head sunk in her shoulders as though it had been hammered in forever, for a cup of hot chocolate at the California Café. And I tried to understand her dreams. But when I laid my hand for an instant on her tense shoulder she started, turned white and ran away. That was how I learned to take care not to touch children. Ludmir stopped talking to me, having come to the conclusion that I had ruined everything and that it was all my fault that he would die lonely. Two years later he forgave me, having come to a different conclusion, that in the last analysis we are all condemned to loneliness. "Noa smoke without a fire" were the words with which he first removed the interdict. But every now and then he shoots me a long wounded glare from those blue, childlike eyes of his that suddenly fill with pain.

Linda went to her kitchen to make another round of coffee and to prepare some fruit and shop-bought crackers. She told us to start the meeting without her, with the door open she could hear everything from the kitchen. I went out too to give her a hand and by the time we returned Ludmir had already erupted and was shouting furiously at Muki – how had we dared to purchase that filthy ruin, on our own initiative, without convening the committee, that whorehouse, that vipers' nest of drug-crazed criminals, without taking the trouble to ask ourselves what the public implications might be: "Not for me redemption's message if it issues from a leper," he quoted, attributing the line to Lea Goldberg. When I pointed out it was actually by Rahel, the molten lava changed course from Muki Peleg to me – such condescension, such arrogant pedantry, what are we here for, an operation to rescue young lives or an academic seminar? Are we a lifesaving team, or mere puppets in the provincial drama of a bored lady who is laying yet another trap to catch herself a new father in the form of a shady arms-dealer, whom she will reduce in his turn to a baby for her own amusement?

So saying he threw the minute book down on the table and walked out, slamming the door behind him. He was resigning. Leaving in disgust. Abandoning Sodom and Gomorrah to their fate. A couple of minutes later he rang the bell and returned. He picked up the minute book in resentful silence and sat for the rest of the evening with his back to us in the corner near the aquarium. It turned out later that he nevertheless made a faithful and accurate record of the whole proceedings, confining himself to adding at certain points in the minutes "*sic*" in square brackets, accompanied by an exclamation point.

Spreading out the notes I had previously prepared before me on the table, I put on my glasses and proceeded from one point to the next. There were various possible ways of calming the suspicions that were brewing in the town. For example, we could offer to treat, at no cost, local youngsters who became addicted. We could agree to give the Education Committee, the managers of the school and the teachers permanent representation on the Board of Governors of the clinic. Or, rather, not so much a clinic as a therapeutic community. It was worth stressing the intention of offering fellowships to some prominent specialists in the areas of drugs and young people, so that Tel Kedar would gradually become a prestigious research centre, attracting up-and-coming scholars and scientists from all over the country. It would make sense to harp on the pioneering theme and on the idea of community involvement. We should try to emphasize the creation of employment for teams of educators, psychologists, social workers, people who would be able to make a contribution to the life of the town. Scientific opinion on the treatment of addiction was divided between a biological and a psychological approach, and here we would be able to combine the two. And why shouldn't we try to involve the local police chief, who could issue a statement recommending that we grapple openly with the problem of addiction among the young instead of sweeping it under the carpet? It would be to our advantage if it was the police who explained to the public that the creation of a closed institute would reduce rather than increase the crime rate in the town. Above all, we must stress the motifs of communal responsibility, civic pride, an initiative that would make Tel Kedar into a model and example for other towns.

Ludmir broke his offended silence to hiss: Stress the motifs, did you hear that?

And when he looked at me, the repressed pain welled up in his eyes again.

Meanwhile, Muki Peleg was dozing on the settee, his artistically tousled head burrowing into an embarrassed Linda's bony lap; he had removed his shoes and put his feet on my knees, as though forming a bridge between her body and mine. He muttered something in his sleep about the need for a personal approach. Ludmir erupted again, his cracked voice rattling the glass menagerie and the collection of dewdrop vases:

Hypocrisy shall not prevail!

I realized it was time to bring the meeting to an end. I proposed that we should reconvene in a week's time, after I had had a meeting with the chief of police. As we were getting up to go, Linda shyly asked if we would stay for a few minutes longer, she had a little piece she'd like to play for us, it wasn't anything special, we shouldn't expect too much, it was really very short. She sat down at the piano with her head bent, as though trying to touch the keys with her forehead. In the middle of her piece she had an attack of asthma and coughed so badly that she could not breathe and had to stop playing. Muki Peleg fetched her little Ventolin inhaler from her bedroom; then, before our eyes, he put a teaspoon in the pocket of his pink shirt and a moment later produced it laughingly from Ludmir's hair. He was the only one to laugh; apologizing, he stroked the gasping Linda with one hand and me with the other.

Linda said, almost in a whisper: We didn't make much progress today.

And Ludmir: Out of the frying pan into the fire.

Tomorrow night I'll go and talk to the police chief at his home. If I can manage to bring him round to our side, I'll try to get him to come to a special meeting with the parents' committee and the members of the Education Committee and I'll ask Batsheva too. And one weekend soon we'll have an open study day with professors, public figures, artists, we'll invite a panel of personalities from Jerusalem and Tel Aviv. The promise of a weekend at the Kedar Hotel will entice them to come, and the promise of well-known guests will entice the Kedar Hotel into making a nominal charge for their stay. I'll type out a concentrated fact sheet for the study day. If the public mood changes, we may be able at least to – At least to what? What's got into you, Noa?

Should I ask Theo to have a word with Batsheva privately?

In actual fact there's nobody in Tel Kedar better qualified than Theo to spearhead this initiative, to allay apprehensions, to influence public opinion. After all, over the years in Latin America he managed to plan and build vast settlement areas, industrial zones, housing schemes, new towns several times larger than Tel Kedar. Two and a half years ago he politely turned down a deputation of teachers, engineers and doctors who came one winter weekend to beg him to agree to stand for the local elections at the head of an independent slate: his qualifications, his record, his confidence-inspiring appearance, his professional expertise, his image. But Theo cut them short with the words: It's not what I want. And he closed his left eye even more, as though he were winking at me above their heads, Thank you, he said, getting to his feet, it was nice of you to ask.

Bitter and hard. Gleam in a blind eye. Or is he simply confined to an invisible wheelchair?

What about me? A bored schoolteacher starting a new chapter? Putting herself to the test? Or am I just provoking him, making a fuss to force him to wake up, if you can say that about a man who suffers from insomnia.

As we left, Muki Peleg made it clear that Linda, apparently, had virtually insisted he stay the night. Perhaps he was hoping I would be jealous. I walked Ludmir back to his immaculate shack overgrown with passiflora, behind Founders' House. On the way the old man said: That Muki is nothing more than an ill-mannered buffoon, and that Linda of his is a sentimental fool. There was once a godforsaken village at the foot of the Carpathian Mountains, a village with thirty hovels and only two clocks. One belonged to the Starosta, who was the headman of the village, and the other belonged to the deacon. One day one of the clocks stopped and the other got lost. Or it may have been the other way around. The whole village was left without the time. So they sent a boy – he was nimble, literate too, beyond the mountain, to the town of Nadvornaya, to bring them back the time and reset the clock that had stopped. Well, the boy rode for half a day or more, he reached Nadvornaya, he found the clock in the railway station, he made a careful note of the right time on a piece of paper, folded the precious piece of paper, hid it in his belt and rode back to his village. Forgive me if I offended you, Noa. I'm sorry. I couldn't stay silent back there and restrain my anger at our futile prattle.

At once he embarked on a muddled apology for using the adjective "futile": he had tried to put things right and he had only made them worse, he had wanted to make peace and he had rubbed salt in the wound. Fire and brimstone is raining down on us all the time, Noa, because compassion itself is tainted with arrogance. There is Noa smoke without a fire. If you can, please forgive me. I cannot forgive myself, but you are still young. Good night to you. Pity on us all.

I got home at ten. I found Theo lying on the white rug in the living room, in undershirt and tracksuit bottoms as usual, barefoot, not reading, no television, he may have been dozing with his eyes open. He kissed me on the cheek and asked how it went and I kissed him on his bristly grey hair with its military cut and said: It was terrible. Ludmir is mad and Muki is a baby and that Linda is pathetic. So am I probably. There's nobody to work with. Insignificant. Nothing'll come of it all.

By the time I'd had a cold shower he had made us some supper, a geometric salad with radishes cut like rosebuds, cheeses and freshly sliced wholemeal bread on a wooden board, the frying pan with a cube of butter in it was waiting on the gas, and there were two eggs and a knife beside it, at the ready for the omelette-making. This is a ritual with its own invariable rules. I poured us both some mineral water. We sat down to eat opposite each other. His heavy, bare shoulders leaned against the side of the refrigerator. I was facing him and the window behind him that was full of desert stars. Theo told me that he'd been out too this evening, he'd been to see Batsheva, he just had a feeling I was going to ask him to talk to her.

I haven't asked anything of you yet. Least of all that you should go opening doors for me.

That's quite true, still, you ought to listen to me: I have the impression that, granted certain conditions, we might have a chance of getting this thing through.

We?

All right. You. I'm sorry. Even so, I think you ought to listen.

I got up in the middle of supper and shut myself in my bedroom. After a moment he knocked on the door. Noa, I'm very sorry, I only thought –

I forgave him. I went back to the table. The omelette was cold, so Theo got up, put a tea towel round his waist as an apron, and started to make me a fresh one. I told him to stop, there was no need, I wasn't hungry, we could drink some herbal tea and see if there was anything tolerable on the television tonight. We switched on, and turned off almost at once because they were broadcasting an interview with the Minister for Energy, who managed to say, Surely it is unthinkable . . . before we silenced him. Theo put a record on and we sat in the armchairs for a while without talking. Maybe at that moment we really did resemble each other as Muki once said about childless couples after years together. Suddenly I got up and went over to Theo, snuggled on his lap, buried my head in his shoulder and whispered, Don't talk. I remembered Tikki, the religious typist from Beersheba that I'd never seen, the one who fell in love with a basketball player and had a "Mongolian" baby by him that he refused to recognize. A live baby, I thought, so what if it's handicapped, it's alive, and just because it's handicapped it needs and deserves much more love. What was Immanuel doing all alone in the dark nurse's room on that grey winter's morning? How and why had he got there? Was he ill? Or had he slunk in to help himself to something from the medicine cabinet that he couldn't do without? How little I knew. Even now I didn't know anything. If I bumped into an addict right now, how would I be able to tell from a distance of four or five feet whether he was drugged or sleepy or simply had the flu? When Immanuel suddenly spoke and asked me, with his shy voice crossing the valley of silence in that room, whether I happened to have anything to write with, what had he really wanted? What was he after? To write something? Or was he just adrift, trying to communicate? And I pushed him away. I barricaded myself in. I failed to grasp that it was a plea for help.

Theo. Listen to me. Kushner the bookbinder wants to give us a two-week-old puppy. Don't worry. I've told him you're not interested in pets. Wait. Don't answer yet. Listen to something else, listen to this farce, Linda is in love with Muki Peleg and apparently he's already sleeping with her but he's still quite keen on me and I still love you. How about you?

Me, Theo said, well, it's like this, and instead of continuing he suddenly raised his undershirt and drew my head inside and enfolded me in the dark hairy cave of his chest as if he were pregnant with me.

WHILE the six o'clock news was on I made a fruit salad. I sniffed the carton of milk in the refrigerator, suspicious as usual both of the milk and of my own sense of smell. Then I started to tidy the kitchen cabinets, from right to left. I hoped she would come back early. Just before seven I went out on the balcony to see how the day was receding. A strange grey dog slowly crossed the garden and disappeared behind the bougainvillaea bower, swaying as though it had been knocked out. There is the dark stone wall between the garden and the desert. And behind the wall and the two cypresses turning black with the evening come the barren hills – not so much hills as notes from a muffled tune. In fact the muffled tune was someone playing a recorder in a neighbouring apartment, not a whole tune but simple scales repeated apparently without any variation. Six times the elevator passed our floor without stopping. I remembered she had a meeting at Muki's Linda's apartment this evening. I decided to go out. To go down and see what there is in the wadi, or perhaps, instead, to go down to the square and take a look at the Alsatian puppy that Kushner the bookbinder wants to give us.

The end of June. The days are very long. The nights are dry and chilly. Outside the front door some youngsters were sitting on a low wall, and they whispered together as I went past as if they had noticed something funny. The one and only police patrol car in Tel Kedar went past me and slowed down without its flashing light. The policeman waved to me and smiled: Evening, Sombrero, why don't we ever see you? And a sudden breeze blew from the end of the street making a low whistling sound. I started the Chevrolet and drove straight to the place the sound came from. There are only nine apartment blocks on the street and straight after the last one the road turns into a rutted dirt track which you can follow, if you like, southwards, then south-eastwards as far as the entrance to the quarries. Once I was out on the plateau I realized that the wind was actually much stronger than it had seemed among the buildings: it was not a gentle breeze but sharp gusts whose roar I could hear above the sound of the tires on the gravel. It was hard to make out the track through the dust that was caught in the headlights and whirled around me, like driving in a snowstorm. Too late I remembered to close the windows of the car. I continued groping my way forward, at a snail's pace, trying to guess from the billows of dust where the slope of Hyena Hill was and where, on my right, was the edge of the wadi. Grains of fine sand whirled across my entire field of vision in their millions until even the sharp horizon dividing the desert from the sky was obliterated. It was like crossing a virgin forest in the middle of the night. I supposed that the dark smudge on my left was the lower slopes of the mountain range and I advanced slowly parallel to it while the westerly wind, from my right, lashed the windows with sand. The headlight beams were broken up by the dust and reflected back dazzlingly into my eyes, as if I were driving in thick fog. The car lurched and bounced about and I realized that it had left the dirt track to the quarries and that from now on I would have to try at least to stay on a parallel course to it on the flat scree at the foot of the cliff. The darkness deepened. I tried driving with full beam, dipped headlights, sidelights, but still the dust continued to break up the light and reflect it back to me beaten, soaked in murky sand.

I decided it was best not to go on. I stopped the engine, got out, and stood waiting for the cloud raised by the tires to settle, but after a while I was still surrounded by thick, soup-like air. I had lost my way. Nevertheless I thought I could vaguely identify the line of cliffs to the left. I started the engine and decided to get a little closer to it and drive along it until it brought me to the electronic fence that the army had put up along the mouth of the forbidden valley, and that would certainly guide me to the curve of the quarries. A low cloud or a tall pillar of dust barred the sky from my eyes. I was struck by a strange feeling, as though I were moving not forward but up and down, swinging in a sealed box deep under the ocean. I enjoyed this feeling until my eyes almost closed, in fact they may have closed altogether as I could see nothing anyway except the convulsive dancing of the dazzling wall of dust in front of my headlights. I considered for a moment whether I was not better off stopping here, lying down on the ground and waiting. On second thoughts I could not see what change might be worth waiting for. I took account of the danger involved in proceeding, as there were some fairly deep gullies that bisected the plain, but I answered myself, Never mind, I can still press on slowly and steadily. So I drove on gently in bottom gear, at 5 miles an hour or less. Stone chips and gravel groaned and grumbled under the weight of the moving wheels. Could I have unwittingly passed the quarries already? Or could I have drifted into the forbidden valley? There was nothing to stop me turning round and trying to drive back. But there was no point in turning round and nowhere to go, because the car's tracks were immediately obliterated by the eddies of windswept sand. Better keep moving southwards, if it really was southwards, until my tires splashed into the Indian Ocean or until at least I managed to fall asleep, and sink down into the depths of that sleep that had abandoned me but still went on calling to me like a will-o'-the-wisp.

Then I made out beyond the murky screen a pale flickering light, the barrier at the entrance to the quarries. I flashed my headlights to the guard, so as not to alarm him, but after a moment I realized that it wasn't the gate to the quarries: what I had done was to drive right round the south side of the town and now I was entering it again from the west, on Ben Zvi Street, in the chic residential neighbourhood. Now there was a paved road surface under my tires, a row of streetlights, and the wall of dust dissolved. I could see tiled roofs, and darkened trees in the gardens. The eerie sound of muffled woodwind music had faded too. The dim silvery expanse and the carpet of ashes had vanished. I felt a momentary urge to turn round and drive back into the fog from which I had come. But what for? So I drove past four identical houses that looked as though they were inspired by an illustration in an old-fashioned children's book: simple, square houses with chimneys, built of red bricks and with symmetrical windows on each side of the door. I parked the Chevrolet outside the fourth house, behind Batsheva's battered Subaru; I got out and, without bothering to lock the car, rang the doorbell. I rang three times, at intervals, but answer came there none, even though there was a friendly little light in the window on the left and I fancied I could hear a faint sound of music coming from somewhere inside the house.

Undeterred, I made my way round the side of the house along a dark paved path almost canopied with wild oleanders. At last I came upon Batsheva in the garden at the back. She and her old mother were sitting enjoying their evening peace by the yellowish glow of a light bulb suspended in the branches of a fig tree. The old woman sat motionless on a stool, erect and ascetic-looking, with a green kerchief on her head and her shrivelled arms held stiffly in front of her on her knees. Batsheva was playing a mouth organ, and this was the melancholy tune I had heard when I pressed the doorbell. She was sitting sprawled in an old claret-coloured armchair with splayed legs that had no doubt once adorned an oriental-style drawing room. Now that the upholstery was worn thin and the stuffing was spilling out in several places, the chair had been consigned to the garden like a magnificent pleasure cruiser grounded on a sandbank. Both their heads were ringed about with brightly lighted moths, and I knew that if I lingered here my head too would be surrounded with a similar shimmering halo.

Batsheva Dinur, the mayor, a woman of my own age, strong, pink-faced, with short-cropped silvery hair, a solidly built, oddly proportioned figure, sitting deep in this armchair, looked like a range of mountains with extensions piled up in every direction, as though she had more than four limbs. Her large horn-rimmed spectacles had slid down her nose. Her solid red arms looked rough, like old bookbindings. She always reminds me of a plump

Dutch grandmother, or an innkeeper's wife ruling with a firm hand all those around her.

When she spotted me, she stopped playing. She shot me a wry look over the top of her spectacles, as though she could see right through me before I had said so much as a word. She said: Look who's come to see us. Come over here, fetch a chair from the veranda and bring it over. Not there. Here.

I took a stool like the one her old mother was sitting on, stiff and unmoving. I remembered to say, Good evening.

Batsheva said: Be quiet, Theo. Let me finish.

She went on playing a tune that I could not identify yet that sounded vaguely familiar and even moving.

After playing for ten minutes she suddenly had enough, stopped, and let out a braying sound, like an impatient mule. She slipped the mouth organ into a pouch formed by the folds of her skirt between her heavy knees.

It won't come right, she said, I keep trying to play it like geometry, to dry the feeling out of it, otherwise it goes all sticky like plum jam, which I hate by the way. You look terrible.

She peered at me for a while, still over the top of her glasses, curiously, thoroughly, without the slightest embarrassment, a redoubtable woman whom no adversary has ever got the better of. And yet at the same time she is generous and vigorous, with an occasional wicked twinkle in her eye, as if someone has just whispered a juicy obscenity in her ear and she is savouring it in her mouth, and putting off swallowing it, deliberately prolonging the pleasure.

I said: Look here, Batsheva. I'm sorry to butt in out of hours. The thing is, I've got a problem I can't really talk to you about at work.

Her old mother said: Here comes that poor Seriozha. He's in love. He's looking for his Anyushka.

Batsheva said: A problem. Yes. So I've heard. Your wife. That clinic of hers.

I pointed out that Noa and I aren't married.

Why ever not? You should get married. Noa's a sweetie.

She winked at me merrily, her broad face lighted up with affectionate, knowing shrewdness.

Give me two minutes to explain.

I know, I know. You've bought Alharizi's ruin and now you're stuck with it. You've come to ask me to meet you halfway. Forget it.

The old woman remarked sadly: Love. They don't eat. They don't drink. Phoo – and the brains go out.

Batsheva said: Ah, thanks for reminding me. I'll put the kettle on in a minute and make us all some tea.

She did not move from her armchair.

I said: There's no need. Don't get up. I've only come for a few minutes.

Batsheva said: Right then. Please, talk. We don't let him get a word in and we keep saying talk. Now you can talk.

Batsheva Dinur's husband was killed in the battle for Jerusalem in 1967. She brought her four children up by herself while working as an electrical engineer specializing in transformers. Nine years ago, not long before we came to Tel Kedar, she put in a successful application to manage the washing-machine factory. Two years ago she was elected Mayor, and since then she has fought valiantly to, as she puts it, clean up the bloody shambles. Her children have grown up and married. She has grandchildren all over the country. Every Saturday evening she goes out with her old mother to stroll up and down the square by the lights. Or else the pair of them sit in the California Café for an hour or so, and a queue of favour-seekers lines up at their table. She is an indefatigable, straightforward woman, always armoured with a casing of witty practical gruffness. Her enemies detest her and her friends would go through fire and water for her. The Tough Old Truck, they call her in the town.

Look, I believe that with proper preparation of public opinion and on whatever conditions you lay down for us, a small medical clinic, something pioneering, experimental, with all appropriate supervision arrangements, could be a boon. It would attract researchers. It would act as a useful focus for voluntary communal activities. There would be a favourable press. And in fact it's just the hook you've been looking for to bring us a university extension or the first nucleus of a hospital. Think it over.

The old woman added: In winter the thermometer drops to forty below, the wolf howls at the door of the hut, *aaaoooo*, like an abandoned baby.

Batsheva said: Drop it, Theo. It'll never happen. But I'll tell you what, there's some iced mint tea in the refrigerator. Why don't you help yourself, and bring us some too. The glasses are in the dryer.

Batsheva. Wait. Try to see it like this. A man who has lost his son turns up here and pledges to give us seventy thousand dollars, with the promise of more to come. He gets together a committee. He's within his rights. A funny committee, admittedly. The committee purchase an abandoned property that was hanging around here like a pain in the backside. They register as a memorial foundation. The people involved show enthusiasm. Dedication. Naturally there are doubts in the town. Some of which are justified. That's perfectly understandable. But with you on our side the doubts will be dispelled.

Who needs it, Theo? For heaven's sake. An opium den. Besides which, he still hasn't repaid you a penny. Do me a favour, bring your chair round to the other side. That's right. Now I can see you without getting the light in my eyes. You really do look terrible.

The old woman intervened: On the stove sweaty peasants with fleas are sleeping in their clothes, and outside the wolf goes *aaaoooo*. And what of compassion? Has it vanished? Disappeared?

I didn't say a drug clinic.

Ah. Something else? Definitely, why don't you set up a memorial in the form of, let's say, a workshop for desert sculpture? The rocks are on me. For free.

But it's got to be connected with the problems of young people, I said. It's in memory of a dead schoolboy.

And Seriozha shivers all night long. Everybody is asleep and he has none.

Young people. By all means. Computers. All you have to do

is persuade your donor. Let's say for instance a centre for young computer wizards. It mustn't be called that, of course. Isn't that right, Mama? Or else what about a hothouse for young researchers on subjects related to high-tech industry? You'd need to get at least another hundred and fifty thousand dollars out of your benefactor for equipment and operating costs, and that's without even thinking about a scholarship fund. If you can come up with some academic patronage then we're talking business. Why not?

That's not what the donor is after.

Well make it so it is, then. Or else get hold of someone else who's lost a child.

I don't think Noa will buy it. Or the donor. It's hard to know.

You take care of it, Theo. Cleverly. Then come back to me. Mama, you've talked enough. And what happened to our iced tea?

Not for me, thanks. I'm off. I'll try to talk to Noa. It won't be easy.

Seriozha will be ill.

Won't you stay a little, Theo? Take it easy? Only don't stop me playing. Just sit quietly, no, why not? You're not a nuisance, is he, Mama? Not a nuisance, is he? On the contrary, you're lovely. Stay.

How about a compromise, Batsheva? Kids with a talent for computing who have got mixed up with drugs?

She didn't answer. She merely puffed out her cheeks, like an elderly baby determined to amuse at all costs, and blew into her mouth organ. She played a tune I remembered from the fifties, "He didn't know her name, but all the same, that pigtail went with him all the way . . ."

As I got up to leave, on tiptoe so as not to disturb her, she stopped playing and said: One more thing, Theo. You've got to be in charge. It's got to be your baby. Be quiet, Mama. Drive carefully. And remember: I've promised you nothing.

MEANWHILE the summer is intensifying. The daylight oppresses us, murky and wearing, and even though the windows are closed tight, the powdery dust manages to get between my sheets. The asphalt road surface melts in the blast, and in the evening the walls release the residue of the heat. A southerly wind from over the hills brings a whiff of burning rubbish from the municipal dump, a sourish, scorched smell like a puff of bad breath. From the balcony I can sometimes see a Bedouin shepherd sprawled on the nearest hillside, a black figure among black goats, and the faint sound of his piping reaching me in broken snatches breeds peaceful detachment. What is he dreaming of, lying there motionless for hours on end in the shade of a sloping mass of rock? Some day I'll go across and ask him. I'll trail him to the caves in the mountains to the place where they say there is a nocturnal smugglers' route between Sinai and Jordan.

My class 12 graduates have started to disperse. Some have been called up early, others are drifting around the town, racing their parents' cars along the deserted streets. Or prowling backwards and forwards in groups across the square by the lights. Five of them turned up in Theo's office to ask his advice, not in his professional capacity but to do with their plans for backpacking in Latin America. There's a story going around in the town about him living alone among the Indians in the jungle for ten years. Some people call him Sombrero behind his back. Although everybody here keeps a respectful distance from him.

The battery and the oil pump of our rusty blue Chevrolet packed up within two days of one another. Jacques Ben Loulou from Ben Elul's Garage said, That's it, you should get rid of her.

Theo screwed up his left eye, with a suspicious, peasant-like smile lurking in his grey moustache, and replied, What's the hurry? There's still some life in the old girl.

Some Tali or another came to see me one morning to show me some poems she'd written. She didn't know whether to call me miss or Noa. I was surprised because I didn't imagine that she or her friends would still be writing poems. I found the poems themselves thin, anemic, and I was looking for a way of saying so without hurting her.

Then I decided that I had no reason to discourage her: let her write. There was no harm in it. Who knew? Had Immanuel written poetry too? She had no idea. She didn't suppose so. But maybe he did actually – before he fell for that addict from Elat who taught him to sniff, he was in love with you up to here, so he might have written poems to you. With me? In love? What? Where did you get that idea from, Tali? Listen, Noa, first of all it's not Tali, it's Tal. Secondly, everyone knew. Knew? Knew what? How did they know? With an embarrassed, or perhaps disbelieving, smile on her lips: That's easy: it was written all over him. The whole class knew. What do you mean, did you really not notice, Noa? Seriously? Didn't you feel his love?

I said no. And I could see she didn't believe me. When she had gone I remembered the wall of the concrete apartment block, so close to the window of the boxed-in balcony that was his tiny bedroom in Aunt Elazara's apartment: a grey, dusty, depressing wall. And I remembered the brown mug. And his clothes. Folding the sweater. The torn blanket at the foot of his bed, where the mute dog slept at night. And the upside-down open book about the end of the Jews of Bialystok.

A couple of days later she turned up again, shy but excited, bringing me a new poem, and this time she agreed to have a cold Coke and some grapes with me on the balcony. She had written this poem under the inspiration she'd received from me the last time she came. She hoped she wasn't really bothering me. She found it quite tricky, this poetry thing, because she didn't have a lot of people she could show them to but on the other hand it is rather strange, isn't it, writing and writing and not showing them to anyone because there aren't a lot of people here to show them to. Apart from me, that is. She hopes it's not too heavy. Is she the only one in the class who tries to write poems? I dunno. I think so. We don't talk all that much. I mean, we talk lots, but not about that kind of thing. No way. So what do you talk about? All sorts of things. It's really hard to say. A bit about the army, about going abroad, about clothes and money, gossip, nothing special, this and that and that's it. Like on Friday evenings, after the disco, sometimes we get round to talking about what we're living for, there's this thing about the Far East and that, but that's just a few of us. Most don't. The boys are hooked on how to get into the real-action units, and what's cooler than what. Even though they're quite frightened about the army, and where it's screwing up most effectively – in the Territories or in South Lebanon, that sort of thing. Then there's the stuff about AIDS. We get to talk about that a bit too. And computers. And motorbikes.

I asked her about drugs. Tal said that they were actually quite in favour of this project, the refuge, that Muki Peleg and I were going to bring here. It'll be a real monument, so people will remember Immanuel, not like just any old pillar with a name-plate on it. We're all really keen on it. But most of the parents are jittery, they're nervous about the image of the town and property values and all that. I asked her if, so far as she knew, there was a real drug problem in the school. Well, it's like this. There aren't many real addicts, but there are one or two who have a smoke on Friday evening. Yes, she said, she had experi-mented herself, slightly, but so far she hadn't managed to get really high, because she always got a headache right away. There weren't a lot of real junkies. At least, not in the circles she moved in. Maybe down in the Josephtal Estate they snort a bit. It's hard to tell. What about Immanuel? Well, it's like this, more or less. At the beginning there was this thing in the Hanukkah break when some of the guys took off and hung around in Elat. He went back there a few times after that by himself, but nobody really knows what happened with that girl, Martha. There are stories going round. That's true. I don't know what really hap-

pened and I think that nobody really knows because Immanuel
was so withdrawn. It got worse after he fell for you. Maybe
there's someone that knows more than I do, but the thing is,
actually I'm not so sure that anyone really truly knows anything
about anybody. At all. In the whole world. How can you? Everyone's on their own private island. There's lots of gossip. That's
true. There's stories going round about you too. And about Theo
and Muki. And Linda. You must have heard them. People talk.
No, I don't want to go into all that now. It's just irritating. Are
you saying you truly never picked any of it up, Noa? Didn't you
spot that he was in love with you? Nothing at all? Never mind.
Nobody knows anything about anybody. Specially about love.
Love is a really destructive condition, she said. Two strangers
who suddenly see each other, or they don't really see each other,
they smell each other, and in no time at all they get more attached
to each other than a brother and sister. They start sleeping
together in the same bed, even though they're not from the same
family. And very often they're not even friends, they don't even
know each other, they just get hooked on each other, and the
rest of the world can go jump. Just look how destructive it is,
really. More people probably die from love than from drugs.
They ought to fix it so there's some way of treating that too.
Every time she thought about how little one person knew about
another she felt like laughing and crying. And the weirdest thing
was that it was impossible to change it. It didn't make any
difference how much you invested in somebody, you could invest
a hundred years day and night without a break, you could sleep
in the same bed as him, it didn't help, in the end you wouldn't
know the first thing about him. If she had any more poems,
could she keep coming? And anyway in a few days Nira was
due to have her first litter of kittens, Nira was her cat, she
was ginger, quite kittenish herself, really funny, had the manner-
isms of a countess, but she was so aloof, even if everybody
pleaded with her, made a fuss over her, adored her, it wouldn't
make a bit of difference – with beautiful stripes like a tigress,
she was so lovely, dreamy, and sometimes she sort of smiled,
grinned to herself in a superior kind of way. And to let her

parents have the kittens put down, it really upset her, so she thought maybe she could bring us a kitten as a present? After all, you haven't got any children, maybe your husband would say yes.

I told her that Theo wasn't my husband, that is, we weren't really married. Tal said, I've heard people talking about it, it doesn't matter, they say all sorts of things, bla bla bla, anyway I feel like giving you a kitten. Well, 'bye then. About Theo, I really wanted to ask you something, I dunno, actually it doesn't matter.

What about Theo?

Nothing. It doesn't matter.

What did you want to say about him?

It doesn't matter. He's a special kind of person.

Special in what way, Tal?

Hard to say. A bit frightening.

She put down the poem and left.

Theo sat the whole evening mending the old typewriter, a forty-year-old Baby Hermes that I found after the second accident in one of my father's drawers. I'd never seen him using it. My aunt sometimes used it to tap out harsh letters to the paper against violence, cruelty or meat-eating. When the house was packed up I took it with me. He sat up till nearly midnight taking it apart and oiling it and putting it all back together again, with the tiny springs that join the arms of the keyboard to the battered keys. He had put on my glasses to help him see better. For an instant he looked to me like a patient Jewish watchmaker from an earlier generation: his slightly cocked head, his partly closed eye that looked larger through the lens of my glasses, his pursed lips under his grey moustache, his greying hair with its military cut, the set of the thick shoulders supporting the powerful neck, everything testified to the immense concentration that he was devoting to his work. I stood quietly behind his back, barefoot, for a few minutes, fascinated by the skill of his fingers. As if generations of fiddlers and scribes had a share in it.

When he had finished repairing the typewriter I made us some herbal tea. Theo said he remembered the clever coffee with which

I used to make men's heads spin in Caracas. Clever? Heads spin? Well, he was referring to the cognac and the Indian powder I laced men's coffee with to bewitch them so that they couldn't resist me. And the cactus essence I used to cure us both of relapsing fever. Listen, Theo, we could go to Galilee this summer instead. Why Galilee? Scandinavia. We could hire a red open-topped sports car and drive around the fjords. Or get a new car? Or adopt a kitten?

He took off the glasses, lowered his head as if to butt, and slowly scratched his neck. He squinted at me obliquely, as though he had managed to decipher a dangerous plot. After a ruminative silence he declared that he had a shopping list in his head. First, a small desk for the corner of my bedroom. Second, a high-powered reading lamp. Third, how about a word processor instead of that wreck of a typewriter that would soon break down again, because its term of office was long since over. Although actually there was life in the old girl yet. And by the way, what did Benizri say when you went to see him yesterday? Same as last time? Or was he prepared to meet you halfway? Sorry. Question abandoned.

I hugged him from behind and enjoyed the warmth of his shoulders against my breasts and the way I made the bristles stand up on the back of his neck. For your information, I said argumentatively, Benizri is beginning to soften. If Batsheva Dinur gives him the green light he is willing to recommend setting up a fact-finding team. If I were you, Theo said, putting his arm round my waist, I would look for a compromise. I might go for a modular concept, a gentle start-up period, with, say, something like seven or eight patients in the first year, not more, running the place as a residential centre, with good fences, and, at least in the first phase, with hardly any link with the community. That way the opposition would die down. And another thing: if I were you I'd insist on putting it on a sound businesslike basis, at least a thousand dollars a month per patient, starting with kids from well-to-do homes, and to keep the town happy we should take in an addict or two from local families, with an eighty percent reduction. And the whole thing has to be subject to rigorous public scrutiny, with a business licence that could follow on a legally binding agreement between the foundation and the Town Council. I would write into the agreement that the Council should reserve the right, on the grounds of public interest, not to renew the licence at the end of the year. What's more, I'd be willing to renounce from the outset, in writing, the right to take legal action if the licence were not renewed. This concept seems to me to be the only chance of making any headway. Let's say, to gain a bridgehead here. That's the way I would couch the proposal if I were in your shoes. And even then it's pretty chancy.

But Theo, you're not in my shoes, I said.

Theo said: Yes. No.

Yes and no?

I meant yes, Noa, I'm not in your shoes.

A girl said to me today that she thinks nobody can know anything about another person.

Know. What does knowing mean?

The water's still boiling. Let's have some more tea. Knowing means getting outside yourself. At least trying to. Now and again.

Do you remember once, in Caracas, you said that a couple of teachers without children would spend their whole time correcting each other. And you said it wouldn't be easy but it wouldn't be boring. That's what you said, Noa. Even so, there are moments when I really am in your shoes and I wish you were in mine.

That's enough talking. Let's make love.

What here? In the kitchen?

Come on. Right away.

I switched off the overhead light and undid his wide leather belt that smelled of old leather and sweat, and snuggled into his hairy chest. My fingers tried to do the same to him as his fingers had done when he was mending my typewriter. Afterwards we stood outside on the balcony in the dark and saw the quicksilver river that the moon was sketching across the hills all the way to the horizon. We were standing very close but without touching or talking, and that is how we slowly sipped herbal tea and listened to the sound of a night bird that we could not name.

AND once she told me about a young traveller from Ireland whom she picked up in the car on the way to a conference of literature teachers near Tiv'on. It was at four o'clock in the afternoon on a rainy December day a year and a half ago. Because it was foggy and the days were so short she had to turn her headlights on early. The moment she did so they picked out a long-haired figure who looked from a distance like a girl, standing by the roadside weighed down by a huge backpack, making a waving sign that is not usual in Israel. When the young man climbed into the car she noticed his boots were full of water. They were large, clumsy boots that reminded her of the lace-up boots that her Aunt Chuma used to wear as she charged around the house or went out to gather medicinal herbs on the slopes of Mount Carmel. As he sat down beside her with his backpack on his lap she noticed a strip of cloth sewn across it bearing the words: "ALL YOU NEED IS LOVE". Both the youth and the backpack were drenched.

He had set out from his home in Galway the previous evening and hitchhiked across Ireland overnight, then flown from Dublin to Birmingham, from where he had arrived two hours earlier on a charter flight. He was on his way now to look for a girl called Daphne who was apparently working as a volunteer in a kibbutz somewhere in Galilee. He did not know her surname, or the name of the kibbutz. Daphne. She was from Liverpool. They had recently spent a single night together. As they were parting she had told him that she was off to Galilee soon. He had not seen her since. She loved sheep and wide open spaces. Her dream was to be a shepherdess. He had never been in Israel before, but he had a map and you could see on it that Galilee was not a very big area. He could go from one kibbutz to another until he found her. He wasn't short of time. In fact, he claimed, being short of time was self-defeating and went against the secret of life. If his money ran out, he would try to get some temporary work somewhere, whatever turned up, he didn't care, back home he was a carpenter's mate, in Portugal he had put up telephone lines, in Copenhagen he had once appeared in a small cabaret singing folksongs from the west of Ireland. Anyone who has some goodwill can find goodwill everywhere. So he said. Noa suddenly noticed that he was ill. He looked feverish. When he stopped talking his teeth chattered even though she had put the heat on. Two winters ago the heater in the Chevrolet still worked. Excuse me, she said sternly, as though reprimanding a lazy pupil, but do you happen to know how many kibbutzim there are in Galilee? Where exactly are you planning to begin this search for this Daphne of yours? He did not reply. He may not even have heard her. The movement of the windshield wipers may have hypnotized him and put him to sleep. It was twenty-four hours since he had left home, he probably hadn't slept all night, yesterday he had had a soaking in Ireland and before he had had a chance to dry out he had got soaked again here. And he looked to her as though he had a high temperature. His head slumped forward on his backpack and his sodden fair hair flopped over his face. She thought he looked like a girl again.

As they entered Qiryat Tiv'on she stopped the car. She woke him up and told him, for some reason, that in the northern tip of Galilee there was a kibbutz called Dafna, and she showed him on his map where it was. Then she dropped him off, with his backpack that looked like a wet mass of rock. After a moment she stopped and looked in the rearview mirror, but she was dazzled by the lights of an oncoming truck, and all she could see behind the car was an unlighted telephone box in the rain.

After registering, she left her things in the bedroom, where two teachers twenty years younger than herself, one of them very pretty, had already settled in, and went to the opening lecture, which was on the subject of whether there is such a thing as women's literature or feminine literature and, if so, what its particular characteristics are. After a quarter of an hour she got up suddenly and went outside to the parking lot in the rain, started the car, and went to look for her hitchhiker at the spot where she had dropped him off, just before Qiryat Tiv'on, because she felt she ought to take him to see a doctor. Perhaps she also wanted to ask him how shortage of time is self-defeating and what he had meant when he said that anyone who has some goodwill can find goodwill everywhere. But when she got there she didn't find the boy, only the unlighted telephone box in the mud by the roadside.

Instead of going back to the conference she turned northwards at the T-junction and drove through the thickening fog along roads she did not know, until she noticed that she was almost out of gas and pulled into a filling station near the village of Majd el-Kurum. The filling station was closed, but a couple of young men were sitting inside under a bright neon light, apparently totting up the day's accounts. Seeing her silhouetted at the locked door they hesitated and whispered to one another, then one of them got up and opened the door, jokingly remarking that they had taken her for a robber, and filled the tank for her. His companion offered her coffee and said, You're not the first visitor we've had tonight, lady, look what we've got here. In a corner of the office, on the greasy floor, curled up and swaddled like a fetus in a grubby blanket, she saw the shock of flaxen hair, and she woke him and said, Let's go and find you a doctor.

He trailed after her to the car, drowsy, silent, feverish, and not at all surprised to see her: as though he had not doubted that she was destined to find him and pick him up again that night. He sat down next to her again, his teeth chattering, his backpack with its love slogan dripping into his lap, and after two minutes he fell asleep. He may not even have waked up when she dragged him out of the filling station. His head landed on her shoulder and his blond hair fell over her chest. His heat penetrated through her sweater and wet the hollow of her neck. At the junction after Majd el-Kurum she turned right, because she had made up her mind to go back to the conference centre, wake up a doctor or a nurse, and in the morning sit down at the telephone and try every kibbutz in turn until she found his Daphne or at least located a place where they would take him in and give him some work. But she lost her way, fog and water obscured the windows on the outside and the inside misted up with their breath, and close on midnight she passed Kibbutz Mazzuva and noticed an illuminated sign indicating a hostel in a few miles. She decided to get them a room for what was left of the night. After a few bends the engine died. She parked in a turnout under tall eucalyptus trees lashed by the winds and sat waiting for morning. His head was in her lap by now. She pulled the blanket off the back seat and spread it over him and over herself, so that he should not freeze to death. Then she fell asleep too. When she was awakened by the grey light of dawn she found that the rain had stopped and the hitchhiker had vanished with his backpack. For a moment she feared for her handbag, which contained her papers, keys and cash, but a short search revealed it in the space between her seat and the door. At half past six a police patrol car drew up. A middle-aged Arab policeman flashed his gold teeth at her, reprimanded her for taking risks, and managed to get the engine started. At eight o'clock, back at the conference centre, she called me at the office and told me her story, and asked me to try to find her sick passenger. Maybe there was a girl from Liverpool called Daphne, working with sheep, on the register of kibbutz volunteers? Or maybe the Ministry of the Interior would have a record of a young Irishman from Galway who had landed in Israel yesterday?

I thought the chances were remote, but something in her voice on the phone made me promise to try. I spent the morning dialling all over the place, I even located a couple of highly placed acquaintances I hadn't had any contact with for twenty years and called them on her behalf, but naturally it was useless. All I got at the other end of the line was perplexity or bewilderment barely disguised as polite surprise. She got home that evening, having abandoned her conference, surprised me in the kitchen, dishevelled, feverish, trembling, seized me, hid her face in my shoulder and started to cry. I took her frozen, veiny, old woman's hands in mine and tried to warm them. Then I ran a hot bath, took off her clothes and put them straight in the laundry basket, soaped and rinsed her, dried her in a thick bath towel and wrapped her in a warm dressing gown. I almost carried her to her bed. I made a pot of tea and poured her a cup, leaving the rest in a Thermos by the bed. Then I rang for the doctor. Noa slept for sixteen hours. When she woke up she stared at me blankly for ten minutes, looking distant and forlorn. I gave her some herbal tea with honey and lemon. She only took a sip, then suddenly she exploded in a rage at me, with a kind of strident hatred she had never displayed before, except perhaps on rare occasions when she tried to amuse me by imitating her father's fits of fury, because I had added a spoonful of cough syrup that the doctor had prescribed and that she had obstinately refused to take. She raised her voice and shouted painfully that I was trying to baby her again, that I was a dead weight on her life, oppressing and depressing her so that she would age prematurely, this apartment was just a cage, Tel Kedar was a penal colony, and I shouldn't be surprised to wake up one morning and find myself alone like an old dog, and maybe that was exactly what I wanted.

By next morning she felt better. Her temperature was down and her joints were less painful. She asked me to forgive her. She apologized. She sat down in front of the mirror and made herself up carefully, much more than usual, and, still facing the mirror with her back to me, told me again about the Irish hitchhiker she had lost. Then she put on a green pantsuit that suited her very well and went to school so as not to have to put off a test. I had intended to stop her, because the doctor had ordered several days' rest, but on careful reflection I decided to say nothing. Still, as she stood in the doorway I couldn't stop myself saying, almost in a whisper, Maybe you ought to stay here. For a moment she looked at me, amused, and suddenly she said, not angrily, Don't worry, I'll come back to you. You took lovely care of me.

Since that December morning a year and a half ago she has never said a word about her hitchhiker. And I haven't mentioned him either. A week after she recovered she called me at work one day and asked me to come home late, at seven instead of five. I got back at seven fifteen to find that she had made us a splendid three-course dinner with sparkling wine and a dessert. But I still had to put the car in for major repairs. Jacques Ben Loulou from Ben Elul's Garage said, Look here, she's really been in the wars, somebody's been driving her over stones and rocks and then got stuck in the mud, and after that she's got bent, here, here as well, because she wasn't towed properly. It's none of my business, Theo, but you can take it from me that whatever the true story is, it isn't a nice one.

At one or two in the morning, alone on the balcony facing the silent plain, I sometimes imagine her solitary traveller wandering still among the empty hills of Galilee. Looking for his Daphne in the sheepfolds, or maybe he's abandoned the search and still travels on slowly, aimlessly, along deserted roads. Anyone who has some goodwill can find goodwill everywhere. I still haven't the faintest idea what this means, but the music of the words pleases me more and more. And now he's falling asleep, his breathing is light and even, he looks like a pretty girl, with his head on his heavy backpack, and his flaxen hair falling like a fine veil over his face that I have never seen, alone in the evening light in an uninhabited place, in a remote and pleasant valley where there are birds and a wood and a spring. Or it's not the carpenter's apprentice from Ireland but me lying there, at the foot of the trees, sleeping in the light breeze among peaceful shadows in a valley where there is nothing but a spring and a wood and a bird, and why should I ever want to wake?

IN the morning when he left for his office I went back to the kitchen and continued reading *Youngsters in the Trap*. I jotted down various details that I intended to follow up. There are three public rehabilitation centres in the Tel Aviv area: one in the Hatikvah district, another in Jaffa, and the third in Neve Eliezer. None of the three is actually a residential centre. Hashish and opium are mainly smuggled from Lebanon. Recently the use of crack, an impure form of cocaine, has become widespread. The hard drug that is most readily available on the market is Persian coke. Most users need one dose in the morning and another in the evening, and its advantage is that its effects continue for several hours and the addict under its influence can continue to function apparently normally. Up to a point at least. As for rehabilitation, some undergo it in prison, whereas other people are actually exposed to drugs for the first time during extended periods of imprisonment. The attempt to keep those undergoing treatment in the company of others who have been cured, and isolated from their usual surroundings, has pros and cons. The dramatic phase of the cure is the "withdrawal", which lasts on average ten days or so but can be as brief as a week and sometimes extends for three weeks or more. The ordeal usually reaches its peak on the second or third day, and is marked by pains, nausea, convulsions and fits of depression or aggression. In extreme cases suicide can occur. Sleeping pills and painkillers as well as intensive massage can alleviate, but do not remove, the withdrawal symptoms. It is recommended to spend the period of withdrawal at home, under constant supervision, with the involvement of the family and an expert team and occasionally also a support group of former addicts who have successfully kicked the habit. This is on condition the family home constitutes a supportive environment and not an aggravating factor, in which case a clean break is preferable. Withdrawal is followed by a period of detoxification lasting six months to a year. During this period it is advisable to keep track of the patient's progress by means of frequent urine tests, although it is possible to cheat the tests by bringing specimens of someone else's urine. It is best not to incarcerate youngsters who have started using drugs but to put them under the supervision of a probation officer and compel them and their families to commit themselves to a custom-built programme of treatment. In the following chapter I read that the heavy addict is someone who lives exclusively on the emotional level, which is why any emotional injury is liable to make him backslide into his old ways. I found the expression "make him backslide into his old ways" wrong and even offensive, while "emotional level" struck me as a crude expression.

Should I go to Elat tomorrow?

Should I look for a girl called Martha?

Should I investigate? Compare testimonies?

And what about the father? Why hasn't he been to Elat? Or has he been and not told me? And why should he have told me?

What did his aunt know? And when?

What was he looking for in the nurse's room? Why did he sneak in there? And why did I freeze up when he hesitantly asked for something to write with? Did he really flutter his eyelids or am I just imagining it now because of Avraham's story?

You can invest all your resources for a hundred years. In the end you won't know anything.

It is better to do the right thing than to try to decipher the truth. Better, like that policeman, to work as far as possible in a drily compassionate way: with the precision and persistence of a tired, experienced surgeon who volunteers for an extra shift because at the last minute as he is driving out of the parking lot of the hospital, on his way home at the end of a long day, he notices that more casualties are being brought in. So he turns round, parks his car, quietly puts on gown and mask again, and returns to the operating theatre.

At the end of July, Avraham Orvieto arrived, alone, without Arbel this time, a lean, ageing, weak-shouldered man in cream-coloured jeans and a crumpled bush jacket. In his quiet, sad voice he promised Theo that he would transfer twenty thousand dollars to him within a fortnight on account for the loan, and that the rest was imminent. Theo said, What's the hurry? Then they talked between themselves about some oversight or error way back in the War of Independence. Avraham hardly said a word to me, except to thank me for the coffee; it may have been because Theo did not let go of him for an instant. I went out to the grocer's and when I got back I found that they had both reached the same conclusion concerning a certain decision taken by Yigal Allon and another famous military commander by the name of Nahum Sarig, nicknamed Sergei. It turned out they had both known him well and been opposed to his tactics, whereas I had never even heard of him, but when they offered to explain to me in what the particular greatness of this legendary commander consisted, and in what way his tactics had been faulty, I said, Thank you, but I am not interested in the subject, and besides, I haven't got the background. In fact I found it pleasant, even enjoyable, to sit between them and listen to them conversing in low voices, like a pair of conspirators hatching a secret plot, as though the War of Independence were still being waged underground somewhere in the Negev Desert, and the blunders and missed opportunities and alternative strategies could be discussed only indirectly, in coded language. Avraham Orvieto mentioned some fortified height by the name of Bir Aslug, and Theo disagreed with him and said, I think you're mistaken, to the best of my recollection that was a little further south, near Kadesh-Barnea. Avraham said thoughtfully, Still, the credit for the flanking movement by way of the ancient Roman Road belongs to Pini Finkel. And Theo said, Permit me to disagree with you there, I think you deserve the credit for that one, Avraham. Pini Finkel was insignificant, when it comes down to it he was killed because of his own superficiality, and by the way he had a son called Nimrod, I brought him up, he lived with me for two years when he was still a wretched youth, I gave him a job, I gave him a hand up, and the upshot was that he was the one who kicked me out of the Development Agency, he didn't do it on his own but he was the one who was behind the cabal. Never mind. It was all a long time ago.

He had never told me. I had never asked him.

I poured them some more coffee and left them alone together. I decided to go and collect a pair of sandals that were being repaired.

I had called a meeting of the committee for eleven o'clock in the morning at our apartment. Theo prepared plates of fruit, glasses for cold drinks, walnuts and almonds, thinly sliced whole-meal bread and a selection of cheeses on a wooden board, and set it all ready on the coffee table. Ludmir arrived twenty-five minutes early, panting, in his khaki shorts and battered flip-flops, and after pronouncing his usual slogan, Noa smoke without a fire, he demolished all the walnuts and most of the almonds by himself. The Ethiopian immigrants, he declared, were being treated here like shit, not that the Russians were faring much better, anyway the Absorption authorities ought to be lined up against the wall and shot, and the quarries ought to be dynamited before they poisoned us all with their dust. Muki Peleg was a quarter of an hour late, looking like that young thinker on the brandy advertisement again, with his flowing locks, and an artis-tic silk scarf round his neck; he told a couple of jokes, apologized on behalf of Linda, who had joined an organized tour in the Jordan Valley, quizzed Avraham Orvieto about the girls over there in the Congo, what's that, Nigeria, same difference, then said, Come on then, Theo, start the meeting and let's get it over with.

Theo said:

Permit me to outline briefly the difficulties we may anticipate. First, Batsheva can prolong the discussion in the Town Council as long as she likes. She can set the subject low on the agenda. She can work against us in the government departments, to prevent us from getting the permits. She can have the matter discussed but delay it indefinitely with all sorts of formal and technical snags. Second, the public is already up in arms. Setting up the clinic will bring property values down, will lead to nuisance from crime and noise, will expose local youngsters to contact with dubious elements. People claim that they have invested their money in an apartment in Tel Kedar to live a peaceful life, whereas the clinic will wreck their peace and quiet, with ambulances in the night, police patrol cars, violent incidents, criminal elements springing up in the wake of the addicts. Anyway, you don't turn a town with hardly any crime into a cuckoo's nest or a refuse heap for the big cities for a fistful of dollars. Who needs addicts here? Pushers? Pimps wandering round the school during break? Fifteen-year-old drug-sniffing hookers? Little junkies robbing homes and stealing cars and mugging old folks to scrape together a few pennies? And dirty needles in our gardens, maybe infected with the AIDS virus? They're already going around from door to door getting Tel Kedar to sign petitions – what's all this about treatment, once an addict always an addict, and there's bound to be someone behind it who plans to make a fortune out of it, and why here anyway, isn't it enough they've saturated us with new immigrants that no other town would take in such quantities? Soon they'll be sending us Intifada kids from the Territories, Molotov cocktail throwers, for rehabilitation. And the more the objections multiply, the more Batsheva will have a field day, dealing with each different objection separately, the procedure will drag on for years, and that's before the residents get organized and start taking legal action. Apart from which, the Town Council is liable simply to refuse outright to sanction the change of use in relation to the existing municipal master plan. Checkmate. And that is only on the local level. But there are other levels too: the Departments of Welfare, the Interior, Health, Education, the police, half the government in fact. And we haven't even begun to talk about the running costs. Shall I continue?

Avraham Orvieto sneaked me one of his winter-light smiles, and said pensively: What then? Should we give up? Make do with a memorial garden with some swings?

Theo said: Compromise.

And Ludmir: Compromise. Compromises stink.

Then Muki Peleg reported to the committee on the sale of the apartment that had belonged to the aunt, Elazara Orvieto, which was henceforth to house a dental surgery. The money that would shortly be received for the sale would, with Mr. Orvieto's consent, go straight into the trust fund and could be used for the renovation of the Alharizi house once love had broken down the barriers of prejudice, as the rabbi said to the nun.

I did not speak.

And so it was decided that Theo would go to Jerusalem with Avraham Orvieto the following week, to try to secure the support of the minister who had served with Theo in a combat engineering unit forty years ago and knew Avraham well from his days as military attaché in Paris. It was further decided to meet with the authorities of Beersheba University and the leaders of the Anti-Drugs Campaign. And it would be necessary to alter the composition of the committee. It was essential to bring in at least a nucleus of influential and well-connected citizens, teachers, social workers, psychologists, respected local personalities, perhaps one or two parents who were progressively minded, or whose children were affected by the problem, and the editor of the local paper, and maybe also an artist or two.

It turns out, said Ludmir blankly, that I am redundant.

And Muki Peleg added: As the husband said when he surprised his wife in his neighbour's arms. Will you leave Linda in, at least? So she can go on doing the typing?

After the meeting, when Ludmir and Muki had left, Muki hurrying ahead in his sky-blue shoes to call the elevator while Ludmir ambled after him with his camel's gait, Theo said: I'm going to leave you here for a quarter of an hour while I pop down and fetch us a pizza from Palermo. We'll save the time we would have wasted making lunch. When I get back and we've eaten we'll go down and introduce Avraham to the place.

After the pizza we showed our visitor Tel Kedar, because Avraham Orvieto had asked to "catch something of the feel of the place". The gasping Chevrolet had trouble starting again, despite the two recent repairs. On the way Theo took it upon himself to explain the misconceived plan on which the town had been built, a conception that was doomed from the start. It may have been these words that made Avraham turn and send me another secret, fleeting smile, as though I were being offered a glimpse of a pleasant, cosy room. Whose shutters were closed again after a moment. A frail, slightly built man, with thinning white hair, his face furrowed and wrinkled by the African sun: the face of a veteran metal engraver who has retired and now divides his time between reading and thinking. He spoke only a little, in a soft grey voice, with self-effacing hesitancy, as though he found the very act of speaking to be something noisy. "And where are we meant to be shining, and by whom is our shining required?" I asked him silently from the back seat.

We drove slowly past apartment blocks and private houses, past palm trees ruffled by the desert breeze, fainting lawns, and poinciana saplings kept alive, as in intensive care, by a drip.

It's beautiful, it's exciting, said Avraham Orvieto, a completely new town, with no biblical or Arab past, built on a human scale, and you don't see any poor districts or any signs of neglect.

Maybe it's wrong of us to take it for granted.

Theo said: Modestly built is not necessarily a compliment.

And Avraham: Not necessarily. But it is.

At the square by the lights we stood for a few minutes in front of the Monument to the Fallen, on which were inscribed, in metallic letters, those words, THE BEAUTY OF ISRAEL IS SLAIN UPON THE HIGH PLAC S, the penultimate letter still missing. In the same letters, only smaller, were the names of the twenty-one fallen, from Aflalo Yosef to Shumin Giora Georg. Old Kushner was sitting, hunched up, on a stool in the doorway of his cubby-hole, reading a thick volume. In the window of his shoe shop Pini Bozo had now placed his lacquer-wood model of a holy ark. Inside the ark passers-by could now see the colour photograph of his dead wife holding the dead baby aloft in her arms, touching the baby's forehead to her own, smiling to it with strong bright teeth, while the baby beamed back at her with its toothless mouth.

Then we had coffee in Theo's office, "Planning", on the top floor of the building to the left of the Town Hall. On the wall there were various maps, views, an enlargement of Ben Gurion staring resolutely towards an expanse of barren gullies. Theo showed his visitor some plans, ideas that he had thought up for an environmentally sensitive development in desert conditions, sketches of streets, squares, vaulted buildings related to one another in a manner carefully calculated to cast shadow and to repel the dazzling light, forming winding alleys like shaded valleys. It was plain that even though the visitor spoke little, his very presence ignited in Theo a sort of electric alertness. After the second cup of coffee Theo even took a blue folder out of a drawer and extracted from it three different sets of plans for the refurbishment of the Alharizi house. Avraham Orvieto looked at them silently for a while, and did not take his eyes off them even when he put a brief, conspiratorial question and received a terse reply. I did not hear what the question was, and I missed the answer too.

I walked over to the window. I could see a torn kite that had got tangled in the power lines and was swinging to and fro in the wind above the run-down billiard hall which also sold lottery tickets. Schatzberg the pharmacist's old dodderer, the one who died recently, was known as Elijah because he was in the habit of asking everybody courteously when Elijah was coming. From a death announcement that was turning yellow on the notice board opposite I learned that his real name was not Elijah but Gustav Marmorek. I suddenly recalled the expression that Benizri from Beersheba had used: "insignificant". I decided to stay there looking out the window, so as not to be in the way. Theo and the visitor seemed to be establishing bonds of closeness and sympathy that did not leave any room for me. I noticed that Theo had twice been treated to the fire-in-the-hearth-through-the-shutter smile. I wished I were somewhere else. In Lagos for instance.

At the meeting with Batsheva Dinur it turned out that Avraham Orvieto had commanded the reserve platoon in which her husband had fought and been killed in the battle for Jerusalem in 1967. Avraham had not forgotten him, Didi, the tall bearded boy who had stretched out on the asphalt in an alleyway while they were waiting, reading a musical score as though it were a thriller.

At the end of the conversation Batsheva asked Theo to put down in writing a detailed memorandum. I particularly need to know, she said, just how secure your stockade is intended to be. And in fact, if it is really to be a closed unit, what good can come of it for the wider community? And how about the staff: are they to be local or imported? And if imported, are they contractually obliged to reside here among us, or are they going to get in their cars at the end of the day, leave a duty officer behind and process in convoy back to civilization? Further, how much money is Mr. Orvieto, Avraham, planning to invest in the project, and how much, if anything, is he going to contribute to the running costs? And if you can't provide a convincing break-down of figures for at least five years, then you might as well not bother to come back. Let's be clear that in all I've just said I haven't promised you anything more than a glass of cold water and a biscuit next time you come and see me, if you do. And by the way, a memorial, a benefaction, I understand that and appreciate it, after all this whole country of ours is a sort of memorial, and I understand that in this case the memorial has got to be something to do with young people, without young people we have no future, even if without a future we have no young people, but why not, say, a sports hall? A clubhouse? Or a swimming pool? Computerization of the educational system? A crafts and hobbies centre? New laboratories? A cinematheque? And, Noa, you say something. Bring them down to earth. After all, you have some influence over Theo, and if I'm not mistaken she has some influence over you too, Mr. Orvieto, Avraham, am I right? Eh?

Avraham Orvieto said that what he wanted to do was to save young lives. He said that his son Immanuel had loved Tel Kedar and that he himself was beginning to understand the personal reasons for this love. He also said that Immanuel had been fond of Noa and now he himself had become fond of her and Theo.

Towards the end of the afternoon Theo drove the visitor to see the empty building.

I've got a headache, I said, I'll stay at home.

After ten minutes I really did have a headache.

I took two aspirin and went and sat in the air-conditioned reading room of the public library, which was deserted. I found a book in English about the history of colonial rule in Lagos and I read it for a couple of hours, then I read about chimpanzees until someone came and touched my shoulder gently and said, Noa, sorry, it's closing time. When I got home I found that Avraham Orvieto had already left for Tel Aviv, asking Theo to pass on his thanks and good wishes. Theo himself was sitting in one of the white armchairs, as usual, patiently waiting for me to get home, waiting quietly yet unrelentingly, unyieldingly, with his bare feet propped up on the coffee table and his undershirt showing off his tough shoulders, his wide belt smelling of leather that has soaked up male sweat, but for once he was not sitting in the dark, he had put the light on so that he could read a book about addiction that he had picked up from my bedside table, called *Youngsters in the Trap*. As I came in he took off my glasses that he was wearing and asked how I was feeling, was my head better?

Absolutely wonderful, I answered.

FIVE to one in the morning. Through the wall the grating of the elevator; with groaning cables it continues without stopping to a floor above. Noa is in her bed, she has washed her hair, she is wearing a white T-shirt and her glasses, her head is ringed with a halo of light from her bedside lamp, she is absorbed in a book, *The Rise and Fall of the Flower Generation*. Theo is lying down in his room listening to a broadcast from London about the expanding universe. The balcony door is open. A dry wind coming from the east from the empty hills slowly rustles the curtain. There is no moon. The light of the stars is cold and sharp. The streets of the town are long since empty and dead but the traffic lights in the square have not stopped rhythmically changing colour, red amber green. Alone in the telephone exchange Blind Lupo, on night duty, listens to the shrill of a cricket. His dog is dozing at his feet but from time to time it pricks up its ears and a nervous twitch ripples its fur. When is Elijah coming? The man who used to ask is dead, now perhaps he knows the answer. At the ultimate limit of hearing the blind man listens to the rustling of the night because he feels that behind the layer of silence and beneath the grating of the cricket the howls of the dead are stirring, faint and heartrending, like mist moving through mist. The weeping of the newly dead who find it hard to adapt sounds feeble and innocent, like the cry of a child abandoned in the wilderness. Those longer dead sob with a continuous, even wail, women's crying, as though muffled in the darkness under a winter blanket. While the long-forgotten dead of bygone ages, Bedouin women who starved to death on these hills, nomads, shepherds from ages past, send up from the depths a desolate hollow howl more silent than silence itself:

the stirring of their yearning to return. Deep and dull beneath it breathes the groaning of dead camels, the cry of a slaughtered ram from the time of Abraham, the ashes of an ancient campfire, the hissing of a petrified tree that may once have flourished here in the wadi in springtime eons ago and whose longings still continue to whisper in the darkness of the plateau.

Lupo stands up, trips on his dog, apologizes, feels his way and closes a window in the exchange. Noa turns out her light. Theo, barefoot, goes to check that the door is locked and turns to investigate the refrigerator. What is he after? Again he has no idea. Maybe just the pale light filtering through the food, or the sensation of cold inside. He gives up and goes back to his bedroom. Forgetting to switch off the radio, he goes outside to sit for a while facing the empty hills.

AFTER the meeting Theo went out to fetch a pizza from Palermo, instead of lunch, to save time. He wanted to be able to take our visitor on a tour of Tel Kedar and also to show him the Alharizi house.

As the door closed behind him, I said: I don't have much to contribute to an argument about the fighting in the Negev in '48. You won that war and all the wars, the few against the many, with or without Pini Finkel's flanking movement, or somebody else's. So now I'm going to bring you the correspondence, the receipts and the accounts, so that you can see what we've done with the money you insist on sending us every month.

Avraham Orvieto said there was no need for that. First of all, for the time being almost all the investment had come from Theo. He would repay him in the coming weeks. There had been a delay in realizing the cash. And in any case it was becoming clear that there were many more obstacles ahead and you might say that the purchase of the building had been a little premature.

But I didn't give up. I had to present to him the accounts and receipts that I had put together, it wasn't all properly sorted out yet, and show him the paperwork and the exchanges of correspondence. He was the one who had given me this job to do, and he was the one to whom I had to report. I'll just go and bring everything I can find. Or rather, I took his hand, let's go to my room, that's where the papers are, and it's cooler there because I don't open the blinds in the morning.

The only chair in my room was occupied by the clothes and underwear that Theo had stripped off me in the night. I sat Avraham down on my bed and placed myself between the bed and the bedside table, trying to hide from him with my body what was on the chair; I put my glasses on and handed him the papers one by one. Avraham Orvieto peered at each document, his warm face radiating sympathy, curiosity and perhaps mild astonishment, and piled the papers in his lap. After a while I did sit down next to him on the bed, because I felt odd standing like that, with my shadow falling on him, almost covering his ascetic form, in this room where the noonday light filtered in softened and distorted between the slats of the blind. When I sat down I found it was even odder to be sitting knee to knee with the father of the boy on the bed where Theo and I last night had made love, lingering on every note, gently holding each other back.

I said, as though I were speaking to an inattentive schoolchild: Are you checking those papers, Avraham? Or are you just browsing? Are you dreaming?

Look, he said, you were the only teacher he liked, and he may have had an ear for literature. If you like I'll try to tell you a story. During the last winter, in December, after his first trip to Elat, I was here for two and a half days. I stayed at the Kedar Hotel. On the last evening after sunset he came to the hotel to take me for a walk. Every time I came on a visit we used to stroll for an hour or two, even though we didn't talk much. He was wearing warm corduroy trousers and a brown leather jacket, a stylish bomber jacket that I'd bought him on my way here, at Rome airport. I was wearing a coat, too. We walked shoulder to shoulder, because we were both about the same height. It was a cold evening and a strong wind was blowing off the hills. If I am not mistaken we went round the smart residential district, crossed the neglected little park behind the health clinic, and came out by Founders' House, whose front was lighted up by floodlights hidden in the bushes. Suddenly it started to rain. You're not comfortable, Noa. Why don't you lie back on the pillow? Yes, like that. Rain in the desert on a winter's night, you know, there is something about it that makes you feel sad. Even more than rain falling at the usual season in places that are not desert: it afflicts you like a deliberate insult. It was half past nine, and the streets were already deserted, and they seemed

even more deserted because they were so wide. By the light of
the street lamps we could see how the wind lashed the rain
diagonally, every drop piercing like a needle, and a smell of
wet dust came up from the ground. All the blinds were down
everywhere. It looked like a ghost town. Two or three figures,
perhaps Bedouins, with empty sacks on their heads for protection
from the rain, ran across the square. And vanished. Immanuel
and I sheltered under the corrugated metal awning of the box
office of the Paris Cinema. The awning was groaning from the
onslaught of the rain in the wind. Then we saw some distant
lightning that made the slope of the desolate hills to the east
flash white. The diagonal rain became heavier and turned into a
thunderstorm. The square seemed to be turning into a dark river
in the mist in front of our eyes, and the buildings seemed to be
floating away from us. The roar of the flood came to us from
the direction of the wadis, although on second thoughts it may
have been just the shaking of the metal awning overhead. For
some reason I found this deluge interfered with my perception
of the desert. When I said this to Immanuel he gave a kind of
twisted grin, though it was hard to tell in that wet yellow light
that could not break free of the faint lamp over the shuttered
ticket office. I don't even know if it was after he got caught up
with drugs, or how deep he was in by then. That's something
I'll never know. Once you said to me that he was very careful
and sparing with words, and you were right, that's how he
always was, and that's how he stood by my side inside that cage
of cold railings under the awning that rattled and creaked in the
rain. In that manly bomber jacket that I had chosen for him,
with its zippers and pockets and metal buckles, he looked less
like a tough airman than an emaciated refugee child who had
been saved from drowning and dressed in his rescuers' clothes.
So there he stood, looking frail and torpid, and as he leaned
back against the emergency exit of the cinema it suddenly opened
wide under his weight. Presumably they had omitted to lock it
that evening. The rain was getting heavier so we took shelter
inside the empty auditorium, which was quite dark apart from
the emergency lighting that glowed faintly behind the word EXIT

above the locked doors on either side. Below and facing us was the pale screen. In here the rain sounded dull, as though it were a long way away, and the thunder seemed to be under water. So there we were, my son and I, sitting side by side, like you and me now, in one of the back rows. And we realized how wet we were. And even though I could feel the warmth of his knee with mine, I suddenly had a strong sense of longing, as if he were not there next to me but, how should I put it, beyond the dark mountains. There used to be an expression like that. Though in fact on a rainy night all mountains are dark. Immanuel, I said to him, listen, now that we're sitting here, why don't we try to have a little chat. He grinned. And asked what about. About your schoolwork? About your mother? Or maybe we should talk about the future? A slight, indeterminate movement of the head. And so, from me, another two or three questions, and from him just a phrase or a mumble. Can you understand that, Noa? There I was, alone with my son on a winter's night in a cold, deserted auditorium, with our shoulders touching, or more accurately with our coats touching. And nothing was said. There was no verbal contact. None. Whereas I belong to a generation that is a very verbal one, if I can put it like that. Even if during my African years I've forgotten what there is to say when it isn't a matter of getting things done. Suddenly he blinked at me, as he did when he was little, took a deep breath, as if to say wait a minute, and pulled out of one of his pockets a magnetic game of checkers, a miniature set that I bought for him once in an airport somewhere. In that gloomy light we played three games, one after the other almost in silence, to the sound of the pounding rain. I won all three. Telling you the story now, I believe this was a mistake. I shouldn't have won all three games. What good were those victories? On the other hand, what use would it have been if I had let him win by lying and pretence? What do you think, Noa? As a teacher? As a sensitive person? Wouldn't it have been better to let him win on our last night together?

Instead of answering Avraham's questions I put my arm round his shoulder. I withdrew it at once because he turned and fixed his weary blue eyes on me and smiled his bright warm-room smile, a smile that flared up and at once faded away among those charming wrinkles, like a curtain being opened and then drawn shut. Then, he said, with his roughened hands moving in front of him as if he were trying to mould into a ball an object that did not want to be moulded, the rain slackened off and my son stood up and walked all the way back to the Kedar Hotel with me. Next morning I flew back to Lagos. I thought of writing him another letter. But there's Theo at the door now; let's go back to the sitting room and eat the pizza he's brought us, and then let's go and look at whatever he cares to show us, even though I have my doubts whether in the last analysis they'll let us build a refuge here. I do find it hard to believe they will, and in fact would it be so terrible if we decided to give up and commemorate him with some other good cause? I'm sorry for making you sad, Noa. It would have been better if I hadn't spoken; you were the one who told me that my son called words a trap, and that we didn't take care. Pity.

IT will cost me six thousand shekels to repair the fence. And it would be worth having a gate put in, to prevent people wandering around there at night. I still think that there won't be a drug treatment centre here, and yet I'm forever trying to devise some sort of compromise. What am I after? I don't know. Batsheva Dinur has called twice to ask where the detailed paper I promised her is. At night I sit and read the pamphlets and books that Noa leaves scattered around, open face-downwards, on the kitchen table, in the passage, on the settee, on the armchair on the balcony, in the toilet. I have already learned a thing or two, but the heart of the matter still eludes me. And meantime I have to protect the property against neglect and against the dubious characters who apparently bivouac there at night. I am starting to like the derelict building itself. I spend half an hour or so there every day with a sketchbook and pencil. Noting possibilities: the north window could be either here or there, and it could be made three times bigger. In the centre of the building, in the hall, if the plaster ceiling were demolished, the distance from floor into roof space would be almost twenty feet and it would be possible, for example, to suspend a gallery with a platform all around, with a spiral staircase and a wooden balustrade.

To Noa I said: Just give me a few more days.

It's not long ago that she begged me, Don't take everything away from me, Theo, yet now she has stopped interfering. As if she's lost interest. When I suggested she come with me to Jerusalem she said, I've got a bit of a temperature, and my head . . . you go and sort it out by yourself. When I got home in the evening and began to explain to her what I had achieved she said: Skip the details, Theo, I really don't care who else still remembers you from the days when you were the gleam in their eye, or what the Palmach got wrong in the War of Independence. Now that there seems to be at least a chance, she has lost that radiant joy that always seemed to well straight up from the core of life. She has lost that sparkle she had in her eye whenever she declared my judgment to be hot or cold, good or bad, or phony, or entrenched, as though she were grading the whole world. Instead of that flash of excitement there's a sort of abstraction that I've never seen in her before: she leaves home in the morning, comes back at midday, grabs something to eat standing up in front of the open refrigerator, leaves me the washing up and goes out again. Where does she have to go to now that the school is closed for the summer holidays and the staff have all vanished to their refresher courses and conferences? I take care not to ask. Or the opposite: she sits the whole morning watching children's programmes on TV, then vanishes in the evening till eleven o'clock. I might have suspected that she's got herself a lover at last, but it's just on these nights that she appears in my bedroom, smelling sweetly of honeysuckle, floating towards me barefoot and silent, in her demure nightdress that makes her look like a girl from a religious boarding school. I stand and kiss the brown birthmark beneath her hairline. My whole body strains to listen to her, like a doctor making a diagnosis, or as if she were my daughter who had suffered an unknown misfortune. I take hold of her hands that have aged ahead of her, and I am filled with a desire that is not made of desire but of a tender affection. I cup her breasts and run my fingers down the front of her thighs like a healer gently seeking to locate the pain. After the love, she falls asleep immediately, with her head in the hollow of my shoulder, the sleep of a babe, while I lie awake half the night, carefully attentive, breathing evenly so as not to disturb her. Though she sleeps deeply.

Sometimes I have found her sitting in the kitchen, or on the balcony, or once even in the California Café, with a dark-haired girl called Tali or Tal, apparently a pupil or ex-pupil of hers. She is a slim, finely sculpted girl, who looks like a little red Indian in her patched and faded jeans. I would have dressed her in a flame-red skirt. From a distance they seem to be immersed in a lively conversation, but as I get closer they stop talking as though they are waiting for me to go away and leave them alone. But in fact I have no desire to go away and leave them. I find there is something spellbinding about that Tali, perhaps precisely because she seems a little afraid of me, retreating to the edge of her chair, looking me up and down apprehensively, like a threatened animal. This has the effect of making me insist on joining them. Their conversation instantly dries up. An unwilling silence descends. A brief interrogation elicited the information that Tal was due to be called up for military service in November. She still had to face the matriculation exam in math, and that bitch Gusta Ludmir was giving her private tuition, but what a drag, logarithms, she wouldn't be able to pass that bit in a million years. I also discovered that she is the daughter of Paula Orlev from Desert Chic, where I almost bought Noa a folksy dress recently. What brought her here? Nothing special. And what did she think about the situation in the Occupied Territories? Or about the future of Israel? Or about life in Tel Kedar? About permissiveness? About life in general? Her replies were wishy-washy, lukewarm. Nothing that sticks in my memory. Except that her cat has had kittens and she wants to give us one. Can I get you a cold drink? No thanks, we've just had one. Some grapes? No thanks. Then I suppose you'd like me to leave you alone? You've left your keys on the table. And take your paper. 'Bye.

But I was in no hurry to leave them. On the contrary. What was the rush? I settled back in my chair and asked what people were saying in town about, say, the new string quartet. Or about the expansion of the parking lot in the square? And what plans did Tal have for the summer? From now till she was called up? Didn't she feel like getting away from the logarithms, getting to see something of the wide world, like the rest of them? Why not? What was wrong with the wide world? Would she be interested in some information about Latin America?

Noa intervened: Batsheva Dinur was trying to get you on the phone.

I caught the hint, and replied: So she was looking for me. Fine. In that case I'll just sit here with you till she calls again. Don't let me disturb you. Carry on. I'll just read my paper.

Once, jokingly, I asked Noa over our morning coffee what exactly she was scheming about for all those hours with her Indian princess. Does she bring you her love problems? Is there another story with drugs? Is there another memorial project in the offing? Noa flushed and said: Theo. That's enough. This is going to end badly. And when she saw that I wasn't letting go, she stood up and started ironing. Even though normally the ironing is my department.

So I decided to retreat, to effect a temporary withdrawal. I might have a chance some time to have a tête-à-tête with Tal. Or I might go to her mother's boutique by myself and buy Noa a surprise present of a light skirt in a colourful geometric print.

Meanwhile I have had worries of my own. Natalia, the young Russian woman who has been cleaning the office on Fridays, sent me the keys and said she couldn't go on. This time I made up my mind not to give in. A little detective work brought me the phone number of the grocer in the prefab complex and they agreed, not without coaxing, to go and call her to the telephone. After a determined struggle against shyness, politeness, apprehension and language difficulties, it turned out that apparently her unemployed husband, in another fit of jealousy, had forbidden her to go on working for me. So I got into the Chevrolet and spent a good half-hour wandering around the prefabs trying to find where exactly the husband hung out. I planned to talk him round, but it transpired from what the neighbours said that Natalia had run away from him and was staying with his father, who lived in a rented room near the square, less than two minutes from my office. A couple of days later the husband also moved into the old man's miserable room. By the time I found the place, Natalia had pulled out and moved back to the prefab. The father and the husband shouted suspicious questions through the locked door for five minutes before they consented to slide the chain and let me in. It turned out I had interrupted them in the middle of a game of cards, two strong, slightly balding men, who resembled each other like brothers, both of them round-headed and big-boned, with hefty weight-lifter's arms, baring rows of sharp teeth when they smiled, both with stubble-covered faces and wearing black T-shirts. For some reason, when I tried to talk to them about Natalia they burst into wet, noisy laughter, as though I had been caught in the act, slapped my back, explained something in Russian and in another language I did not recognize, and in Russian again, then they had another good laugh, revealing their predatory teeth, and begged me with enthusiastic gestures and almost violent heartiness to join them in a game of poker. I stayed an hour or so, in the course of which I drank two vodkas and lost forty shekels.

Since then I sometimes drop in on them in the early evening, when Noa is out, of course, and as for poor Natalia, she has apparently gone, or escaped, to her sister in Hazor in Galilee. That much I managed to get out of them after two more lost games. I enjoy spending an hour or two in the company of these rambunctious men. I can hardly understand their language, but I like their thunderous laughter, their shoulder-slapping, their roars, their elbows jabbing me in the ribs, the shabby, low-ceilinged room with the greasy smell of frying coming from the tiny kitchen For some reason it reminds me of the fireside nights with strangers, in the courtyards of country inns in remote regions near the shores of the Caribbean. They treat me to spicy, wonderfully tasty pickled fish and a glass of vodka, I lose fifty or eighty shekels, and sometimes I am caught up in their raucous laughter over some joke that I cannot understand. I forget that my initial object was to try to dissolve their jealousy, to get the husband to take Natalia back and to get Natalia to come back to me and clean my office on Fridays. I had the impression they were trying to show me with roars and comical rounded gestures that Natalia was pregnant, so there was no point in my running after her, and that her sister in Galilee was expecting a baby, too. But it is hard to know if I understood correctly or if I simply put together a story of my own on the basis of their gestures and laughs. And, in fact, what business was it of mine?

At certain moments I can almost see her: hardly more than a girl, about seventeen, golden-haired, slim, shy, silently fearful, her waist and breasts are those of a woman but she has a smile of sweet confusion or childlike wonder on her face, even when she thinks I am not looking at her. Between smiles her lips purse as if to weep. Whenever I put a perfectly simple question to her, such as whether she has parents, or whether there is any water left in the electric kettle, she turns white and trembles, as if she has committed a serious breach of polite behaviour, or as if I have made an obscene suggestion, and she whispers a faint apology and makes me give up on the answer and regret asking her in the first place, and turn my back to hide the lust that has suddenly transformed me into a rhinoceros. When I found out that her husband and his father had both been mechanics back in Moldavia, and that they had both been unemployed since arriving in Israel, I rang Muki Peleg and asked him, as a personal favour, to see if he could find them something temporary at least. Perhaps with one of the earth-moving contractors he sat with every day at the Council of Torah Sages in the California Café. Muki promised to fix it for me, what a question, like a rocket, even if I didn't really deserve it after throwing him and Ludmir off the committee; in fact, he wouldn't do it for me but for the sake of the Ingathering of Exiles, as the air hostess said to the Jewish passenger who begged her to lock herself in the toilet with him on the jumbo. And he went on to offer me a story about a little ballpoint pen factory that he was planning to set up here in partnership with Dubi Weitzman and Pini Bozo from the shoe shop, something really pioneering, the pens have an electronic device in them so that if you forget where you've put them all you have to do is whistle and they chirrup back at you, and Batsheva was finding them another investor – perhaps Orvieto and would I like to come in on it? We would double our money in three years, maximum, that was being cautious, because in fact the chances were we could double it in two and a half years.

On Saturday I started to jot down the headings for my paper. I found out from one of Noa's pamphlets that in Scandinavia they have had residential centres for under-eighteen-year-olds for some time, and precisely in small towns, far from the big cities, and there were mounting indications that they were successful, even representing a social and educational challenge that focused the life of the host population and sometimes produced a "thriving example of a therapeutic community", a supportive milieu that developed a sense of purpose and a feeling of local pride. The framework that seemed to me best suited to Tel Kedar was that of a social experiment coupled with an academic study, not just another supply station for drug substitutes like adolan or methadone. As for the economic aspect, of course we can't be Scandinavia, but it made sense to begin with kids from wealthy families in central Israel, and, as I had suggested to Noa, we would do well to add in two or three locals, from needy families, for a token payment. That should clear the ground here a bit. It might strengthen our public opinion rating. But when I asked Noa to go over these notes she said, Don't give me drafts to read. Don't give me anything to read right now. Not just now, Theo. Can't you see that I'm trying to listen to some music quietly. Do me a favour and start the record over again, would you?

For a moment I had an urge to remind her that she was still getting a check for three hundred dollars every month from Orvieto, via his lawyer, Arbel; it would be interesting to know what for actually, and somebody might well ask one day just exactly what she did with the money. She spends half her time nowadays with her Indian princess, Tal or Tali. From my office window, I can see them going to the hairdresser together, coming out of an afternoon showing at the Paris Cinema, sitting whispering at the lovebirds' table behind the pillar at the California Café. Sometimes I get up and lock the office, buy a *Ma'ariv* at Gilboa's, and go to the California myself. I do not join them but secure a lookout post on one side near the cash desk. Dubi Weitzman, if he has no work on, arrives a few minutes later, paunchy, hairy, sweaty, with dusty sandals, always wearing a peaked cap like a Greek sea-captain's with gold braid all round it and a shiny anchor at the front; he sits down, orders us cold Cokes and a plate of cheese and olives, sighs and declares:

A casino, Theo, that's what'll save us here. Stop Tel Kedar from being a graveyard. A casino will bring us tourists, holiday-makers, girls, the big money will come pouring in and culture will follow. For me, you understand, the casino is just a means to an end. Culture, Theo, that's the object. Without culture we're living here like animals. Don't take it personally. Take it as food for thought.

A couple of days ago he said to me: Every time I go to Tel Aviv I notice the city has moved a bit closer to us. Holon is attached to Rishon Le-Zion. Rishon is creeping towards Ashdod. Ashdod will link up with Qiryat Gat. In another hundred years Tel Aviv will reach all the way to here, it'll knock on our door at five o'clock one morning and say, Good morning, dear friends, wake up, I'm here, and that's that, the exile will be over. But in the meantime we are stuck here beneath the mountains. Blast them. You could choke because of those mountains. Forget it. Let's have a game of chess. Don't you get fed up sometimes, Theo? Take it as food for thought.

Ludmir sometimes intercepts me in the square or outside the post office, promising to move worlds and to fight to the death against the nest of maggots that I am scheming to plant here, Sodom and Gomorrah, he is utterly ashamed of succumbing to the temporary blackout that made him join our committee, and he warns me, as though from pity, that there's "Noa smoke without a fire". Several times, in the kitchen, I've felt an urge to say something that would really hurt her, like a slap in the face. Something like, Tell me, have you ever actually seen a drug addict? Just one? From a distance? Through a telescope, per-haps? Like your father who used to sit in his wheelchair on his roof keeping an eye on the world through his telescope? And, as a matter of fact, tell me truly, could you actually tell the difference between someone who was drugged, sleepy or just plain moronic? How did you have the gall to take on a project you understand less about than I do about Eskimo cosmetics?

And which has never really interested you for a moment, deep down? Was it just a pretext for getting out of the house? Was it just because you were fed up with teaching literature all day? What got into you to make you drive the whole town crazy and, the moment it was time to roll your sleeves up and get down to work, decide to change games and leave me to put your toys away after you?

I restrained myself.

No point in getting into an argument.

Particularly since I've abandoned her, too. I spend my time with the husband and his father over the pickled herring and vodka that I've got into the habit of taking with me. I wolf thick borsch and stuffed dumplings. Suddenly I find myself presenting a survey, in orderly instalments, without language, in pantomime and broken words, of the history of the Zionist endeavour, the swamps, the underground, the illegal immigration, the British, the Nazis, the victories, the Western Wall, Entebbe, the West Bank settlements. The two of them look at me without surprise but without much interest either, without interrupting their steady munching, occasionally bursting into fierce laughter that I am unable to relate to my exposition. Last time I went I managed to win fifty shekels from them at poker, and they both choked with laughter, slapping their knees and the back of my neck, thumping my back, they could hardly stop. Nevertheless, on Tuesdays I still settle down in the California for a couple of hours, playing chess with Dubi Weitzman, as I've done for years. And almost every afternoon I walk round the ruin on my own. Though I don't carry the sketchbook and pencil any more. As if I've lost the thread.

Muki Peleg phoned excitedly: he'd managed to secure a trial period for my two muzhiks, a week, with Jacques Ben Loulou from Ben Elul's Garage, that saint, admittedly for nominal wages, so he could show what they could do, as the Queen of Greece said to her three Turks. You don't know that one, Theo? Okay. I'll teach you some time. Just bear in mind that a Turk and a Greek woman is a bit like Ludmir and a quarry. The point is, tell them to be there at seven o'clock tomorrow morning.

What do you think of me? Aren't I just Albert Einstein disguised as a village saint?

I said: There's no one else like you, Malachi.

And Muki: Just as well.

Despite the cracked tiles, the cobwebs and the thick dust, the missing windows, the broken cabinets, the smashed or stolen washbasins and toilet bowls, the roof groaning under the ravages of the desert wind, the dirty syringes and bloodstained wads of cotton wool and the stench of urine and the dried damp patches, I am gradually becoming convinced that the house was an excellent buy because it was built honestly. Solidly and generously. The rooms are spacious and tall. The walls are thick. All the rooms open onto a central space, a fairly extensive hall in the middle of the building. This central space is dark and pleasant, storing a gentle coolness even in the worst heatwave. Something in the way it is built reminds me of an Arab or Armenian house from before the wars. Or the German Colony in Jerusalem. The depth of the arched windows. The curve of the corridor. The flagstones. In the big garden a score of tight-packed pine trees grow, their trunks bent northwards by the southerly winds. The trees overhang the tiled roof and besiege the house with their shadows. Every breath of wind makes the shadows quiver slightly. A subdued light filters through the pine needles, a hushed murmur behind your back, and an ever-changing stream of shadows dappled with patches of light, plays on the walls. Sometimes this movement gives you the tense feeling that there is somebody walking around on tiptoe in the next room. All round the pine wood the white-hot summer light beats down, but the garden and the house stand separated in shade, like an enclave of winter. Plunging to his own seabed, Noa said, and Avraham Orvieto felt the windowsill and said nothing.

Yesterday at six o'clock in the morning I loaded a shovel, pruning shears and a saw into the Chevrolet, borrowed my two Russian weight-lifters from Ben Elul's Garage, and for seven hours we cleaned all the filth out of the pine wood and trimmed the trees. When Linda and Muki appeared after lunch, saying that they had just heard I was planting a tower-and-stockade settlement here and were enlisting to help, everything was finished. We had even propped up the trunks of the trees that I thought were too bent. On Thursday a Bedouin contractor is coming, a friend of Dubi Weitzman's, to start putting up the new fence and to fix a wrought-iron gate.

Then I shall have to renovate the whole structure and adapt it for its new purpose.

But what is its purpose? I don't have a clear idea any more. I haven't finished writing the memorandum either. I've lost the thread.

Linda still types on a voluntary basis the letters I dictate to her at the office, and we send them off to various authorities. But the idea is becoming vague, as though the meaning has faded. And meanwhile we have attracted the wrath of the volcanic Ludmir. In his column in the local paper. "A Voice in the Wilderness", he calls me a shady character. He terms Avraham Orvieto's benefaction the tainted money of a pedlar of weapons of destruction. I should have published a rejoinder, but I couldn't think what to write. I've lost the thread again. As for Orvieto, he has vanished. He may have gone back to Nigeria. This time he has apparently taken his lawyer with him. The money still hasn't materialized. Perhaps it never existed. But Natalia suddenly came back to us from Galilee, pregnant and even prettier than I remembered her; with that expression of innocence and wonder she served me a glass of very strong, very hot tea, which for some reason made her husband and his father choke with laughter, which this time, to my utter astonishment, carried me away, too, and she burst into tears. But instead of getting involved, instead of trying to protect her or comfort her, I was smitten with desire. For some reason I was reminded of the broadcast I'd heard from London, about the life and loves of Alma Mahler. The presenter was going to explain to listeners what she was really like. This notion of "reality" seemed to me ridiculous but I couldn't decide what to replace it with. How can one know?

On a scrap of paper I jotted down: Furnishings. Equipment. Problem of heating in winter. Kitchen or catering? Interior alterations. Plumbing. Wiring. Drainage. Water supply. Roof. Floor tiles. Bars on the windows? Fitted cabinets. Telephone line. A treatment room? A classroom? A space for TV and video? Computers? Clubroom? Library?

All this before we get to the actual plan of operations. But what operations? And who with? Here a curtain comes down inside me, like a monsoon. As if the empty building has become an end in itself. Maybe it's time to sit down for a tête-à-tête with Orvieto. To try to fathom his aims once and for all. In Tel Aviv? Or perhaps in Lagos? Maybe very soon I'll fly out to see him for a couple of days. Without telling her. But for some reason I still shrink from this thought. If I try to imagine the two of us meeting behind her back, the picture arouses in me a mixture of dread and shame. As if I were plotting to deceive her. As if I had woven a tissue of lies so as to be alone with another woman.

So I rang Dubi Weitzman and told him to put off the Bedouin contractor and the workmen for the time being. Thursday is too soon. Even next week is too soon. What's the point of putting up a fence round something that doesn't exist? Round a dream? Still, I haven't forgotten her paralyzed father sitting on his roof in a wheelchair for years on end, getting heavier and heavier, like a defeated wrestler, and following what went on in the world through the lens of his telescope. If only that roof had had a proper parapet, the old man might have been alive today. The bulldozers wouldn't have demolished the house on the edge of the village. The collection of picture postcards would not have been donated to the Tolstoyan farm. And she would still be there, not here, still looking after him no doubt, worrying about him, singing to him, feeding him, putting him to bed, changing his diaper, five times a day.

The new dress we bought her in Tel Aviv the day we signed the contract has a tiny defect: it doesn't hang straight over the hips. We shall have to ask Paula Orlev to alter it after all. For some reason the thought that her fingers will touch this dress disgusts me. I wonder whether the Indian girl Tal has learned from her mother how to straighten a waistline. Or maybe by some miracle Natalia, my pregnant virgin, can handle a needle.

But Noa didn't notice the fault when she wore the dress this evening. We went to hear the new quartet in a private recital at the home of Dr. Dresdner in the chic residential district. As we were setting out, I nearly stopped her and pointed out that the waist was not straight. I finally decided to say nothing, so that we wouldn't be late but also because there was something delightful and touching in this almost invisible defect. And it's possible that I'm the only one who can see it. If it really exists. Never mind, let it go until Noa notices it. And if she doesn't, it doesn't matter.

H E wears a rough elastic bandage on his left knee, because of an old injury. At midnight, when we got home from the musical evening at Julia and Leo Dresdner's, the pain started up again. It's only midsummer, yet he is already picking up signals from the distant winter. I sat him down in an armchair, removed the bandage and tried to disperse the pain with massage. He laid his fingers on my shoulder and said, Yes, go on, it's working. Theo, I said, this knee is a little warm, warmer than the other one, you should pop into the health clinic tomorrow. What's the hurry, he said, it comes and goes.

He got up and made us some herbal tea, and switched off the overhead light. We stayed sitting for a quarter of an hour by the soft glow coming from the kitchen. The windows and the balcony door were open to catch the night breeze. From the direction of the hills to the east came the dim sobbing of a fox and at once self-righteous dogs began howling around the buildings. Then I washed the elastic bandage in warm soapy water, confident that in the desert air it would be dry by morning. After that I took a shower, and Theo took one after me, then we went our separate ways to sleep. When I was almost asleep, or even already sleeping, a hushed woman's voice, suppressing a vague excitement, came to me from his bedroom: the late-night news from London.

Next day I went to an afternoon showing at the Paris Cinema with Tal. The film was about treachery and revenge. Afterwards we sat in the California for an hour and a half drinking iced coffee. Then I took her to Bozo's shoe shop, because I had made up my mind to buy her some new sandals, with heels. Sometimes she looks just like a ten-year-old child, especially when you look at her from behind. That Indian princess, Theo says, what are you scheming about all day long, hasn't she got any friends her own age?

We chose a pair of light-coloured sandals with a buckle on the side in the form of a butterfly. Tal refused to let me pay for them but I insisted.

Pini Bozo said: I've got something terrific for you, too. Try these on. Never mind, just for size.

In the end I bought myself a new pair of sandals too. They were flat and cream-coloured, with plaited straps.

A little later we met Theo in the square. He offered to treat us to iced coffee at the California. We burst out laughing and said, You're too late, that's where we've just come from. I asked him what he thought of our new sandals. Theo shrugged his shoulders, said, Nice, great. He screwed up his suspicious eye, just like a miserly peasant: Where are you going now? Then he shrugged again and summed up, All right. I'm sorry. I didn't ask. Only don't neglect your math exam. Logarithms. Actually I could prepare you for that exam myself sometime. I think I can still remember a thing or two. 'Bye.

What does he do all day long? He hardly seems to get any new commissions. It's summer. He still has a few old jobs to complete. Every morning at half past eight he opens the office, switches on the powerful light and sits down alone at his drawing board under a photograph of Ben Gurion staring resolutely into a desert landscape. He scribbles geometrical shapes. Or stands at the window watching the life in the square. At ten o'clock he goes down to Gilboa's to buy the paper. Then he walks round the square and returns to his office. Not long ago he told me that he had offered to take care of a family problem for his cleaner: he fixed up her husband and also her father-in-law with temporary jobs. In fact, all he did was to pick up the phone, it was Muki Peleg who arranged it. I didn't ask about the details even though I wanted to know, so that he wouldn't have the feeling I was watching him.

In the mornings I sit for an hour or two at my corner table in the library, facing the air conditioning, while the old librarian,

Amalia, dozes behind her counter, shrivelled, grey, wrinkled, her lips sucked into her jaws as if she is mocking me; every now and again she lets out a faint snore, wakes up, gives me a wistful glance and then her chin sinks again and her eyes close with an expression of repressed pain. Once she was the director of the municipal gardening department, it was she who planted the avenues of palm trees and initiated the Founders' Garden; she adopted a Bedouin orphan who eventually grew up and emigrated; she got into an argument with Batsheva and took early retirement, fell ill with diabetes, and at the beginning of the year she volunteered to help refurbish the library. But the numbers of readers are declining. Amalia has filled the neat, well-lit reading room with dozens of well-tended indoor plants in hydroponic containers full of fine, brilliant gravel, watered by test-tube drippers with a mixture of fertilizers and minerals, as though the place is gradually changing from a library into a hothouse or a dense tropical forest, with creepers and ferns branching out, climbing in and out of the shelves, pushing their way among the volumes, translating the neon light into dark vegetal sap. But nobody ever comes here except for me and some pensioners and a handful of weird youngsters. Empty. Most mornings there is just the ailing librarian and myself.

The books about drugs, addiction and treatment that were kept on a special shelf for me all these weeks have been dispersed and returned to their places. Now I have to prepare for the coming school year. But what's the hurry? Instead of the poems of Bialik I have selected a few books about the lives of musicians. Maybe because Julia and Leo Dresdner from the dental surgery telephoned to ask me to serve on a committee for helping immigrant musicians from Russia to settle in. There are plans to found a small music school with the co-operation of the high school, the Workers' Council and the municipality. It may be possible to bring in the Ministries of Absorption and Culture too. A meeting has been scheduled for next week with Batsheva. I have been asked to draft a letter addressed to a handful of classical-music lovers, to find out who will contribute. Linda has volunteered to type it, and Ludmir and Muki Peleg will distribute fifty copies.

I sit in my corner near the window at the end, wearing a flowery summer dress, leafing through the books and stopping here and there to read two or three pages about the strange love of Brahms for Clara Schumann, the illness and death of Mozart, and plump, shy Schubert, whom it is doubtful any woman ever loved except his mother, and who described his own compositions as mediocre and ephemeral; he appeared in a public concert only once, before dying of typhus at the age of thirty-one. My eyes stray from the book to the shady plants. I remember my father's collection of postcards. Amalia is staring straight ahead with hollow eyes, huddled as though in pain. Her hair is thin and dry and her cheeks in the neon light are sunken like the face of a corpse. Muki Peleg told me that once, in the fifties in Beersheba, she was the beauty queen of the desert, she divorced, remarried, separated, danced on a barrel in a bathing suit at the wine festival procession, turned all the men's heads, seduced the drilling workers, lived with a well-known poet. The years passed and illness ravaged her and now behind her back they call her "the witch".

The air conditioning hums and grates a little. From far away, in the direction of Sharett Street, comes the rumble of heavy road-digging machinery. Despite which, miraculously, the reading room is full of a deep and total silence: when I leaf through a book you can hear the rustle of each separate page. Outside the drawn curtains the sun is blazing fiercely. A tyrannical light lies over everything. The ring of mountain peaks faints in the scorched dust. In a book called *Words to Music: The German Lied from Mozart to Mahler* I came across a poem entitled "Moonlit Night" by Joseph von Eichendorff that was set to music by Schumann in 1840:

> The breeze was lightly straying
> Thro' cornfields waving light;
> The forest leaves were sighing,
> And starlit was the night.

And my rapt soul her pinions
In eager joy outspread,
And over Earth's dominions
As homeward on she sped.

I close the book, lay my arms on the table and cover my face.
Noa: smoke without a fire. Amalia the librarian comes across,
bends over me, touches my shoulder, looking like a dying bird,
with a sort of floppy crop hanging under her chin, but her voice
is gentle and anxious: Are you not feeling well, Noa? Shall I
make you some coffee?

I say: It's nothing. Don't bother. It's over now.

She grins at me without lips, the grin of a skull, and I have to
remind myself that it is not a contemptuous grimace of irony
beyond despair, but simply the shrivelling of the cheeks owing
to illness and old age. Tal will join the army Avraham will vanish
in Africa Theo will close his office and give himself over to Radio
London day and night, the days speed past the summer will end
years will pass and I shall be in her place behind that desk in
the deserted library which will have turned into a jungle whose
foliage will gradually swallow everything up.

In the meantime Linda and Muki came back, suntanned and
giggling, from a short holiday near Safed. Muki has cut down
on his jokey pursuit of me. Perhaps he finally fell in love with
Linda there. Or am I beginning to lose whatever it was that
attracted him? The change saddens me, even though I never liked
his courtship. I joked about it to Tal, who said, Rubbish, Noa,
forget it, it was all just a little game, still it's a pity you've had
your hair cut so short. Before, when your hair used to fall to
one side of your face sometimes, it was much prettier.

What about her? Why did she decide to have her hair cut
short?

Because she didn't "go a whole load on that whole thing any
more". All she wanted was peace and quiet. She had split up
with someone barely two months ago; one morning she woke
up and found she was attracted to an ass – "just like when we
studied *A Midsummer Night's Dream* with you". Now she was

simply tired of it. She felt like taking time out at least until the army. It'd be good if she could find part-time work in the meantime, like half a day in some office. She was turned off by boys who have nothing in their heads but combat reconnaissance and cars and motorbikes. And that's more or less all there is in stock here. The truth, since we're talking, is that what she finds really attractive is a more mature kind of male. More along the lines of someone who knows how to give a lot and wants to receive a lot. Somebody like Theo, only not so old, if I didn't mind her saying so. Theo struck her as someone who was inward-looking and sad. And that's what she found most beautiful and attractive in a man. Only with him it comes with the cold, indifferent bit, sort of, sorry to be blathering on.

I said: Look here, Tal, with Theo, and I stopped. Even though actually I wanted to go on and on.

But not now. It's too soon.

Muki grabbed me as I was coming out of Schatzberg's pharmacy, which still had a faded notice of the death of the late Gustav Marmorek: Listen, lovely. A consultation. Have you got five minutes to talk to me in the California? When Linda and I went on holiday to the Mount Meron Hostel, the first day she got sick on me. Food poisoning. Serious. I'll spare you the details. At first I thought, that's it, you've really landed in it; that's all you need, pal, changing her diapers instead of having fun, rushing to fetch her hot tea, boiled potatoes, medicine from the clinic in Safed, washing her underwear because naturally she hadn't packed enough. But in the end, you'd be amazed, I even ended up enjoying it. Perhaps I've become a masochist. It's not that we didn't have fun, don't get me wrong, by the third day she was as fit as a tigress and then I started striking sparks off her, if you know what I mean. Only, it's a funny thing, while she was sick I suddenly felt really close to her. How do you explain that?

That evening I told Theo about it. I reminded him that he'd offered to take me to Galilee. How about us going north too? To Safed? Or the Golan Heights? Mount Hermon? Not in your beat-up Chevrolet. This time let's hire a car. We'll share the driving. And shall we take Tal with us? If she wants to come?

Theo said: It's possible.

But the days are passing and neither he nor I has raised the subject of our trip to the north.

Last weekend we went to the funeral of Batsheva Dinur's mother. She died in her sleep. She was buried in the last plot in the row underneath the pine trees, past old Elijah and beyond Immanuel Orvieto and his maiden aunt Elazara. Kushner the bookbinder gave the address, and he mentioned that before she fell seriously ill she had served for decades as a history teacher and a devoted educator in the school for workers' children in Givatayim and indeed was a regular contributor to the *Education Echo*. He sketched her later years delicately, by means of hints, and joining together two halves of two different verses of the psalms he said, Cast me not away in the time of mine old age and take not thy holy spirit from me. Most of his words as well as the prayers were swallowed up in the roar of jet planes that circled low overhead, chasing each other in the dusty-looking sky.

A couple of days later we went to offer our condolences to Batsheva. We had difficulty squeezing in. The house and the garden were packed with visitors, her children, grandchildren, daughters-in-law, brothers-in-law, friends, cousins. Through the door that was permanently open flowed the whole of Tel Kedar, and Bedouins from round about, and neighbours, like a huge wedding. Women I did not recognize controlled the kitchen and dispatched convoys of refreshments into the garden and the various rooms. We had a job pushing our way through to Batsheva herself; we found her sitting on her throne in the garden, in the shade of the dense fig tree, surrounded by a turbulent throng of relatives and friends. There were large numbers of children running around in the garden, chasing each other noisily, but Batsheva looked as if she enjoyed the commotion. A bearlike, freckled woman, in a threadbare velvet-covered armchair. She was calmly conducting four or five different conversations simultaneously, in every direction, about roads, births, party politics, her mother's childhood in Smolensk, budgets and recipes. When our turn came to express our sympathy, she said:

Hey, look who's here, my pair of addicts, grab a couple of chairs, and hold the cake for a minute, you must try these olives that a good friend brought me today from Galilee, from Deir el-Asad. Come, come here, Nawwaf, show yourself, these aren't olives, they're pure ecstasy, soul olives. If Mama could only taste them she'd eat a whole jar in no time. She was simply addicted to spicy crushed olives, with some fancy cheese and a glass of wine. Anyway, we ought to have parties like this for people before they die, not afterwards, so they realize what a silly idea it is to go – so people start dying less. By the way, the project, I had a phone call the day before yesterday from Avraham. What a noble, tragic, enchanting man, I'm already in love with him. Didn't you know that he was involved in rescuing the prisoners from Syria? And gathering information about soldiers missing in action? We chatted to each other for half an hour on the phone, and I think I persuaded him to drop the drug addicts and computerize the school instead, and that'll be his memorial to his son, such a pity I never knew him, I might have managed to get hold of him and prevent him killing himself. The problem is that you're stuck with the Alharizi house. You can't swallow it and you can't spit it out. But don't worry, it'll resolve itself; I think I've found a way of getting you out of it without leaving you out of pocket. We'll talk about it next week. Not that cheese, Noa, Theo, try the salty one first, my grandson from Rosh Pinna made it himself. It's not a cheese, it's a symphony. Where's the sweet boy who made it for me? Etam? Call him to come and take a bow. And here's Ludmir, come and sit down, Voice in the Wilderness, sit on the ground, you deserve it, and first of all you must try these olives that a good friend of mine brought me from Deir el-Asad.

That's how the fencing of the Alharizi house came off the agenda. There won't be any renovations either. A new dental surgery called Ivory has opened in the aunt's apartment, but it turns out that it's Dr. Dresdner and Dr. Nir again: they've moved out of their old premises next to Theo's office. And old Kushner has hung a sign outside his place, "SHOP FOR SALE", they say he's decided to leave Tel Kedar, he hardly has any customers left, and that he's going to go and live with his daughter and his grandchildren in Gedera, though others say he's moving into the Golden Age Home there; he put his name down for it ten years ago and now his turn has come.

Heavy bulldozers are roaring from six in the morning to nightfall and raising a cloud of dust at the end of Eshkol Street: they're connecting it at last to Ben Zvi Boulevard by a new road that runs round to the west. A whole throng of crows is hovering over the cloud of dust. In the square by the traffic lights they're putting up pillars for a new lighting system, like the ones they have in big cities. Julia Dresdner is calling the first meeting of the Public Committee for the Absorption of Immigrant Musicians. Violette and Madeleine, the hairdressers who are sisters-in-law, are expanding the Champs-Elysées Salon which henceforth will include a sophisticated beauty parlour. A snack bar is opening soon in Founders' House, and they may decide to have a permanent display of minerals in glass showcases. In the autumn there'll be a shop for musical instruments by the lights. So there are new things happening in the town. And Theo and I received a registered letter from Ron Arbel, the lawyer: in view of the opposition and the complications, it has been decided to put the memorial project on ice for six months. Alternative options are being examined concurrently. Mr. Orvieto will write separately. The project has not been shelved. As for the financial matter that remains open between us, it will be settled very soon, in a mutually satisfactory fashion. The various parties concerned will soon convene with a view to a revised appraisal of the situation and a comprehensive assessment of the various possibilities and alternatives. And we were warmly thanked and congratulated for our efforts.

Meanwhile Muki Peleg has been talking to an ultra-Orthodox group from Beersheba, who it turns out are keen to buy the Alharizi house for a boarding school to inculcate Jewish values in the children of the Russian immigrants. They are willing to pay us a sum identical to the original purchase price. Naturally the whole business has not been finalized, Muki explained. In the meantime, everything is open, and the negotiations with the Men in Black are only in case it turns out that our God is truly repenting, there in Africa, of all that He has decided to create here and is leaving us hanging between heaven and earth. As things stand at the moment, we are in a bit of a fix: the building is registered in the name of our fund, the money is yours, Theo, all we've got from Avraham is a verbal commitment, there's a letter from his lawyer but I really don't know what it's worth from a legal point of view. If we decide to sell to those holy men, I won't take any commission for this deal either, even though I'm actually quite short of cash at the moment, because Linda and I are planning a pleasure trip round Italy in the autumn. Why don't you two get married too? Then the four of us can paint Rome red and show them over there what *dolce vita* really means. Flowing with milk and honey under the Arch of Titus, if you get my meaning. The truth is, hand on my heart, if the three of us, four of us, decided not to give up, come what may, I believe the refuge would happen, whatever. Shall I tell you something straight from the heart? We ought to push it all the way. We ought to fight for it. We ought to turn the town upside down. It's needed a thousand times more than a holy boarding school that will start drugging our youngsters with the coming of the Messiah, and all that, instead of rescuing them from drugs. We ought to be looking for investors. Or donors. Organizing public pressure on Batsheva and the bureaucrats. Not giving up. Enlisting good people. Of whom there is actually no shortage here. And shall I tell you something else from the heart? Our real tragedy is that we're not truly desperate to do anything. That's the real disaster. When you're not burning to do anything any more, you cool down and start dying. That's what Linda says and I think I agree with her. We've got to start wanting things. To hold on with both hands so life won't run away, if you get my meaning. Otherwise it's all over.

Theo said: Meanwhile don't sell yet. If Avraham Orvieto drops out your trust will find another buyer.

What buyer? How much for?

Me. And we'll agree on the price.

When I got home in the evening Theo said, It's odd I said that to him. I don't know what I was thinking of. We're attracted by the house but what'll we do with it? Can you understand it, Noa? Because I haven't got the faintest where I got the idea from.

I said: Wait. We'll see.

On Saturday, at seven o'clock in the evening, as the light was softening and turning blue, we felt like going there. The groaning Chevrolet wouldn't start again. So we walked. Not through the square by the lights but the roundabout way, along the dirt track, along the foot of the cliff that shuts off the forbidden valley. A few dark, windswept bushes were stirring on the hill-tops, because a fierce southerly wind blew up every now and again and filled the world with millions of sharp specks. As if it was about to pour with rain. Violent gusts periodically shook the bushes at the top of the line of hills, forcing them to bend, wriggle and stoop in a contorted dance. The piercing sand pene-trated to our skin under our clothes, filling our hair, grating between our teeth, hitting us straight in the eyes as if it was trying to blind us. From time to time a low howl crossed the empty plains. And stopped. And started whipping and torment-ing the long-suffering bushes again. We progressed slowly south-wards, as though fighting a way upstream. We made our way round the cemetery. The wail of pine trees shaken by the wind rose from the direction of the graves. It is a small, new town, and the dead are still few, a few dozen, perhaps a hundred, and apart from Bozo's baby none of them was born here or buried with their parents. My father and Aunt Chuma, his sister, are buried among the nettles under dark cypresses in the neglected cemetery at the edge of the village where I was born. My mother is presumably in New Zealand, where it's winter when it's summer here and night when it's day here, and maybe the drizzle drips on her grave in the dark, and trees I do not know the name of whisper to each other and stop. One Saturday, when we went for a walk in a wadi on the northern side of town, we came across a Bedouin burial ground, heaps of grey stones that the sand was gradually covering. They may have been the remains of ancient nomads who lived and died here exposed between the mountains and the sun long before the Bedouin came.

When we reached the turning for the quarries we took the path to the west among the rocks. The wind, which had been blowing in our faces, now struck us from the left, pushing us towards the edge of the ravine whose bottom was already dark. The light faded and grew murky; curtains of dust obscured the sun and painted it with a strange grey redness tinged with purple flares; it sank until we could look at it without being dazzled. A glimmering, lethal mantle was spreading across the west, looking like burning chemicals. Then it sank and was swallowed up beyond the edge of the plain.

We reached the ruin as the remains of the light were still flickering. There was a sour, damp smell, even though the building was open to the four winds. We groped our way from room to room, stepping over heaps of rubbish until we imagined we could see shadows flitting in front of us: the reflection of the wind-lashed treetops in the garden on the walls in the remains of the light. But no: this time we really did seem to have disturbed a pair of uninvited guests, a girl and a boy, blurred, slow, we had apparently woken them from a deep sleep; they stared at us for a moment as if we were ghosts, then they slipped out through a window frame on the eastern wall and disappeared silently among the trees in the darkened wood.

Theo touched my back with outstretched fingers: Look here, Noa, you must understand, that boy is dead. I answered in a whisper, I know. Know? Then say it. But why? Say it, Noa, so that it is in your own voice.

And we stood there waiting for it to get cold.

We got home at ten o'clock. We went back through the town, crossing the square that was completely empty by now and lashed by the wind with tattered newspapers and salvos of sharp sand. I put my arm round his wide belt and sensed the smell of old leather and sweat. We hurriedly closed all the blinds and windows against the dust storm. Theo made a fine salad with a radish cut in the form of a rosebud. He made an omelette and put out sliced bread and various cheeses on a wooden board. I made two glasses of herbal tea. We put a record on, Schubert's Mass in B Flat Major, and we sat in the kitchen till late. We did not speak. Maybe we'll hire a car and go for a trip to Galilee. We'll stay in village inns and go and see the sun rise through the dense tangle of vegetation near the sources of the Jordan. When we come home Tal can bring us the little kitten she has promised us. Theo will give her a part-time job filing in his office, until she joins the army, and meanwhile he will prepare her for her math exam. We'll buy her a pretty blouse and skirt instead of the worn jeans with the rips at the knees. I thought about the shadows we had disturbed this evening in the ruin. They might have gone down into the wadi under the cover of thick darkness, and by now they'd have got as far as the flank of Hyena Hill. Or they might have taken shelter in the wood. Or they might have sneaked back inside after we'd gone and now they'd be lying in the gloom under the crumbling wall, head on thigh, drowsing in the peace of a silent dream, far from themselves, far from pain and sorrow, listening to the gusts of the southerly wind that blows and fades and rustles again through the tops of the twisted pine trees in the garden of the ruin from where it carries on to sweep the whole of the town and gropes at the outside of the shutters we have closed. If you like, you can hear it whistle through the low bushes. If you don't, you don't have to listen. In another two and a half weeks the summer holiday will be over. Whoever has some goodwill can find goodwill everywhere. Maybe this year I'll agree to be a form teacher. Meanwhile, tonight, I'll make him give up London because I'll have a shower and go to him in the darkness.

The Cast

Theo (of Planning Ltd.)
Noa Dubnow (teacher)
Malachi (Muki) Peleg (estate agent and investment consultant)
Avraham Orvieto (defence adviser or perhaps arms-dealer)
Erella Orvieto (his wife)
Immanuel Orvieto (their son, former secondary school pupil)
The Orvieto family's chimpanzee
Immanuel Orvieto's dog
Elazara Orvieto (aunt and former bank clerk)
Ron Arbel (lawyer)
Ludmir (retired employee of the electricity company, member of many committees)
Gusta Ludmir (his wife, gives private math coaching)
Larlach Ludmir (his granddaughter)
Linda Danino (clerk, divorced)
Nehemia Dubnow (retired employee of the water company)
Chuma Zamosc Bat-Am (militant vegetarian and pacifist)
Yoshiahu (Yoshku) Zamosc (born-again Jew)
Peeping Gorovoy (former champion weight-lifter of Lodz)
Ezra Zussman (poet) and his wife
Batsheva Dinur (the Mayor)
Didi Dinur (her husband, killed in the Six Day War, apparently a musician)
Batsheva's elderly mother (retired teacher)
Etam (Batsheva's grandson)
Nawwaf (who has brought olives from Galilee)
Julia and Dr. Leo Dresdner, and Dr. Nir (the last two are dentists)
Dubi Weitzman (notary and accountant)
Yehuda and Jakki (Hollywood Photos)
Kushner (bookbinder)

Schatzberg (pharmacist)
Avram (falafel seller, lately also shawarma in pitta)
Shlomo Benizri (from the Department in Beersheba)
Doris (Benizri's secretary)
Tikki (a typist)
Pudgy policeman (from the road accident at Ashkelon junction)
Martha (from Elat, apparently a drug user)
'Aatef (a Bedouin tracker)
Alharizi (formerly a house owner in Tel Kedar, now an importer
of televisions in Netanya)
Natalia (immigrant, a cleaner)
Her husband and his father (immigrants, mechanics)
Gilboa (newsagent and stationer)
Limor Gilboa (assists her father, cellist)
Pini Bozo (sells shoes)
His wife and baby (killed)
Albert Yeshua (the soldier who killed them)
Blind Lupo (from the telephone exchange)
Anat and Ohad (a young couple)
Bialkin (sells furniture)
Gustav Marmorek (alias old Elijah)
Violette and Madeleine (hairdressers, sisters-in-law)
Hungarian cantor
Paula Orlev (Desert Chic Fashions)
Tal Orlev (her daughter, between school and military service)
Jacques Ben Loulou (Ben Elul's Garage)
Bargeloni Bros (estate agents)
Pini Finkel (killed in the War of Independence)
Nimrod Finkel (his son, head of the Planning Agency)
Cherniak, Refidim and Arbel, Lawyers (90 Rothschild Boule-
vard, Tel Aviv)
A professor and piano tuner (writing a book entitled *The Essence
of Judaism*)
Amalia (ailing librarian)
Young man from Galway (travelling around Galilee, looking for
a girl named Daphne)
String quartet (immigrants from Kiev)
Man crying in Jeep